PRAISE FOR ARKANSAS BLACK

"... visceral realism that puts flesh on the bones of Ozarks history."
—**Brooks Blevins, author of *A History of the Ozarks***

"It is one of those books with an ending that will linger like the taste of the last apple of the season, sharp, bittersweet, and unforgettable."
—**Shanessa Gluhm, author of *A River of Crows***

"An eloquently cinematic Southern Gothic tale, ... *Arkansas Black* depicts a world where blight destroys the land and infects the hearts of humans."
—**Kathy Maresca, Christy Finalist author of *Porch Music***

"... a transportive historical novel crafted with equal parts poetic prose and propulsive pacing. ... Blevins gives us characters as real and raw as the rural landscape they inhabit."
—**James Wade, Reading the West Award-winning author of *Narrow of the Road***

"... magnificent look into early 20th century Ozark Mountain life."

—**Scott Lenoir, author of *The Amendment***

"Intricate layers of betrayal, loyalty, and redemption unravel with a pace that is both deliberate and gripping."

—**Johnnie Bernhard, author of *Hannah and Ariela***

"The conflict between the brothers is both moving and heartbreaking. This is a damn fine novel."

—**Tom McGraw**

"... a masterful work of historical fiction. ... a slow-burn of familial tension that leads inevitably to violence."

—**Bruce Leonard, award-winning and best-selling author the *Hadley Carroll Mysteries* and *Hard Exit***

"... brilliantly written, sweeping historical drama that follows an American family whose bonds are tested by love, ambition, struggle, and betrayal."

—**Rob Samborn, best-selling author of *The Prisoner of Paradise***

"Executed with authentic dialogue and extraordinary sensory detail ... a compelling story that will long be remembered."

—**Vallerie Winn, Author of *The Dance Between***

"... a combustible story, whipsawing the reader between what the characters want and what they feel obligated to do ..."

—**Drew Estabrook**

Also by Alexander Blevens

Bycatch

The families of two Vietnam veterans are reunited and must heal old war wounds to find peace.

60066

Ark, Black
Mr. C. Bingham
St. Thomas,
Franklin Co.,
Pa.

A. A. Newton
10-18-12
10-28-12

ARKANSAS BLACK

Alexander Blevens

LOST MERIDIAN

Book Cover by Srdjan Vukovic / WolfBell

Edited by John J. Ledwith

Illustration: U.S. Department of Agriculture Pomological Watercolor Collection. Rare and Special Collections National Agricultural Library Beltsville, MD 20705

First edition 2025

Printed in the United States of America

Library of Congress Control Number: 2025914174

PAPERBACK ISBN: 979-8-9990794-0-4

EBOOK ISBN: 979-8-9990794-1-1

For my sons Christopher and Andrew.

"There is little choice in a barrel of rotten apples."
—William Shakespeare

ONE

Benton County, Arkansas–April 1927

THE SUN ROSE ABOVE the gray-green silhouette of Elkhorn Mountain into a pale, unblemished sky. Jesse watched its rays march across the orchard, igniting a hundred thousand apple blossoms encased in ice. Crystal globes twinkled in the brilliant sunlight.

He turned against the glare and retraced his steps through the frosted grass to the hardwood forest at the edge of his family's land. His breath hung in soft swirls within inches of his face on calm, crisp air. A flannel field coat draped his broad shoulders, cutting the chill of the late spring freeze. Jesse glanced again at the long rows of apple trees—icy mint-green leaves glistened in the sunshine and hung heavy on black branches bent toward the earth—then he walked home down a well-worn path to his wife and son.

Marybeth did not move when he entered the kitchen. She stood with her back to the door, her pelvis pressed against a bone-white porcelain sink, his gift to her in better times. Through a window, the morning's first light had also revealed the blanket of ice to her. She knew and could not bear to turn and look at her husband.

Jesse pulled up a pressback chair and dropped his hat on a wooden table. White flour from rolling the morning's biscuits dusted its smooth, worn surface. He looked at his wife; her long brown hair, held back with a red ribbon, rested between her shoulder blades. Apron strings pulled tight to the shape of her hips accented her slim waist. A plain cotton dress fell to her mid-calf, just above her brown leather shoes with blocky heels, needing repair. Jesse knew what Marybeth was thinking. He knew why she stood with her back to him. He did not want to say anything, either; he did not want to discuss the inevitable.

Marybeth reached for a blackened kettle on the woodstove and tipped steaming water into the sink through soft white suds. She then dipped her hands into the warm water to continue her chore.

To Jesse, the room was quiet except for a melodic hiss and pop of the woodstove, the scrape of a broom-corn brush against cast iron, and his own deep breaths.

"Coffee?" Jesse asked when he felt they had reached the limit of their silence.

"Bit left," she said, not turning.

Marybeth worked a skillet, then placed it on the drainboard for rinsing. She pried the wooden stopper free from the bottom of the sink and turned to face her husband while wiping suds off her forearms with the bottom of her apron. Their eyes met, just like they had dozens of times each day during the past ten years of their marriage. She knew what he needed to say. If only she had the words to soften the blow, ease some pain, and offer hope. Nothing.

She pulled a red enameled cup from a shelf, lifted a coffeepot off the stove, and poured out the last of the dark liquid.

"It's old. Want me to make more?" she asked.

"No."

Marybeth set the cup on the table and pulled up a chair beside Jesse.

"Where's Levi?" he asked.

"Coop."

Jesse nodded, understanding. Steam rose off his coffee, spinning toward the ceiling.

With her hand, Marybeth swiped at the flour on the table. She should have cleaned this before her husband sat down, she thought. But how silly to let that enter her mind when so much more was at stake. She then focused on Jesse and what she expected he would say.

"We're done here. Can't make it work no more," he said.

"No." She shook her head, not believing her own response.

"I'm gonna tell Silas today we're done." Jesse thumbed a tear from her cheek, then took her hands in his. "Crop's gone, Marybeth. It's gone everywhere. Ain't gonna be no fruit on them trees this year."

"It can't end like this."

"I don't see any way out."

"Can't you talk to the bank again?"

"Sure. But it ain't gonna work."

Marybeth felt the strength and roughness of her husband's hands in hers. Thick, dry calluses covered his fingertips and the arch of his palm. The meaty base of his thumb quivered as it warmed. "What do you reckon we do?"

"I don't know."

"West?"

He nodded. "They'll have apples to pick out West."

She turned from Jesse, perhaps to hide her disappointment in their predicament, glancing at their simple kitchen: a splay-legged wood stove, a punched-tin pie safe, and shelves of old apple boxes holding meager supplies. "What about Paps?"

"Don't know if he'll come."

Marybeth pulled her hands from his and stood when she heard their son land on the wooden porch outside. Seven-year-old Levi pulled the latchstring and pushed the wooden door open. He was about to speak when he sensed the tension in the kitchen, froze in the doorway, and lowered a wire basket of smooth brown eggs to his side. He had his mother's handsome face with high cheekbones and wide, almond-shaped brown eyes but his father's sandy-blond hair. He shared an athletic build with his father and uncle, even as a child.

"Put 'em on the table, Levi," Marybeth said. "Get going. You've got more to do."

"Yes, ma'am. Yes, sir," he said, even though his father had not spoken or barely looked in his direction. Something was wrong. Levi set the basket on the table and scurried outside, gently closing the door behind him.

Jesse drained the last drops from his cup and said, "We've no choice."

Marybeth stepped away, facing the window. She placed both hands on the sink's front edge and watched her son lead their only cow, a common red-roan breed, toward a small shed-roofed barn. Vapor spilled from the cow's nostrils with each breath. Large bony hips stretched with steaming hide, tipped from side to side, and lumbered forward, swinging an engorged udder. Marybeth then pumped the black iron handle on the spigot several times before a gush of clear, icy water splashed into the sink.

Jesse scooted his chair on the bare wood floor, set his hat, and stood to leave. The prospect of upending his family and forsaking his ancestral land, his grandfather's land, was daunting. He knew the day would come when he had to make this decision; he did not expect it to happen so soon from an errant late spring frost. But he had given this possibility ample consideration before, rehearsed it in his mind, ironed out the details, cataloged the process, and inventoried their assets. He believed he was prepared to start a new life in a distant land, however difficult it might be. What remained outside his capacity for understanding and reason were the hurdles he would face in cleaving the conjoined life he shared with his brother.

Two

Jesse pulled the canvas brim of his hat over his neck, then stepped into the fresh morning air. He passed through a garden gate and out to the orchard's edge. A magnificent apple tree, twenty feet tall, broad at the base—an Arkansas Black—blocked his view of the rising sun. Jesse and his twin brother, Silas, tended hundreds of *Blacks* just like this, planted forty feet on center by their father years ago and covering nearly all the flat land their grandfather had homesteaded before the Civil War. The sun was up a quarter; most of the ice had already dropped from the apple blossoms and outer twigs. Still, a frozen film remained on the top surface of the branches and in the forks where they met the trunks. Under the trees, bright green grass blades bent by the overnight frost sprang skyward, rejuvenated as if the dark, frigid assault had never happened. Jesse dug his hands deep into his coat pockets and turned downhill, skirting the orchard.

The land his family had farmed for the past seventy years was part of the Springfield Plain, an ancient mesa forced out of a primordial ocean with the Ozark Mountains by the collision of continents. The rolling tallgrass prairie, covering the northwestern corner of Arkansas where Missouri and Oklahoma met, was the ancestral hunting grounds of the Osage Indians. Bison, black bears, elk, and puma once roamed on the grasslands and among the temperate hickory, chestnut, and oak forests.

Through the millennia, abundant rainfall impacted the land: carving the edges of the plateau into gullies, channeling small streams over dark, moss-covered cherty limestone ledges, and exposing the embedded fossils of primeval creatures. The rivulets from Jesse and Silas's eighty acres ran north in wet weather, where they joined Spanker Creek coming out of Pea Ridge. The water from Spanker cascaded off the plateau year-round into the Little Sugar Creek, then meandered northwest into Missouri before turning south into Oklahoma to mix with the Arkansas and Mississippi Rivers on its way to the Gulf of Mexico.

Jesse marched down a cart path. Manure littered the grassy strip between iced-over muddy ruts. He jumped from edge to edge as he walked, continually trying to find solid ground on which to step. A dogtrot cabin came into view a hundred and twenty yards down the road behind an enormous white oak, dripping with yellow catkins and late to leaf for the season.

Partially hewn timber walls, chinked with cement, lay on a slate stack foundation. One continuous rusting corrugated tin roof covered a generous front porch and an open breezeway between two square rooms. The homestead was nestled in a low spot near a natural spring that bubbled out of the bedrock. Jesse did not know how old the home was or who built it—it had always been there. His grandfather, J. R., used to live in the house before he passed, and now his father did.

Jesse paused in the cabin's dooryard and looked through the open section to the deciduous forest, growing in the steep ravine beyond. Blankets of white flowers layered on a dogwood's delicate, arching limbs claimed the dark void between the crown canopy and the rocky slope. Farther downhill, in an unrivaled spring show, cotton candy-pink flowers encased a redbud's vertical trunk and splayed branches. Above, in a chestnut tree's upper reaches, a gray and white mockingbird ran through his repertoire of plagiarized songs. Behind Jesse, from atop a split-rail fence, a blue jay answered with a scolding rasp. The muted and melodious tinkle of water from a springhouse filled the brief intervals between the staccato blast of bird song.

Jesse called out to his father without generating a reply. Two wooden rocking chairs and a stack of empty apple boxes sat on the porch. A frayed horsewhip, a rusted pruning saw, a soiled woolen coat, and a broken pump handle hung haphazardly from nails driven into the timbers under the eave. Next to the porch, Jesse noticed a discarded brown glass bottle in the grass. He picked it up, bringing the open neck to his nose: applejack. Jesse inverted the bottle and shook out a dollop of golden-brown sludge. He stood the bottle on the weathered porch boards and stepped under the roof's edge. The blue jay continued to scold.

"Paps," Jesse called out again.

The wooden door leading to the kitchen room was ajar. His father, eyes closed, lay on his side, half under a farmhouse table with its bench tipped over. Bile-colored spew covered the front of his pants and shirt sleeves. Oily curls of long gray hair draped from his head and chin to the wooden floor.

"Paps!"

Jesse nudged his father's thigh with his boot. He bent down, wrestled him from under the table, and slid his hands under his arms.

"Come now. Stand up," Jesse said as he dragged his father across the breezeway and into the other room. Paps collapsed onto a horsehair tick when released, still unconscious.

Jesse returned to the kitchen and stoked the stove, kindling cedar splits until the hickory staves burned hot. He snatched a tin pail off the floor and headed to the springhouse. Again, the blue jay scolded with a rasp. He opened a small door and stepped into the damp hutch. Cold, clear water trickled from the side of a rock outcropping through a one-inch lead pipe. Jesse reached down and let the water fill his cupped hands, water that he thought must have flowed continuously for at least three generations, if not since the beginning of time. He drank and savored its purity.

Jesse's father, Paps, was born and named Levi Fitch in the Boston Mountains sixty-five years prior, during the Civil War. Levi's father—and Jesse's grandfather—J. R. Fitch had just come with a young wife from Illinois to Northwest Arkansas five years before the war to work a small parcel of flat land. They grew no cotton, no tobacco, no sugarcane. They had no slaves and had never even seen a colored man in this part of Benton County. When the chatter of secession in Little Rock from politicians and planters percolated, he considered it simply crazy talk. The Confederacy was not a cause J. R. and his wife could support.

By July 1862, gray-clad soldiers rode through Bentonville's streets five miles to the south, conscripting all men with clear eyes and a sound back to take the fight to the Yankees. Then, J. R. Fitch abandoned his crops and moved his pregnant wife south to wait out the war in the safety of a deep hollow in the Boston Mountains. They took only what they could carry.

Early in the civil conflict, the Union army met the Confederates in a Northwest Arkansas field within a cannon shot of nearby Pea Ridge. The Southerners sustained a decisive defeat, assuring neighboring Missouri would remain in the Union. After the rout, the Federals took what they wanted in the Fitches' isolated corner of the state and destroyed the rest. Only freezing winter weather and rugged mountains stopped the Union army from pursuing the Confederates further south—and only after Bentonville and Fayetteville lay ransacked and burning. Even among northern sympathizers in Arkansas, resentment built against the foreign occupiers of their land.

Some men are born with solid convictions, knowing right from wrong. They cling to generational norms as if they are God-given truths. J. R. was not one of those men. He was pragmatic, adaptable, and lived on his own frontier. Though he grew up listening to his Illinois Methodist preacher decry the sins of slavery from north of the Mason-Dixon Line, he had never seen it with his own eyes, never believed God's children could be so cruel to each other. Before the war fell to Northwest Arkansas, he could put the slavery question out of his mind and not have to reconcile with it being right or wrong.

When the cotton growers on the Mississippi River alluvial plain in Southeast Arkansas sounded out and ginned up a secession fever in Little Rock, J. R. paid them no mind—crazy talk. When Confederate conscription forces combed the state for able-bodied men, J. R. hid in the mountains. But now that Federal troops had burned his adopted homeland, raided his neighbor's grain stores, slaughtered all livestock, and needlessly torched any structure that would burn, J. R. found his conviction. *Now* he had a cause to fight.

Leaving his wife and a newborn son behind, J. R. returned to Benton County with only a bedroll and a squirrel gun to muster into the Thirty-fourth Arkansas Infantry Regiment, Confederate army.

Months later, on a frosty December morning in 1862, Federal troops charged J. R.'s regiment, dug in on high ground near the Prairie Grove Presbyterian Church, ten miles west of Fayetteville. The Union ranks met a withering barrage of rebel fire. In the end, however, the Yankees prevailed. His unit was in shambles and making a hasty retreat when J. R. deserted the battlefield. A bloody cloth wrapped the remaining three fingers of his right hand, all that was left attached to his palm after a nearby cannonball explosion. Feeling unfit for battle, he spent the rest of the war in the Boston Mountains with his family, hiding from Union scouts and Confederate bounty hunters. In those mountains, his son, Levi, took his first steps.

By April 1865, when word of the Confederate surrender from Appomattox reached Northwest Arkansas, J. R., his wife, and his son had already returned to their original homestead near Spanker Creek. Having no mule, he plowed his fields by hand. Soon, bright green cornstalks poked through the tilled dirt, giving J. R. hope for a new life of peace. His son's world could only improve.

Jesse tipped the pail under the waterspout in the springhouse and watched it slowly fill. He had only one childhood memory of his grandfather: J. R. was sitting on the cabin porch on either a pine box or stool, peeling a dark red-black apple in one continuous strip with a pearl-clad pocketknife. His father, Levi, was also there, sitting on an upended barrel with Jesse's twin brother, Silas, on his lap. Jesse's eye-minded image was of his grandfather holding the fruit in his right hand while paring the skin with a tiny blade in his left. His right hand was claw-like, with only a thumb and two small fingers pinching the apple. In the center of his deformity was a jumble of scarred and contracted skin, sliding over bony nubbins. As a young boy, nobody else Jesse knew held an apple on the right and their knife on the left. Nobody ever offered him an explanation.

His only other memory of this time was watching cold, wet rain come down in sheets on freshly dug earth. A dozen people stood about with oiled slickers on their heads while a preacher mumbled. He was sure this was at the Post Oak Graveyard, up the hill on the other side of the orchard. At first, J. R. FITCH was scratched on a simple wooden cross, marking his grandfather's grave. Jesse believed someone was supposed to replace the marker with a stone headpiece, but it never happened. The cross and all tangible relics of his grandfather's life were now long gone. Jesse often wondered if his father, Levi, was like his grandfather, J. R. Were sons images of their fathers?

Back in the kitchen, Jesse poured the pail of water into the stove kettle and went to the bedroom to undress his father. Jesse pulled a woolen blanket over Paps's naked body and gathered his soiled clothing in a tub. He scalded the garments with boiling water and lye soap, then beat them clean on a rub board. Once rinsed and wrung, Jesse draped the white muslin shirt, button-fly trousers, and long underwear over the split-rail fence to dry. He returned to the dogtrot and closed the doors.

This was his father's land, family land inherited from his grandfather, Jesse thought. Fitches had been born, raised, and buried here for almost seventy years. The land had provided—not every year, not every crop, but consistently enough to sustain the growing Fitch clan. The apple trees were entering their prime and could continue to produce for another thirty years. The trees had weathered unpredictable droughts and freezes before. They had fought off disease and pests, proving the strength of their roots in the fertile Arkansas soil. The Fitches had always invested in the land and trusted it. These eighty acres were as crucial to Paps, Silas, and him as a leg or an arm. Tending the farm was as natural as breathing. How could he now think of leaving? He knew no other life. But leave, he must.

Jesse closed the door and crossed the porch, stopping at the brown bottle resting on the edge. An ant trail had found the remaining sweet sludge stuck to its opening. The insect convoy pulsed with activity, moving in both directions at once. Jesse cocked his right hip and kicked the bottle with his boot clear across the yard and into the brush. He would stop by later to check on his father, perhaps with supper.

THREE

JESSE STEPPED AROUND THE side of the big barn the moment Silas's hatchet sliced through a hen's neck and wedged into a blood-soaked stump. The chicken's head kicked out to the side with a sanguine squirt. Silas flicked the headless amber-feathered body to the grass, where its legs and wings jumped in reflexive spasms. Life fluid pulsed from its severed neck with the fading rhythm of its heart. Silas wrenched the hatchet blade from the stump and looked up to see his brother.

"Hey."

Jesse nodded as he watched the headless bird flop on the ground and finally come to a halt. Silas picked it up by its legs, bound the feet with a quick wire whip, and hung the carcass from a nail on a post. Dark red blood dripped from its neck and soaked into the dirt.

"Anna Lee's making meat pie for supper. You and the missus and young Levi are welcome," Silas said.

Jesse did not answer.

A feral tabby cautiously slipped from under the house, following her nose to the dripping blood.

"Silas," Jesse led off. "We can't do this no more."

"What?"

"I said, can't do this no more."

"What the hell you talking about?" Silas shooed the tawny-brown tabby with a hatchet swing, and the cat ducked to safety behind a barrel.

"You know what I mean. It's time you faced it," Jesse said.

"You and Marybeth, you just got no faith. Paps made good on this land. Grandy J. R., too. The land's good."

"I ain't saying that, Silas. I ain't saying the land's no good. What I'm telling is, we can't borrow no more. Can't pay what we owe."

The tabby lowered her head and gingerly ventured out from behind the barrel toward the chopping stump. Breaking into a sprint halfway across the yard with an uninterrupted stride, she snatched the chicken head in her mouth and darted behind the barn.

Silas swung the hatchet again, much too late. "We'll do okay this year. Almanac sez plenty of rain through September."

"You even look at the damn temperature last night? And glaze-ice this morning? What about the two weeks of rain since the blossoms set?"

"I know how much rain we've had. I saw the ice. Not too bad."

"Not too bad? Not too bad? Silas, there ain't gonna be no fruit on 'em trees this year. Not ours, not the Jacobssons', not the Phelpses', not nobody's. Even if we had a crop, there ain't gonna be no market this year."

"They'll set. You watch. We ain't gonna have a full crop, but enough."

"It's not gonna happen, Silas. I'm telling you, it ain't happening. Blossoms froze through and through before the ice came. Twenty-five degrees. Did you even look?"

"Ice'll protect 'em."

"You didn't hear me, Silas. Was twenty-five *before* the ice fell. It's too late." Jesse raised his coat collar and tucked the lapels under his chin. "I'm gonna go to Washington, taking Marybeth and Levi. Leaving as soon as I can. Maybe Paps, too. You need to come."

Silas did not believe his brother. He had heard the same the previous year and probably the year before. Their father planted every one of the Arkansas Black trees at the turn of the century when he and his twin were just little boys. There was plenty of market for good Southern fruit, at least until the last few years. It will come back, Silas thought. "How you figger Marybeth will take to losing a sister?" he asked.

"She'll take it fine. Better than starving."

Silas watched the last drops of blood drain from the bird before he lifted it off the post. "Anna Lee's got a pot going on the stove. You wanna come in, warm a bit, and tell her what you just told me?"

"I'll wait. I got more to say outside," Jesse responded.

Silas took the headless bird by its feet and stepped into a clapboard house. The three-room farmhouse sat atop a rise overlooking the orchard. In front of the main door, simple steps led to a small landing. Above the door, in the triangular space beneath the high-pitched roofline, a window supplied light to a cramped sleeping loft. Across the yard, the large barn was clad in vertical, weathered planks. To the side of the barn were two black and white shoats in a primitive sty. Next to the pen, a half-dozen hens pecked corn scattered across the ground, oblivious to one of their own's recent fate.

Silas returned with the freshly scalded bird; steam pumped from its wet feathers into the calm, brisk morning air. He hung it on the nail again and pulled the dark feathers off the tail, gradually working down the body to the wings. The vaned quills fell to the ground while the white down stuck to the back of his hands and arms. Finally, he worked the hackle off the severed neck.

"Help me out, would ya?" Silas asked while gesturing toward a wooden pail of water by his side.

Jesse poured icy water over his brother's forearms and hands, rinsing off the last feathers and blood.

"Don't think I'm serious, do you?" Jesse asked.

"No, you ain't got the balls to leave. You ain't taking Paps either. He ain't going."

"I'll leave 'im then."

Silas dipped the chicken carcass into the bucket of remaining water and then rubbed and pulled at the hair-like feathers still stuck to the yellow skin. Blood from the neck tinted the water pink.

"Paps's gone back to applejack, passed out as we speak," Jesse said. "I stopped by on my way over. Checked on 'im like you never do."

"So? You still ain't leaving 'im."

"Will if I have to."

Jesse abhorred confrontation, especially with Silas. It was easier for him to back down than to challenge his brother. In these situations, he often thought about their older sister, Achsah, and how she always stood up for him. When he was a child, Achsah was his only advocate; their father was consumed with raising apples, and their mother was consumed with sickness.

Jesse and Silas were identical twins on the outside but could not have been more different-minded. When they were younger, they had often assumed each other's identities to suit their purpose or fancy. Only when they spoke was their charade exposed. Achsah told them they were Siamese. "Look at your pinky fingers," she had said. "See how they're both crooked? You were joined at the finger when you were born, Siamese. Grandy had to cut you two apart with his pocketknife." When the boys were still too young to be significantly helpful on the farm, Achsah would bring them along with her to School #17, three miles from home. She was an excellent student; the boys at age five were not.

One warm spring day, the three children hiked up the road to the schoolhouse. Silas was out front while Jesse hung back with Achsah to repeat a story he had told her the day before. The smell of the morning sun warming the earth portended an explosion of apple blossoms soon to come. Achsah's mind was far from Jesse's story, and she hardly noticed him by her side.

Silas spotted the snake first—three feet long and stretched across the road. It had a muscular brown body with dark-brown saddlebag-shaped markings on its back. Silas fetched a stick from the road's edge and cautiously approached the snake, warrior style. Crouched over, he held the stick in front like a spear and closed in silently. The snake sensed his presence and immediately curled into a defensive posture. Silas hurled the stick, grazing the snake's midsection with its blunt end. The snake turned its head and slid toward the side of the road with powerful waves. Silas retrieved his weapon, pursuing his prey.

When Achsah noticed the commotion, Silas had the snake suspended on the end of the stick as he ran back down the road.

"Silas, drop it. Now!" she yelled.

But it was too late. The snake slid down the stick to Silas's hand and embedded its fangs deep into the base of his thumb. Stick and snake scattered as Silas dropped to his knees in pain and disbelief. He did not cry out.

Achsah ran to him, grabbed his wrist, and squeezed tight, causing blood to fill the veins on the back of his hand. She rattled a cough as she tried to catch her breath. Red blood dotted two tiny puncture wounds in the fleshy part of her brother's hand. She squeezed his wrist and put her mouth on the blood to suck. Nothing came out.

"Jesse, git Paps," she screamed.

Jesse spun home.

The color drained from Silas's face. Achsah lowered her head and shoulders to the ground and continued to pinch his wrist. With her other hand, she felt his clammy forehead and cheeks. She moved her hand to his chest and sensed the rapid beat of his heart and quick, urgent breaths.

Silas looked up at his sister, trying to understand her panic, but did not speak. His thumb throbbed with pain, and his fingers tingled. She had a vice-like grip on his wrist.

Quiet surrounded brother and sister as they lay on the dusty road. Apple orchards spread to the south; wheat fields spread to the north. Sunshine beat down from above. The snake was long gone. A green dragonfly, iridescent in the sun, darted and hovered, then landed on a nearby fence post, motionless as if to study the intruders. The sound of cicadas, like the continuous ringing of a child's bell, wafted from across the adjacent field. A calmness of resignation enveloped the siblings. Nothing to do but wait.

The echo of hoofbeats preceded the sight of the buckboard wagon. Paps sat on a spring bench with reins in one hand and a horsewhip in the other. Jesse crouched in the box behind the seat, holding the sideboard with both hands. A harnessed black mule with erect ears and large brown eyes stirred up dust as it approached at a trot with the cart.

"Copperhead got 'im," Achsah shouted when her father drew near. She held Silas's blue hand by the wrist, then coughed into her elbow. She coughed again, spitting blood-tinged phlegm into the dirt.

Paps jumped off the wagon, sprinted to his son, and touched his face.

"Is he dead?" Jesse called out from on the buckboard.

"No. He'll be fine." Paps pulled a small penknife from his vest pocket and opened the blade. He took Silas's hand in his and sank the tip of the knife into a puncture hole. Blood spurted out, and he did the same with the other. As Paps tried to draw venom from the thumb with his mouth, Jesse climbed down from the wagon with his eyes fixed on his brother. Achsah stood with Jesse and watched their father work on Silas's wound for several minutes. Silas remained awake, shocked, but did not utter a sound.

Paps wiped blood from his mouth and chin with his arm sleeve, then wrapped Silas's hand in a kerchief and lifted him into the wagon bed. Jesse climbed in and set his coat under his brother's head. Achsah sat on the spring seat next to her father. Paps then turned to Jesse. "See how strong Silas is? See how he takes it. Hasn't uttered a word. Takes it like a man, something you could only hope to do. Takes it like a man." Paps snapped the reins, and the mule trotted home.

Before laying the chicken carcass out, Silas splashed the top of the bloody stump with fresh water. He rinsed the bucket and filled it again at the well.

"Watch. That cat will be back," Silas said to Jesse.

"Keep feeding it like you're doing, and you're gonna have a whole yard of them beggars."

"Anna Lee and the girls won't let me put a bullet in it. Real problem is, the more I feed it, the less it mouses."

Silas pulled the windpipe and stomach tube an inch or two out of the chicken's neck, then cut them off with a Bowie knife. He flipped the bird on its back and brought the blade around the vent and up the soft abdomen. While holding on to the lower intestines with one hand, he ran his other hand up and around the organs, separating them from the abdominal and chest cavities. Silas scraped the remaining lung tissue off the ribs with his fingertips, cut off the feet at the ankles, and dropped the body into the bucket of water. The tabby reappeared at the yard's edge and inched closer to the remaining entrails.

"We can't pay off what we owe from last year. When you're out of hens, what're you and the girls gonna eat?" Jesse asked, while watching Silas separate the liver from the gallbladder. "Teague Brothers are still looking for their money from two years ago. They ain't oil spraying scale for free. You thought they were bad last year? You wait a couple months, and they'll be scale on every damn twig in the whole damn orchard. I can't for the life of me figger what you're thinking. Them trees not surviving two years without oil."

"Watch this," Silas said. He tossed the gall sack to the cat. The tabby pounced on the yellow-green organ, then recoiled when it sensed the bile. "Can't never fool them cats."

"I'm serious, Silas."

Silas salvaged the liver, heart, and gizzard and slung the rest of the guts and feet into a galvanized pail for the pigs. "Well, I'm serious about meat pie, too," he said.

"Take my share to Paps."

Silas stuck the knife tip into the stump. He looked at his brother. "Why the hell you name Levi after Paps?"

"Cuz, he's my son. I can do as I please."

"You named 'im Levi Fitch, so he'd know where he's come from. He'd know his great-grandy cleared this land, fought for it, and raised Paps, his grandfather, his namesake, on it."

"Where're you going with this?" Jesse asked.

"What I'm saying is that you got a duty to stay here and raise Levi here." Silas pulled the knife free by its handle and held the blade up.

"Ain't got no duty." Jesse took a step backward.

"This's family land, Fitch land. I can't expect my girls to stay when they're grown." Silas stepped toward his brother.

"Don't know that. This next one could be a boy."

"Think I have more seed for a boy? Five girls, I'm likely to kill Anna Lee trying to git me a son of my own," Silas said. He tapped the tip of the knife on Jesse's chest. "You can't take Levi from me."

FOUR

ACHSAH DIED THE SAME year the copperhead bit Silas. It happened later in the fall when the apples were filling out in the trees, bending the limbs. Their mother said the consumption got her, but Jesse believed otherwise. "She never spits out the poison in her mouth," Jesse reasoned to his brother. "I saw Paps suck and spit, suck and spit. Achsah never did. The poison killed her."

During the preceding summer months, Achsah became weak and overcome with coughing fits. At first, she lost interest in school, then spent days in bed at their mother's instruction. Jesse found himself drawn to her side and sat for hours, stroking her hand, telling her stories, and trying to lift her spirits. Silas could not. He could not face the pain in Achsah's sunken eyes. He could not watch her flesh waste, leaving bony joints to connect reed-thin arms and legs. The sicker Achsah became, the more Jesse wanted to stay with her, and the more Silas was repulsed by her.

Paps sent for a doctor the night Achsah's breathing became labored and her lips and cheeks lost their rose. Doc arrived in a black lacquered runabout hitched with a singletree to a blood bay steed. He rushed into the house while Jesse and Silas waited outside on the wooden landing, studying the buggy and horse. They figured that any doctor with such a carriage was a good doctor and could save

25

their sister. Paps allowed Jesse and Silas inside to eat, then told them to grab blankets, get outside again, and sleep in the barn. The doctor remained at the house well past supper and into the night. Mother stayed with Achsah behind a partition while Paps and Doc discussed her condition over an open bottle of whiskey.

Achsah was not yet dead when the doctor stumbled out of the house into the night air and climbed into his buggy. The bay needed no instruction to head for town.

"It was consumption," Mother said, fitting a cough of her own between strident breaths. "Nothin' nobody could do." Mother's eyes were puffy. Dust on her cheeks showed streaks of dried tears.

As the sky turned pale blue above the mountain, Paps changed his shirt, saddled the mule, and headed out to find a preacher.

Jesse had seen no one die before except for his grandfather. Achsah's death was different. She left with a big part of him. She left him alone. After she died, Jesse realized how little he had in common with his twin beyond sharing a face. Achsah had filled a maternal role their mother had vacated. At six years of age, Jesse found himself isolated and alone. Feelings of abandonment, which he did not fully understand until he was much older, shaped the rest of his childhood.

Silas handled Achsah's death differently. He continued to embrace adventure and seemed to relish risk-taking. The copperhead was the first of many poisonous snakes Silas hunted down to test his mettle. When he was ten, he found a diamondback rattler, four inches thick, coiled behind the big barn and spinning out a whir. Silas taunted the snake with a spade, slapping its triangular head full of venom from side to side. The snake repeatedly struck at Silas, who reacted with quick backward hops. Most boys need an audience to propel them into reckless behavior, but not Silas. The game was for his enjoyment alone and ended when Silas brought the shovel's sharpened edge down on the snake's fully extended neck, just inches from his bare foot.

As the boys grew through adolescence, Jesse pulled into himself, while Silas became gregarious, confident, and daring. The family expected both boys to help with orchard chores during the growing and harvest seasons. Book learning was for the rare time between putting the apples up in the fall, pruning limbs in the late winter, fertilizing in the spring, and spraying fruit in the summer.

During the fall harvest, men came to the Fitch orchard from downstate and all over the Midwest, looking for day labor. They hand-picked the tall trees from fifteen-foot tripod ladders by gently lifting and turning the fully ripened fruit to keep the stem attached, thus avoiding tearing the skin and inviting spoil. The men used both hands to gather apples and carefully release them into a chest sack suspended from their shoulders or a basket hung from a nearby limb.

Women and children sorted the apples in the field on a culling table. They packed the choice fruit in barrels destined for storage at the co-op icehouse in Bentonville and then for transport by rail on the San Francisco Line. They carted culled and dropped apples to the pressing house to be fermented for cider or vinegar or to the evaporator to be sliced, sulfured, and dried.

Colonists planted apple trees in the South as early as the 1600s, with many varieties producing superior fruit to northern orchards. Because early farmers had limited ability to store and transport the enormous number of apples harvested simultaneously, they primarily selected types that either kept or processed well to satisfy an English taste for cider. By the 1840s, nurserymen throughout the South peddled catalogs of grafted fruit trees, chiefly red apples, such as Ben Davis, Winesap, and York Imperial. After the Civil War, Northwest Arkansas saw a boon in orchard planting and apple production. The Springfield Plain's fertile soil, mild winters, and abundant summer rain produced the perfect environment for growing Southern apples.

In 1881, the San Francisco Railroad connected Northwest Arkansas to markets in the East and ports in the South, and apple demand exploded. By 1910, Arkansas had over seven million apple trees, with Benton County alone having two million, more than any other county in the nation.

In this cash crop frenzy, Levi Fitch planted eighty acres of apple trees on his father's land. By 1915, he grew Arkansas Black apples almost exclusively. The medium-sized fruit was nearly round, with yellow skin covered in deep red streaks, especially on the sunny side. The pale flesh was hard when picked, crisp and juicy with a lively acidic taste. The apple was ready to be harvested in October or November, depending on the season's rainfall. The fruit kept well for several months as the skin darkened to an almost black color and the flesh softened and sweetened. The apples were edible in February but could be stored until June. Its tart, firm flesh made it a popular choice for cooked pies and cobblers. Paps sold most of his choice-grade crop for three dollars a barrel in Bentonville, ten times the cost to grow it.

What Levi Fitch could not predict, and his sons, Jesse and Silas, could not overcome, were the ravages of disease and pests such as fire blight, apple scab, hawthorn fly, San Jose scale, curculio, cedar-apple rust, and the codling moth. Without expensive annual spraying of insecticides and fungicides, these afflictions rendered the fruit underdeveloped, blemished, and wormed. Spraying cut into the profits of growing apples for fresh markets in distant cities. In the 1920s, collapsing apple prices, extreme and unpredictable weather, and increasing production in the Pacific Northwest pushed the Arkansas apple industry into rapid decline. Many orchardists abandoned their trees and switched to a new up-and-coming industry, poultry.

By the late 1920s, Jesse foresaw the inevitable end of an era that had sustained his family since the Civil War. Silas did not. For Silas, the trees planted by their father would always be in his future; they would still produce. Silas thought the market would return, making the increased cost of growing a crop profitable again. This was family land. It had provided for three generations of Fitches and would give again if he could keep it.

FIVE

LATE SPRING HEAT ROSE from the moist soil, carrying a musty organic scent into the humid air. Life seemed to pulse in wisps on gentle breezes that found their way into the open window and doorway of the kitchen.

"Levi, grab that basket for your mother," Jesse commanded while Levi shifted in his stiff shoes and pulled at the starched neck of his buttoned-up shirt.

Marybeth finished packing blackberry preserves, a pan of fresh cornbread, pickled snap beans wrapped in wax paper, and a jar of honeycomb into the wicker basket and covered it with a cloth. She hoisted the basket off the kitchen table, handed it to her son, and then looked around the room to see if she had forgotten anything. Jesse held the door as she stepped out into the warm midday sun.

"Jesse, this is right-nice for Silas and Anna Lee to have us over for Sunday dinner," Marybeth said. "It has been a while."

"Been a long while."

"Quite unusual. What do you think this is all about? You think Silas is up to something? I think he wants to talk. He wants to get us all together. Silas is going to try to convince us to stay. I know it."

"I dunno what my brother is thinking—if he thinks at all," Jesse said.

"Maybe this is Anna Lee's doing. What do you think?"

"Probably."

"She's conflicted. This whole thing's been eating at her for the past few weeks." Marybeth lifted the hem of her skirt and petticoat with both hands.

"How's that?" Jesse offered his arm as he helped his wife down the porch steps.

"You know . . . the farm, the crop, the bank. I don't know. She says Silas is talking crazy. Anna Lee has always been able to keep him under control. But lately, he has gone mad," Marybeth said to Jesse in a hushed tone that did not reach Levi.

"What's Silas talking crazy about?"

"She doesn't say. She doesn't know. Just that he seems preoccupied, distracted, distant. Talking like nobody's taking the farm from him. Anna Lee's a little unnerved," she said. "Does Paps even know what's going on?"

"No, no idea, and I'm not inclined to tell."

"Don't you think he'd notice? Are you going to tell him?" she asked.

"No."

The three strode down the cart path to the lower edge of the orchard. Jesse could not help but stop and examine each apple tree along the way, looking for developing fruit that were not there. Six weeks prior, the frost had destroyed this year's crop and any hope he and Silas could stave off their creditors. The trees looked healthy to a novice eye, with sturdy limbs and green fleshy leaves soaking up the late spring sunshine. Jesse knew otherwise.

As they approached the dogtrot cabin, Jesse said to Levi, "Give me that basket and run on down to Paps and make sure he's gitting ready for dinner. Don't take no for an answer."

"Yes, sir." Levi spun to the right at full speed with energy only a seven-year-old boy could muster at a moment's notice.

Jesse called out, "Wait."

Levi braked hard halfway to the cabin and turned, catching himself from falling backward in the dirt with a quick hop.

"In the springhouse, your Uncle Silas has three bottles of root beer, cooling. Bring 'em up with Paps."

Again, Levi took off in a sprint.

"Marybeth, this is hard . . . for everyone. I don't expect Anna Lee to take it well." Jesse reached over and took her hand as they continued to walk.

"Silas doesn't want us to leave," she said.

"I know. But Silas don't understand there's nothing to stay for." He turned to Marybeth. "The bank's got it all. We own nothing. Nothing. I can't tell Paps."

The cart path bent left as it climbed up the back edge of the orchard. Silas's house came into view at the top of the crest. In the yard next to the house, Anna Lee flung a red and white checkered cloth into the air with both hands, letting the breeze open it up before guiding it back onto a kitchen table set in the grass. Four girls, stair-stepped in size wearing white cotton dresses, buzzed between the kitchen door and the developing picnic outside. The three youngest, Sussie, Vesta, and Mayel, had pale blonde, wispy hair needing a barrette or ribbon, as it drifted about in the air with each movement. Only the oldest, Nancy, who was just coming into womanhood, had her mother's richly hued blonde curls draped to her exposed shoulders.

When she spotted them trudging up the path, Nancy ran to Jesse and Marybeth. "Uncle Jesse," she said, turning her head as she careened into Marybeth's midsection with both arms out wide.

"Well, that's some welcome, Nancy," Marybeth said, catching her breath. "You'd think we just traveled from Kansas City to see you instead of just across the field. You remember, we live over there," she motioned with her chin, "and see you every week?"

"But Aunt Marybeth, this is just a special day. Mama's got all the fixings for dinner. We got ham, store-bought."

"Now, Nancy, let me look at you a little." Marybeth held her niece at arm's length. "My, how you keep growing up. I think you have gained an inch since last week. Are you doing what you can around the house to help your mother?"

"Yes, ma'am."

"Have you finished *The Story of Doctor Dolittle*?"

"No, ma'am, not yet. You mean reading it again? No, I haven't finished it the second time. Oh, how I love the doctor. Right now, he has arrived at the monkey kingdom, and he's treating the sick monkeys but has not yet met the *pushmi-pullyu*." Nancy looked at her aunt. "You know of the *pushmi-pullyu*, don't you?"

Marybeth nodded and looked at Jesse.

"Don't ask me," Jesse said, shrugging his shoulders.

"The *pushmi-pullyu* is a fantastic mythical creature that is only found in the deepest of jungles in Africa. It has no tail but a head at either end with sharp horns like an antelope's. They're very rare and very shy. Doctor Dolittle wants to bring one back to England and put it in a circus. But he has to worry about the king of Jolliginki again and pirates before he gets home. You know he can talk to animals, don't you?" she said to her uncle. "I want to be a veterinarian, too. Do they let women become veterinarians? If not, I want to be Doctor Dolittle's assistant."

"I'm sure you can be whatever you want when you grow up," Jesse added.

"You know, with a *pushmi-pullyu,* you can make a lot of money. They are sooo rare," Nancy said.

Jesse whispered to Marybeth, "Maybe we can find a pushy-pully to save the farm," then he smiled.

Marybeth elbowed her husband without giving his comment any credence. She focused on Nancy. "When you're done with this book, I'll find you another. *Anne of Green Gables.* It's your mother's book from when she was a little girl, but I still have it. I think you are old enough for it now."

"Oh, I can't wait. Come, let's go." Nancy grabbed her aunt and uncle's hands and led them up the path to the house. As they arrived, the three younger girls broke away from their tasks and flocked over to welcome them.

"Levi's coming with root beer in a minute," Jesse said to Anna Lee, who also met them at the yard's edge. "I sent 'im down to check on Paps. I'm looking for a push-me-pull-you. You seen any around here?"

"Pardon me?"

"Ignore him if you will," Marybeth said to her sister. "He knows not the boundaries of civility."

"I was hoping Paps would come, and I'm so glad you're here." Anna Lee undid the strings of her apron and pulled it over her head.

She positioned her pregnant abdomen to the side, hugging her sister around the neck.

"Don't believe you're gonna last three more months," Marybeth said, placing her hands on Anna Lee's belly.

"I have a choice?"

"Not now—Jesse, go put that basket on the sideboard," Marybeth said. "We brought some bread and beans. There're sweets, too, for the girls," she said to Anna Lee.

"Come to the kitchen. We've so much to talk about," Anna Lee said, pulling on her sister's arm and backpedaling toward the house.

Jesse wandered up to the big barn at the side of the yard and found Silas sitting on a bench.

Before Jesse could speak, Silas said, "Where's Levi? I ain't seen 'im come up with you." Silas adjusted a pocketknife in his hand and continued to whittle on a stick. Wood shavings littered the dirt between his boots.

"He's on his way with Paps."

"You're keeping 'im from me. Why you wanna take that bastard child off his homeland?"

"Bastard?"

"Bastard. You heard me, bastard."

"Levi is hardly a bastard child. I'm gonna pretend you never said that. And for the rest of the day, try to enjoy your family's company despite your crude comments."

"You're right, not proper. Just don't take to all your talk about leaving," Silas said.

"We don't have no choice. Gave it a shot. Things are different these days. We can't compete with the West. You have to be able to see it, don't you?"

Jesse sat down next to his twin. They both had an unobstructed view of the house and the dinner table on the grass. Beyond the house were the verdant crowns of hundreds of apple trees. A deep ravine, supporting a forest of oak, hickory, and chestnut, separated their orchard from another barely visible to the north. The blue sky above yielded to a dark thunderhead towering over the horizon and threatening the festivities with a far-off rumble, like an uninvited guest mumbling its displeasure.

"If you leave, you're not only gonna hurt Anna Lee but also their father. You know that. He raised them girls right. They're to stay in Benton County," Silas said.

"Their father don't care one bit about our wives. I don't know why you'd say that."

"I can say whatever the hell I want." Silas leaned in.

"Okay, let's talk about the farm," Jesse continued.

"There ain't nothing to talk about. Nothing. I'm staying. Anna Lee's staying. And next year, we're growing apples—again. You're the fool who's leaving."

"The fool?"

"You're gonna kill Anna Lee if you take her sister. How can you do that when she's six months with child?"

"Anna Lee will be fine. We might wait to leave until she delivers. But only because of her."

"You can't separate sisters."

"Marybeth's agreed to honor my wishes. She told me this again last night and will follow wherever the Good Lord takes us."

"Bullshit."

Jesse looked across the yard to where Anna Lee and Marybeth were busy setting out food and dishes. Though they were sisters, they looked nothing alike. Marybeth was tall, lithe, and with dark hair. She shifted with the natural grace and fluidity of a dancer. She seemed to move in synchrony within her world, or perhaps the world moved in response to her.

Three years her sister's senior, Anna Lee, was the same age as Silas and Jesse. She was short, stocky, fair-skinned; some would say sturdy, solid, built-to-last. Both sisters possessed a sharp intellect and a fine wit.

Their father raised them in Bentonville, town-style, with books in the family home, fine Sunday dresses to attend the Calvary Baptist Church, and afternoon teas at Madam Filigrane's School for Proper Girls. Like good young Edwardian-era women, they studied drama, music, and recitation at the Bentonville Academy. At age eighteen, Anna Lee left her home and took a teaching job at School #17, five miles northeast of town, halfway to Pea Ridge.

"I should've waited for Marybeth. That's what I should've done," Silas said, watching his sister-in-law glide about the yard.

"You can't be talking like that to me. She's my wife and probably never would've had someone like you. The way I see it, you're lucky to have Anna Lee. Luck not shared by her." Jesse had always sensed jealousy in Silas over Marybeth. Both sisters were excellent wives, beautiful, and provided loving, well-run homes. It had been ten years since he married Marybeth, a time that only seemed to intensify Silas's jealousy.

Silas never made it through eighth grade at School #17; sometime between conjugating verbs and long division, he and his teachers had lost interest in his education. He only became drawn to school again when he was eighteen, and Anna Lee moved into a spare bedroom at an adjacent farm and took over instruction at the one-room schoolhouse. Their courtship was brief, intense. Country life fascinated Anna Lee—the nearby mountains' ruggedness and the eat-or-starve balance of the harvest season. Silas was a diversion from the imperious mindset of town life found in the debutante balls, the white kid gloves, and the feathered hats. But most prominently, Silas was a conduit of escape from her overbearing, widowed father. Their first child, Nancy, was born three months after their elopement.

"You have a wonderful wife who has blessed you with five beautiful daughters. So beautiful, I have doubts you could even be their father," Jesse teased. "Who's that good-looking stud who keeps slipping into Anna Lee's bedroom when you're out?"

"Don't joke on things you know nothing about." Silas barked, shutting down the conversation. He turned his attention to the slope beyond his house.

Levi, Paps, and a gaggle of girls came into view. Levi had divided the three root beer bottles among his girl cousins to carry. Paps held a clear quart bottle by the finger hole; he leaned on his grandson's shoulder with his other hand.

"We best be joining the others. Looks like dinner's set," Jesse said, getting up from the bench.

"You don't think the bank will make another loan?" Silas asked.

"No, but I'm gonna go to town tomorrow to ask again."

Silas stood, put his hand on Jesse's shoulder to brace himself, and looked directly at his twin, like looking in a mirror. "I'm telling you now, I ain't never leaving this land, ain't never leaving. The soil here's soaked with Fitch sweat and Fitch blood. If the bank ever gets this land, it's gonna have Fitch bones in it, too. My bones, my dead body."

The twins ambled across the barnyard toward the house.

Marybeth and Anna Lee spread dinner down the center of two tables set end-to-end in the lush spring grass. Silas sat in a ladderback chair at one end; Jesse sat in a matching chair at the other. Two benches stood along the tables' uphill side for the children—the four girls in white dresses and Levi in what the men wore: dark pants and a white shirt.

Paps also wore a black coat buttoned at the waist and a black fedora covering gray hair. He sat near the center of the tables, opposite the children. An empty chair remained on either side for his daughters-in-law. To Jesse, his father looked small and fragile, slumped in the low chair on the downhill side of the tables. His curved back and sloped shoulders barely brought his chin to the level of the plate before him.

Anna Lee and Marybeth busied themselves with last-minute details, concluding with bringing out a baked ham on a platter and a woven bassinet with a light cloth draped over the handle to shade Polly, Anna Lee's fifth and youngest daughter. Following the scent of the ham, the tabby cautiously emerged from under the porch.

"You've outdone yourself," Jesse said, looking at Silas and the dinner dishes running the length of the tables.

Silas nodded, then said as the women joined the table, "Just wanted to git the whole mess of us here today to break bread together. To remind all of us who we are and where we belong. We are Fitches. We're Fitches, and nobody, nobody is going to take that away from us. Nobody is going to take our land and—"

"Silas," Anna Lee hissed.

"I just wanted to git us all together. Altogether, so you'd know who your family is."

"Hell, I know who my goddamn fambly is," Paps blurted out. "Let's eat. I'm hungry." He leaned forward and pulled the lid off a casserole in front of him.

"Paps," Anna Lee said, "We will thank our Maker first. Thank you." She gave a short, standard prayer, one her family had used her entire life. "Amen."

Conversation pulsed around the table as the two families passed white ceramic dishes filled with mashed potatoes, cornbread, turnip greens, white gravy, and sliced ham. The scent of garlic, honey, cloves, yeast, and butter outcompeted the pungent smell of the farm. Soon, only the sounds of clinking forks and smacking lips emanated from the table. The children had never witnessed a buffet this size.

"Anna Lee, everything is delicious," Marybeth said, breaking the silence.

"My pleasure."

"I thought you were saving that cured ham for the Harvest Feast," Marybeth said.

"Silas insisted we have it now. Share it with y'all." Anna Lee looked at her husband to see if she had said the right thing.

Silas smiled at his wife.

The women passed seconds and even thirds around to the children and men. Lively banter picked up between the older sisters and Levi as their stomachs filled. Leftover food on their plates became play-toys and, eventually, projectiles.

"All you, up," Anna Lee said to the children. "Take up your plates into the kitchen and run along." The children stood in unison, knocking a bench backward as they did.

"But Mama," eleven-year-old Sussie said, "we haven't had pie."

"Later, run along."

The children hustled into the kitchen with their plates. Nancy and Sussie, the two oldest, returned to clear the serving dishes and refill glasses with lukewarm tea.

"Mighty fine young girls you have there," Jesse said to Silas as the children finally left the table.

"My darlings."

Paps picked up his glass and dumped the freshly poured tea onto the grass. He reached down between his boots, pulled out the quart bottle, and placed it on the table. Marybeth looked at Anna Lee with astonishment, then at Jesse. Paps uncorked the bottle and poured the clear liquid into his glass.

"Excuse me, Paps, that's not welcome at our dinner table," Anna Lee said to him. She then looked at Marybeth and Jesse for confirmation. Both nodded.

"Woman," Silas said, "a man's entitled to wet his whistle after a fine meal like you served."

Anna Lee spun her head and glared at her husband.

"Paps, pass that likker down here," Silas said. "You got plenty."

Paps lifted the bottle and tried to pass it in front of Anna Lee.

"Help me out," Paps said.

Anna Lee crossed her arms over her chest.

"Anna Lee, pass the damn bottle," Silas barked.

Polly, sleeping in the bassinet at Anna Lee's feet, cried. Anna Lee scooted her chair in the dirt and retrieved her toddler.

"Come," Marybeth said to her sister as she also stood. "That was a lovely meal." She gathered the last dinnerware and napkins from the table and climbed the kitchen steps. Anna Lee followed with Polly on her hip.

Silas stood and reached over the table for the bottle. He tipped a generous pour for himself, took a taste, then wagged the bottle in Jesse's direction.

"Pass," Jesse said, shaking his head.

"Good stuff. Your loss." Silas took another swig, pumping the hot fluid down his throat, and sat back down.

Paps slid over to the chair once occupied by Anna Lee, closer to the bottle, and refilled his glass.

"Paps, Jesse here wants to leave the farm. Go to Washington State. He told you yet?"

"Nope."

"Now is not the time to be bringing this up," Jesse said, looking at his brother. "I think we need to hold off on that."

"No. We're talking about it right now," Silas said. He upended his glass and slammed it down on the table. "We're talking now."

Jesse turned to Paps. "Me and the missus are just discussing. Paps, things aren't too good lately. I'm not sure we can make it work much longer."

"The hell you talking about, son?" Paps asked. He looked at Silas.

"The farm, dammit. Tell Paps how you done think this land is no good no more. Go on, tell 'im," Silas said.

"I didn't say that."

"That's what I heard." Silas spun his glass with his fingers, feeling the whiskey invade his mind, stretching out time and bending his notions. "This's good corn mash, Paps. Where'd you git this shit? I thought you were down to just *jack*."

"Benoit brothers."

"You wanted to talk about the farm," Jesse said to Silas.

"No, shit. When did they start moonshining again?" Silas poured more liquor into his glass.

"I said did you want to talk about the farm?" Jesse glared at his brother. "You brought it up, so let's get this out." Jesse turned to his father. "The farm ain't worth shit. The bank owns it."

"Couple months past," Paps said, answering Silas. "They're looking to move around here. Gave me a sample. Last week."

"No kidding? Free?"

"Out of their kindness," Paps said.

"No shit? Interesting," Silas said, studying the clear liquor in his glass.

Jesse slammed his tea down on the table and looked at Silas. "You're not fooling me with this charade. Benoits don't give this shit out for free. You're a fool, Silas, to git messed up with the Benoits. You want to talk about the farm, then I will. If you want to get yourself killed bootlegging, I'll have nothing to do with you."

"Who said I'm dealing with the Benoits?"

"You're a fool," Jesse said. "A fool."

"I'd be a fool to listen to you. You, yourself, said the crop's a bust. I'm looking for opportunity, brother."

"Opportunity is making an honest living. Whatever you have in mind to do with the Benoits will get you locked up or, more likely, shot."

"I can handle myself. This doesn't seem to be of your concern," Silas said.

"Anything you do on the farm is my concern."

"Only if you're here to make it your concern. You leave, what do you care?

"Come on, Paps. Dinner's over." Jesse rose and grabbed his father by the shoulder to help him up. "Let's go."

Silas reached for the bottle, filling his glass before corking it and pushing it down the table. "For later, Paps."

Paps stood with Jesse's help and snatched up the half-empty bottle.

Jesse called into the kitchen through the screened doorway to his wife, "I'm taking Paps home."

Marybeth appeared on the landing, wearing an apron and wiping her forearms with a towel.

"Be back shortly to help collect our things." Jesse guided his father down the hill.

"Don't you go telling Paps stories about me," Silas slurred from his chair. "You're the one causing trouble here. You'll see."

Marybeth looked at Silas and pulled off her apron. "Levi," she called to her son, who was engaged in a free-for-all game of tag around the big barn with his girl cousins. "Let's go."

Marybeth bid her goodbyes to her sister and gathered her woven basket, leaving behind the preserves and jarred honeycomb. She hurried down the cart path after her husband.

Silas stood, kicking over his chair and finding his balance with a hand on the table. He looked behind as Levi ran by to catch up with his mother. Silas lunged forward and grabbed him by the shirt sleeve.

"Come here, boy," Silas said, spittle running down his chin.

Levi spun and brought the side of his fist down hard on his uncle's forearm, breaking the grip on his sleeve. Silas rotated on one foot, the other searching for solid ground before he landed on his back in the hard dirt. Levi tore off after his parents.

"My bones ain't never leaving . . . this land. You hear that, Jesse?" Silas yelled, lifting his head slightly off the ground. "Jesse . . . you hear that? You can take that to the bank." His head fell back on the dirt, eyes gazing at the clouding sky. "I ain't never leaving."

SIX

JESSE PULLED ON THE brake lever, locking the rear wheels of a 1920 Dodge Brothers truck on the macadam street. He looked out the flat glass windshield, over the barreled engine cowling and muscular front fenders, to Bentonville's main square. The one-ton flatbed was the only possession he and Silas owned that had not been set as collateral. The orchard could not operate without it. He rolled up the canvas flaps covering the sides of the square, boxy cab and slid off the bench seat. The black front of the truck rested on a rust-covered steel frame supporting a wood-planked bed. Red-brown mud caked the heavy-duty rubber tires, announcing to the observant that the vehicle had just come in from the countryside. Like the truck, Jesse felt he looked out of place in town.

He walked past a grocer with *DRINK Coca-Cola* painted in massive white script on the red background of a building. The hustle and energy of the city were taxing, bringing hesitation and uncertainty to his step. He passed the Elkhorn Barbershop, alive with the sounds of gossip, and detected the oily scent of pomade and the tang of witch-hazel astringent drifting out the open doorway. It had been years since Jesse afforded himself a proper haircut; Marybeth did her best to keep him adequately groomed. He paused at his reflection in the shop windows, straightened his coat, and adjusted the tie under his vest. He then turned and walked past the Royal Theater and down Central Avenue.

Four red granite columns with bell-shaped Corinthian capitals, reminiscent of an Athenian temple, supported the impressive edifice of the Benton County Bank. Jesse climbed the broad white marble steps and pushed open one of the large double doors. Tellers stood on either side of the room behind paneled counters with frosted glass partitions. In the center of the white marble floor was a single, round wooden table with a black inkwell and a chained dip pen. Amber light filtered through a stained-glass circular dome in the ceiling.

"May I help you?" a young man behind the counter on the left asked.

"I'm hoping to speak with Mr. Cavness. You can tell 'im Jesse Fitch is calling."

Immediately, a heavy-set man in his early sixties emerged from a back office. He wore a bow tie and dark-blue double-breasted wool suit that stressed his girth. Cuffed hems danced on the top of his polished wingtips as he walked. A gold watch chain hung from his belt. "Jesse, come in. We need to talk."

Jesse pulled off his hat and followed Mr. Cavness into a private room; someone closed the door behind him. The room was lit by a large arched window covered with delicate, sheer curtains. Cavness motioned for him to sit in a padded burgundy leather chair at a polished wood table.

"Mr. Cavness—"

"Jesse, I know why you're here."

"We need some time. Silas and I have a plan."

"You don't understand, do you?" Cavness sat directly across the table from Jesse and leaned forward. "Your farm ain't worth what you owe."

"Last year, we borrowed to spray. The crop was good, but you know, the prices dropped again. Couldn't make back the money. This year, the buds were aplenty. Nobody predicted the frost. I couldn't do nothing about that. You know everyone's hurting, don't you? Even though we ain't got no fruit, we gotta spray. Mr. Cavness, if I can't pay a sprayer, they're gonna cut my trees down," Jesse said.

Cavness leaned back and reached behind him to an ashtray on a side table, picking up the remnants of a cigar. He puckered his lips around the end, lit a match, and pulled a flame into the ash until it glowed. Blue smoke played out in the sunlight, slanting into the room.

"Not much I can do about that, is there, Mr. Fitch? I would advise you and Silas to start making some payments on your account, 'less you want the sheriff to come pay you a visit."

"You can't do that to us. We got dealt a bad hand this year. Everyone."

"Everyone, you're right. But everyone don't owe me money, more than their land is worth," Cavness said. "You will think of something."

"We'll do all we can, sir. Please, this land has been in the family for a long time. My grandfather fought in the war for this land."

"Do I look like I care how long the Fitches have been farming in Benton County? I don't. Paying back those who lent you money is something I care about. I will foreclose if I have to."

"Please—"

"Don't please me, Mr. Fitch."

"Silas's wife's expecting a child soon. I ask you for some kindness for her. We're gonna make good on our promise. Please—"

"I think we're done here, Mr. Fitch. You figure it out. The bank is not lending you another cent."

The office door opened, and the young teller stood at the side of the doorway. Jesse read the cue and rose from the table. "Mr. Cavness, you'll drive the last of the Fitches from Benton County." He grabbed his hat and stepped toward the door, turning sideways to pass the teller and leave the bank.

Cavness blew a long stream of blue cigar smoke across the table and said to the teller, "Don't ever admit him into this bank again."

Jesse returned to the town square and found shade on a bench under a beech tree. He needed to collect his thoughts. He had expected Cavness to be unsympathetic, but he did not expect him to be wholly dismissive. Operating the farm in the last several years had become progressively expensive. There were trucks to hire, to spray insecticides and fungicides in order to fight the increasing threat of pests and disease. They would need workers to spread fertilizer and till the soil between the apple rows to keep the trees strong and healthy—and to prune and shape the branches to maximize yield. It was a task too large for just him and Silas. And the cost of it all far outpaced what they made from the apples they harvested and sold in the past few years; they had looked to the bank for relief.

Jesse did not blame Cavness for cutting off their credit. He would have done the same if he had been in the banker's position. All he really wanted was a little more time. Time to let Anna Lee deliver her child. Time to get their affairs in order and make plans to leave. Or perhaps, time to start something new on the land. Silas would be no help; he proved this the day before with his utter denial that the farm was bankrupt and that there was no future in growing apples.

Leaving Arkansas would not be easy. He knew no other life. His wife and sister-in-law knew no other life. Benton County was their home, his father's and grandfather's home. It just didn't seem fair, Jesse thought. But what else could he do? He would have to get Silas and Paps onboard with any new plans for the use of the land. Paps actually owned the orchard; he was the one who had the title, which had been passed down after his grandfather died. But lately, and for the past several years, he and Silas have been running the farm, splitting the profits and debts between them. In many ways, just packing up and leaving with his wife and son would be the easiest.

He could get a fresh start somewhere, move out West where the valleys were carpeted in lush green lettuce, celery, and carrot tops, and the gentle hillsides were splashed in the multi-hued glow of apples, oranges, and cherries. The sun would warm the earth through clear skies, melting the winter's snowfall in the surrounding mountains and sending pure icy water cascading down to broad rivers, aqueducts, and canals to satisfy thirsty crops. A man could raise produce out West without fear of drought, hard winter freeze, or disease. A man could buy a house there and raise a family. His children could become engineers, doctors, or even bankers if they did not want to harvest the cornucopia that California, Oregon, and Washington provided. Jesse slapped his knees, arched his back, and looked up with the sureness that his decision was made. There was nothing left in Benton County for him and his family. Out West was where he belonged. If Anna Lee and Paps wanted to come with, it would be okay with him. Jesse rose from the bench and stood with newfound confidence. The hell with Silas.

In front of him stood a granite obelisk supporting a generic Confederate soldier's statue at parade rest, facing west. Jesse always thought this figure, with a cavalry hat, was what his grandfather must have looked like—brave, stoic, a man of conviction—ready to fight for what he felt was right. Jesse walked over to the twenty-foot monument and looked up at the soldier. He had a bedroll slung over one shoulder and a cartridge pouch over the other. Both hands supported the barrel of a rifle propped before him. Knowing eyes with pupils drilled into stone perched above his sturdy nose and shapely Vandyke. Jesse walked around the monument and ran his fingers on the granite plinth, reading the inscription:

> THEY FOUGHT FOR HOME AND FATHER-LAND. THEIR NAMES ARE BORNE ON HONOR'S SHIELD. THEIR RECORD IS WITH GOD.

Jesse knew little about his grandfather, except that he came from Illinois and fought for the Confederacy. He must have had good reason to fire upon his northern brethren. Jesse assumed he had lost his fingers in the war, but nobody ever spoke about it. Jesse thought, what a betrayal to his grandfather's memory to walk from the land he cleared and fought for. What a cowardly act to not fight for his heritage. Silas was not giving up and said something like the land was the "hill he was to die for." His *raison d'être,* Marybeth would say.

Goddamn, he thought. Hadn't he just made up his mind to leave? Hadn't he justified his departure by reconciling that he had done everything humanly possible to save the farm, and that unlimited opportunity existed on the West Coast? Hadn't he come to terms with splitting his relationship with his twin? Perhaps Silas was right. Maybe he could muster the conviction to fight back, cast off his defeatism, build back their livelihood, turn a profit, and continue to do what Fitches had done on the land for generations. Jesse looked at the statue again, finding strength. He spun on his heels and headed down Southeast A Street.

Massive elm trees lined the newly paved road as the commercial town center yielded to a residential neighborhood of stately homes. A gray squirrel darted across the street and ascended a dark trunk. It paused with its claws spread-eagled on deeply furrowed bark with untidy ridges. The rodent seemed possessed, with a staccato chirp and the Tourette tic of its crooked, body-size tail. When he approached, it darted around the trunk, then continued its chatter and jigging from an overhead limb.

Jesse came to a two-story house with white siding. Pale pink roses, climbing a lattice, framed its broad front porch. Lush maidenhair ferns spilled over the side of a brass urn by the entry. He strode purposely down the walkway, rehearsing his pitch. He climbed the steps, crossed the porch, and rapped on the door.

A young Negress with a white apron covering her modest black dress appeared in the doorway. She had coffee-brown skin, piercing obsidian eyes, and black hair pulled into a crochet net. She looked at Jesse but said nothing.

"Delilah, who's there?" A man's raspy voice came from inside.

Delilah stepped aside to let Jesse enter, taking his hat and coat.

Someone had elegantly decorated the home in the latest style, he thought. A quartz crystal fireplace anchored the inside wall of the sitting room. Double-hung windows with heavy drapes pulled to the side made the space look imposing. Jesse ventured toward an oriental carpet in the center of the room to speak to the man seated in an upholstered wing chair facing away from the door.

"Sir," Jesse said, his hands nervously looking for a home.

"Jesse? This is unexpected." The man had a narrow, straight face with sagging jowls, cleanly shaven. Long gray strands of side hair partially covered his balding head. He wore a dark coat with a thin braided leather bolo cinched to the top of his buttoned-up white shirt.

"I was in town on business. Please excuse me to assume that you'd accept me today."

"Is this about Marybeth?"

"No. . . . Yes," Jesse said.

"Sit down." The man pointed to another upholstered chair a few feet away. "Delilah, bring me some tea," he called out to the hallway. "Get ice from the box."

Jesse sat at eye level with his father-in-law. "We're gonna lose the farm. Silas and I were expecting a decent crop this year. The almanac predicted. We got struck by the freeze. The trees are barren."

"You're here alone?"

"Silas don't understand the predicament we're in, Mr. Suggs. I'm doing what I can to ease the situation."

Delilah appeared with a tall glass of tea on a silver tray. A matching bowl in the center held chips of ice. She set the tray on a table near Suggs and tonged ice into his glass.

"What's it that you want?" Suggs asked Jesse.

"I was hoping you could speak to Mr. Cavness."

"Cavness? About what?"

"Silas's not thinking right. I'm scared when the bank comes after the land, Silas will be stupid. I worry about Anna Lee and the girls."

Suggs studied Jesse for several seconds, then reached over to his glass of tea. Condensation from the humid air wetted the surface and ran down in beads. He placed a cloth napkin on his lap to catch the drip.

"I'm taking Marybeth and our son to Washington State," Jesse said.

Suggs took a sip of the red-brown tea. "When are you leaving?" He put his glass back on the tray.

"Soon as I git our affairs in order. Marybeth wants to wait until Anna Lee births. We can do that."

"Pregnant again?"

Jesse nodded.

"You know I have no desire to invest in apples."

"Yes, sir. I'm not here asking for money," Jesse said. "I just need time to convince Silas."

"I told you, I want nothing to do with apples."

"These daughters are yourn, sir."

"If their mother were alive, she might care. I don't."

Jesse shifted in his chair, taking in what he had just heard. An awkward silence filled the room before he responded, "I'm hoping you can put in a word with Mr. Cavness. . . . Tell 'im we'll make good on what we owe."

"You said that already."

"I'm leaving . . . mind's made up. It's Silas and the girls I'm worried about. Silas ain't thinking right. He thinks he can save the farm. Heard yesterday about the Benoits. They're back in business. Dropped some corn mash by the farm. I think Silas might think to run likker or something. I'm just looking after the girls and Anna Lee. This ain't gonna turn out well for nobody if Silas hooks up with the Benoits. You know if the sheriff comes evicting, Silas'll fight back, said so hisself yesterday. We're in a hole right now."

Suggs nodded while looking right through Jesse, his mind lost in thought.

"Silas will fight. A bullet through the chest is the only thing that will convince 'im he's lost. He's likely to take others with 'im." Jesse stood. "I have ast nothing of you except for Marybeth's hand. Nobody coulda predicted the problems we've—the whole county—had. It's not our damn fault blight has run through the crop. It's not our damn fault we can't compete with the Northwest. Hell, last fall, you could buy apples in Little Rock from Washington State cheaper than we can grow 'em here." Jesse balled his fists. "We're in a bad spot right now. I need a little slack. I don't know what to do. I should leave the farm right now, but I can't."

Suggs snapped back and focused on Jesse, but showed no emotion. He propped his elbows on the chair and interlaced his fingers.

Jesse continued, "You're our last hope. You think it was easy for me to come calling on you? Do you? I've got pride. I've tried to provide a proper home for your daughter and Levi. But things are out of my control right now. We lose the farm 'less we pay the bank. They ain't waiting no longer. I can't control Silas."

Suggs looked at his son-in-law, then picked at his teeth with a fingernail. "You think I'm a rich man?"

"Why, yes, Mr. Suggs. You're wealthy." Jesse motioned to the well-appointed room.

"You think I'm a generous man?"

"No, Mr. Suggs, I can't say that I believe that."

"You're right, I'm not. But I'm a calculating man. A man of opportunity. A man of complexity. You see, Jesse, if I were generous,

I would bail Silas and you out, loan you the money to keep your farm, and help ensure that my investment paid off. But I already told you I'm not interested in apples. A bad bet."

"Mr. Suggs, I don't understand where you are going with this."

"You wouldn't because you are a simple man and I'm a man of complexity."

Jesse took a step toward the door. "I think I'm done," he said indignantly. "I'm sorry to have imposed on your time this afternoon."

"No imposition. No, none at all. In fact, you may have just opened up an opportunity for me."

"Sir?"

"You wouldn't understand." Suggs straightened the bolo under his collar. "Say, I thought you were leaving for Washington."

"We is."

"What are you waiting for? What do you care about what happens to the farm?"

"I don't know what I want." Jesse continued toward the door and turned. "I want what I can't have. G'day, Mr. Suggs."

Delilah had the door open with his coat and hat ready. Jesse took them in his arms and marched down the walkway to Southeast A Street. It always amazed him that sweet Marybeth and Anna Lee could come from such a miserable man. They must have taken after their late mother, a woman he had never met.

SEVEN

LEVI SLID DOWN THE dirt embankment on the uphill side of
Spanker Creek Road. "Come on! Hurry up," he called out behind
him to his cousins then darted across the gravel. On the other side,
he ducked and rolled through the barbed-wire fence, then scooted
off the creek bank on the seat of his pants, landing on an exposed
rock beach at the edge of the water. "You're so slow."

Levi unfastened the strap clips of his overalls and wiggled the
tight denim off his hips. Hopping on one foot toward the water,
he slipped a leg out, then the other. Wearing only white drawers,
Levi balanced on moss-covered rocks as he waded into the pool up
to his knees, then turned around.

Vesta was already behind him on the beach, pulling her dress over
her head. Sussie was at the dirt bank helping Mayel climb down.

"Watch this," Levi said as he tipped backward into the shallow
pool, completely submerging himself, then jerked up to stand.
"Whoa! Water's cold as a witch's tit." He brushed droplets off his
shoulders and arms. "Come on, git in."

Vesta stood in three inches of water, naked except for white
bloomers dropping to her knees. She tightened the drawstring at
her waist and pensively stepped forward. "Levi, you're such an
animal."

"*Haa oooowl!*" Levi howled, then slapped the water, sending a splash into the air toward Vesta.

"Knock it off," she hissed.

Sussie helped six-year-old Mayel out of her dress, then stripped down to bloomers herself. She held her sister's hand as they ventured to the edge of the rocky beach. Levi palmed the water's surface again to splash them.

"Stop it, Levi!"

The pool was in a sharp bend of the creek, fifteen feet wide and three feet deep. Bottomland trees covered the surrounding floodplain and offered welcome shade over the water. Levi had seen a river otter in the pool the week before but did not expect it would hang around today with all the noise the four were making.

Vesta joined Levi in the deep water and then dunked entirely under. Her blonde hair fell over her face when she rose back up. "*Roooar!* Sea monster!" she screamed at Levi as she lifted her arms in a menacing posture.

Levi pushed her over; she went under again, then swam off.

Sussie found a slider hiding behind a boulder and reached down to pick it up. Flames of bright red fringed its yellow and green head. "Look, you want this?" she asked Mayel as she held out the three-inch turtle. "Take 'im and keep 'im. It won't bite."

Mayel waved her off and poked at the water with a stick.

Sussie eased the turtle into the stream, where it swam off, finding shelter under a log.

A car coming up the river road caught all their attention. The creek was on private property, and they were not sure they should swim there. Crouched low, the four children remained quiet as the car continued past without slowing on the road above.

Once the car's sound faded, Levi said, "Watch me." He climbed the creek's far bank, gripping the end of a rope hanging from an overhead limb twenty feet up. The rope was an inch thick and had a large, sloppy knot tied above its frayed end. Holding the rope, Levi scrambled onto a fallen tree trunk to gain height. He then secured the rope with both hands and jumped into the air, wrapping his legs around the knot. Momentum took him across the pool to the rocky beach, then reversed his course, allowing him to plunge into the pool's center like a cannonball.

"Me next!" Vesta shouted as she climbed the bank using a root handhold. "Git me the rope," she said to Levi. Vesta then swung from the lower bank and dropped directly into the water. "Sussie, come on," she said to her older sister. "Just cuz you're eleven don't mean you can't have some fun."

"I don't have to," Sussie said.

"You do."

"Nope." Sussie picked up a flat rock the size of a silver dollar and flicked it across the smooth water with her wrist, skipping it several times before it landed on the opposite bank. She looked for another.

Levi repeatedly climbed the bank, pulled the rope up to the fallen trunk, and delivered a splashing cannonball into the water.

Twenty minutes later, the four cousins sat on the rocky beach in a small frame of sunshine to warm up and dry their undergarments.

"Pa went to town today. Business with the bank," Levi said. He watched a black ant wander from the stones to the top of his foot.

Mayel watched the same. "It'll bite ya."

"It don't bite." Levi reached down, placed his hand in front of the ant, and let it crawl into his palm. He held it up to his face and pretended to kiss the insect before flicking it off with a finger.

"So?" Sussie said. "That ain't nothing. Our father went to town three times last week."

"Did he bring ya anything?" Levi asked. He looked for another ant among the stones.

"Don't need to. We got everything we need already," Sussie bragged.

"I don't think so." Levi picked up a rock and tossed it toward the pool. When he turned to watch the splash, he noticed a boy he did not recognize sitting on the fallen tree trunk across the creek. The boy was about fifteen years old with curly red hair, and he shifted a rifle in his lap and stared at them.

"What you want?" Levi called out.

"Nothing. Just enjoying the view," the boy answered.

"Who are you?" Levi asked.

"No name. But my daddy owns this property, and you're trespassing."

"Ain't nobody owns the crick bed. We can swim here anytime we want."

The boy stood and took a few steps toward them, stopping at the top of the opposite bank. "Where's your sister?" he asked. "I know you got a sister. I seen 'er."

"I ain't got no sister."

"They look like sisters to me," the redheaded boy said, referring to Sussie, Vesta, and Mayel. The girls were still in their wet bloomers and blouse-less.

"These're my cousins."

"Okay, where's your cousin? The older one. What's 'er name?"

"Her name is Nancy," Vesta shouted.

Levi and Sussie glanced at Vesta, shook their heads, and whispered, "No."

Sussie pulled a camisole over her shoulders, conscious of the boy's attention toward her.

"Nancy. Yeah, Nancy. Where's Nancy? I'd be happy to let Nancy come a swimming here," the boy said. "Now, she's welcome."

Levi got an uncomfortable feeling from this boy across the creek. He had been swimming at this hole for years; his father, uncle, and grandfather had probably done the same. Levi did not know who this boy was or where he came from. "We're leaving," Levi said to the boy as he stood and picked up his clothes.

"Come on, let's git out of here," Sussie said, grabbing her two sisters by their arms.

"No, you stay right there." The boy leveled his 22-caliber lever-action Winchester at Levi. "I was out hunting vermin this morning, and I think I found some." The boy lifted the barrel and fired into the trees above Levi's head.

Sussie, Mayel, and Vesta scampered up the bank to get back to the road. Levi gathered up their remaining clothes to do the same.

"Stay right there, you," the boy screamed, training the rifle at Levi again.

Levi stopped at the bottom of the bank and faced him.

"Next time y'all come a swimming in my crick, you bring Nancy with ya. You hear? This here land belongs to my daddy, and I gets to say who gets to swim. . . . On second thought, send Nancy by herself next time."

"There ain't gonna be a next time, and you can just go to hell," Levi answered before beginning his climb. Levi reached up for a handhold and saw a man standing above him. The man pulled him up with a powerful grip, then guided him through the barbed-wire fence. The redheaded boy fired another shot into the air, then wandered off.

"Mr. Jacobsson?" Levi said to his neighbor.

Lars Jacobsson was a big man, a Dane, and a relative newcomer to Northwest Arkansas, having arrived from Wisconsin ten years before to grow Ben Davis apples in warmer climes. He farmed the flat land just to the east of the Fitch homestead.

"You stay away from that boy," Jacobsson said. He then led Levi behind his truck, where all three girls huddled on the road.

"How?"

"I heard the shot. Stopped to see what was going on. That's all. You done nothing wrong."

"He don't own that crick. You can't own a crick," Levi said. He handed the girls their clothes.

"No, he don't own the creek. In fact, his daddy don't even own the land. They're tenant farmers. Just moved here, and I don't expect they're gonna stay long. First flood will wipe them out."

"It ain't right he talks to us that way. You heard me tell 'im to go to hell. Please don't go telling my pa I spoke that."

"That's where a boy like that belongs," Jacobsson said. "You spoke right. I won't go telling your pa."

"Appreciate that, Mr. Jacobsson." Levi stepped into his overalls and flicked the straps over his shoulders, snapping the clips to his chest. "I don't git why he was talking about Nancy like that. What'd he want with her?"

"Nothing good. You stay away from here 'till they move on, you hear? Nancy, too." He turned to the girls. "You, too, Sussie. You watch yourself around that boy. He is nothing but trouble." Jacobsson lowered the tailgate of his truck and lifted Mayel in. "You get in. I'll run ya home."

EIGHT

JESSE WORKED THE CLUTCH and shifter to set the flatbed truck in low gear before climbing the two-track dirt road leading from Spanker Creek up the steep ravine to the gentle slope of the Fitch orchard. Washouts and rocks from the uphill bank rutted the washboard road. A dark-green deciduous canopy sat atop fifty-foot black and gray hardwood trunks scattered across the rocky forest hillside where lichen and fern competed for brief arcs of sunlight. Another gray squirrel worked the fallen leaves, searching for autumn nuts overlooked during winter. Rounding the last switchback with the engine whining against the grade, Jesse saw the glint of shiny black paint between the trees at the edge of the woods. A late-model Chevrolet sedan sat in front of his father's dogtrot. History predicted visitors arriving in a fine car like this were not welcome.

Jesse cut his engine when he pulled close to the Chevy and hopped out of the cab. Two men, drawn from the woods by the sound of his truck, emerged from behind the cabin. Both men appeared to be middle-aged, trim, and confident, with dark city suits and black felt fedoras.

"Howdy," Jesse volunteered.

"You the owner of this here farm?" the tall one asked as they approached through the ankle-high grass.

"Yeah, it's family land. Help you?"

The man pulled open his coat to reveal a silver star and holster clipped to his belt. "We're from the Bureau."

"And?"

"Just looking around."

Even before they spoke, Jesse figured the men were revenue agents. "We have nothing of interest to you here," Jesse said.

The second man then spoke, "Kinda secluded up here. Real quiet, lots of privacy. You got any neighbors nearby?"

"Couple."

"We drove around a little. What you got, three houses on this farm?"

"Three," Jesse said, not knowing where this conversation was going and feeling irritated by the intruders. "What is it that you want?"

"There's likker moving down in Bella Vista. You know anything about that?" the tall man asked.

"If that's what you're looking for, you're wasting your time up here. We grow apples," Jesse said.

"I ain't seen no fruit on them trees when we drove up. Looks like y'all could use a little cash income this year."

"We're doing fine. Trees have been providing for twenty years. We'll git through this one."

The two agents now stood only a few feet from Jesse and spread out to either side; Jesse twisted his neck to see each.

The tall man said to his partner, "You believe this shit? Boy thinks we don't know what's going on."

"Maybe we need to do some enlightening," the second man said. He crossed over to the sedan and reached through an open window, pulling out a clear-glass bottle. "Recognize this?"

The revenuer held a bottle, much like the one his father had brought to the picnic the day before.

"Never seen it, sir."

"Well, we found it next to that old man passed out down by the springhouse. You ain't kin to 'im, are you?"

Jesse nodded and then shifted uneasily on his back leg. A blue jay glided down from the top of the white oak tree, back-tilted its wings, and landed its spindly legs on the split-rail fence. It let out a squawk to mark its presence.

"Corn mash, good stuff. I ain't seen no cornmeal around here, so I'm taking you ain't cooking nearby," the second man said. "I figured you're the cider type, but then, again, you ain't got no fruit."

Jesse was confident these men would not find more than the one bottle today, a gift from the Benoit brothers, his father had said. Still, these agents snooping around the farm disturbed him. They must have had some reason to come up here first; finding the empty bottle would only reinforce their suspicions.

"What makes you think we got anything to do with what's turning up in Bell' Vista?" Jesse asked.

The second man undid the buttons of his jacket and propped his palms against his hips, pushing his coat back, his turn to flash his badge and sidearm. "Drunk folk say it's coming down Spanker Creek. We tasted the water on the way up; don't taste like corn likker. Figured some cat is bottling it up nearby instead."

"You take your bottle and leave us alone now." Jesse was getting impatient with these government men. "There's no stilling here, no bootleg passing through this farm. Time for you to go."

It seemed to Jesse these two agents were not used to not having the last word, especially when they came up empty-handed. They glared at him and squared their shoulders. The tall man readjusted his fedora before walking back to the car to join his partner. As he got into the driver's seat, the second man stepped behind the sedan and popped open the trunk. He tossed the empty bottle in, then lifted a Remington 12-gauge short-barrel shotgun from the boot. He dug into his coat pocket, retrieved an orange-colored shell, and fed it to the breech.

"We're not going far. You'll see this again," the second man said, raising the gun.

The blue jay then sprang from the fence with one last screech, beating its wings in the air toward the crown of the oak. The revenuer brought the gunstock to his shoulder in one smooth sweep and squeezed off a shot toward the bird. Gray and blue feathers burst into the air, releasing a mangled carcass to arc across the field.

The man reloaded the shotgun, slammed the trunk closed, and walked around to the car. Before getting in, he said from the other side of the roof, "This trail leads to the Benoits. You best git off it while you can."

Jesse watched the sedan maneuver down the drive into the woods and turn into the first switchback before he went to fetch his father from the springhouse.

Marybeth dropped her laundry basket full of wet sheets in the grass when she saw the flatbed come over the rise on the dirt road. She ran to the truck when Jesse pulled it to a stop in front of their house.

"Jesse, I heard the shot," she said. "What's going on?"

"Nothing. Someone trying to sell Paps a shotgun." Jesse climbed from the cab and embraced his wife. The clean smell of lye soap lifted from her wet apron. "He's gone now. Paps's resting. I'll check on 'im later."

"What's he shooting?"

"A bird, that's it. He left."

"Lars dropped the kids off with his truck this afternoon. Said some boy down at the crick was causing some trouble."

"Everything ok?" Jesse asked.

"Fine, no problems. . . . How'd it go at the bank?" Marybeth took Jesse's wrists and held him out front where she could look at his face.

"Not good," he said. The afternoon sun was still high in the baby-blue sky, thick with humidity. "Come." Jesse led her to their covered porch, carrying the basket for her. "Town square was bustling. *Flesh and the Devil* is playing at the Royal."

"Greta Garbo?"

"Yeah." Jesse dropped the laundry and motioned for Marybeth to sit on a rocker in the shade. He took another and scooted over to where he could touch her shoulder. "I wish I could take you to the motion-picture show. Someday."

"That would be lovely. I'll look forward to it. What else did you see?"

"Lots of pretty dresses and hats. Everyone's hair is done up on top of their head this year, like a cyclone. Busy."

Marybeth gathered her long brown hair and spun it playfully above her head. "Like this?" she said before letting it cascade down her shoulders. "What's the season's color?" She pulled at the top of her dress sleeves and coquettishly rotated her shoulders like a schoolgirl.

"Let's see, yellow, pink, lavender. I don't know. I'll have to take you for yourself next time."

"Like rose?"

"Yeah, like rose. Pink rose."

Marybeth stood and spun around, letting her cotton dress fill with air. She stopped, facing her husband, rested on her back foot, and pointed the other. She gave him a seductive wink with both hands on her hips and pursed her lips. "You know I would look ravishing in yellow silk." Marybeth spun one more time, then sat again next to Jesse. "You stopped by the bank?"

Jesse looked to his left, across the yard, and down the rows of apple trees. "I met with Mr. Cavness."

"Cavness?"

Jesse nodded his head with his gaze fixed on the orchard. "He won't budge."

"You told him the truth? Told him about Anna Lee?"

"Marybeth, I laid it out plain as day. He's gonna send the sheriff out to collect what's his unless we can make payments." Jesse looked at his wife.

A long moment of silence passed while they contemplated their grave situation and lack of viable options. Nothing had really changed in their predicament since the late freeze. However, hearing the bank decisively shut off their last avenue of hope was devastating to both.

"Anna Lee says that Silas has some money to put down," Marybeth eventually volunteered.

"He don't."

"You saw that spread yesterday? Ham and all the fixings? I don't know where he's getting it, but it's there," she said.

Jesse pushed himself out of the rocker and walked over to the edge of the porch. The sweet aroma of the moist earth decomposing in the sun's warmth filled the air. The clittering sound of katydids drowned out the light rustling of leaves from an early evening breeze. Jesse turned toward his wife and leaned up against a post. "I called on your father."

Marybeth recognized the magnitude of Jesse's admission. Only in desperation and as a last grasp to save the life they had would he reach out to her father, a man they both despised. "What was your request?"

"I ast if he would speak to the bank. Give us some time," Jesse said.

"And his response?"

"No."

"No. Of course, no. I'm surprised he even gave you an audience," Marybeth said. She wrung her hands, then placed them firmly on the rocker's arms, with her elbows poised to lift her frame from the chair. "I want to wait until Anna Lee delivers before we go," she said forcefully.

"Yes. We'll wait," Jesse said, "if we can." He then slapped his knee and grinned at Marybeth. "Where's Levi? I almost forgot." Jesse sprang from the porch and dashed across the yard to the truck. He reached into the cab and grabbed two fluted, gourd-shaped bottles capped with caramel-colored liquid.

"Levi!" Marybeth called out toward the shed barn. "Levi, come here."

Levi appeared in the doorway, saw what his father was holding, and ran toward him. "*Coca-Cola.*"

Jesse handed both bottles to his son. "Now, one's for Ma. Careful."

Levi ran to the porch with a bottle in each hand. He placed both next to his mother and sped into the kitchen, looking for a seldom-used opener.

When Levi returned to open his drink, Marybeth said, "Put mine to cool in the cistern. We'll have it later."

Levi did as he was told and returned to the edge of the porch, where he sat and prized open his cola, taking only a tiny sip. Before he took another, Jesse reached down and grabbed Levi's chin between his thumb and forefinger, holding his head up so he could see his face. "Son, things' about to change around here."

Levi failed to grasp what his father had just said. He rested the soda on the porch while keeping one hand securely on the bottle's neck.

"Your ma and I are gonna move from the farm soon. You'll come with us. We can't grow apples here no longer. We're moving to Washington."

"Moving?"

"Going west, all the way to Washington State. A long ways."

"Who all's going?" Levi asked.

"Just us, son. Just you, me, and your mother."

"What about Aunt Anna Lee? Nancy, Sussie—"

"No." Jesse shook his head.

"Paps?"

"Don't know yet," Jesse said. He let go of Levi's face and sat back down in the rocker.

"Levi, everything's gonna be all right," his mother said. She got up from her chair and sat on the edge of the porch next to her son. "Your father's a smart man and will care for us."

"But why do we have to leave and not Nancy, and Sussie, and Vesta, and Aunt Anna Lee? Uncle Silas?" Levi asked his father. He twisted his body to face him.

"Don't know."

Levi nursed his soft drink, taking only tiny sips of the warm, sweet syrup. Nothing he was hearing made a lick of sense to him. *Of course, they could grow apples. They grew every year.* "I'll be big enough this year to pick. I'll pick 'em all."

"There'll be no apples this year to pick, Levi," Jesse said. "The cold got 'em."

"The cold got 'em," Levi repeated. "Next year?"

"Next year will be too late," Jesse said. "The bank will come and take the farm before then."

A long silence brought out the insects' trilling sound in the grass and adjacent woods. Jesse knew his son did not understand the difficulties they found themselves in. He did not know about bank loans, collateral, interest, and deeds. He did not know how much it cost to spray the orchard for pests and fungus. He did not understand the mountains of regulation upon regulation passed down from the federal government, like those in the Pure Food and Drug Act of 1906. Nor did he have knowledge of fines, fees, confiscation, and arrests for wholesalers, shippers, and growers. The cost of raising apples in Northwest Arkansas was near surpassing the potential return.

"Where's Washington at?" Levi asked.

"I said, a long way away, my son." Jesse looked across the yard to the apple trees, quickly losing their verdant hue in the evening's waning light. He knew it was hard for Levi to comprehend what was happening. Marybeth seemed to have a good grasp of their predicament. Everything would work out, he was sure. Jesse thought about his encounter with the revenue agents at his father's cabin earlier in the afternoon. Silas would have some explaining to do.

NINE

"DAMN, MR. B, SCAIRT the living shit out of me," said a young man crouched behind a wooden cask. "Didn't expect nobody coming around tonight."

"Knob, level that gun somewheres else, would ya?" Jean Benoit barked as he let himself down the steep bank, holding onto saplings and roots. Loose rocks and forest debris slid downhill with each footfall.

Knob pointed the Remington rifle into the night's dark sky and stood the barrel against a post. "You gave me a startle, boss. Didn't expect nobody." He ventured from behind the whiskey still and extended his hand.

"Take?" Benoit asked, ignoring the young man's gesture.

"What?"

"What's the goddamn take?"

"When?"

"Tonight, you jackass. What's the goddamn take tonight?"

"Seventeen and a half."

"Twenty. I'm looking for twenty." Benoit walked around the small clearing next to a noisy creek tumbling off the mountainside. He approached the still, reached up, and threw a knife switch mounted on a post. A dim electric light hanging from a rafter pole came alive. He poked his head into the crude tar-paper shack, where a boiler stood atop a low fire. A conical apron topped the iron tank and led to a copper worm coiling down through a cooling box at the side. Clear liquid dripped in metronome constancy from the end of the tubing into a gallon glass container. The yellow electric light flashed in each bead as it formed and dropped.

"Rain held me up, Mr. B." Knob shifted from one foot to another, mustering the courage to explain himself.

"I didn't ast you no questions, 'why?'"

"Yes, sir, boss."

Benoit finished his cursory inspection of the operation, then sat on a double stack of boxes. He pulled a pouch from his vest pocket, rolled a generous pinch of tobacco, fixed the cigarette between his lips, and looked at Knob.

"Yes, sir." Knob hustled over to the boiler, dipped a twig into the fire, and reached it over.

Benoit pulled flame into the tobacco until the end glowed. He fingered the cigarette between his index and long, taking a deep lungful of smoke in a distinctly feminine manner. "Terrell's muling corn up here tomorrow. You best get it cooking right away."

"Is he staying? I could use some help."

"I decide if you needs help." Benoit blew smoke in Knob's direction. "You're not my only concern. What you're to worry about is doing what you're told."

"Yes, sir, Mr. B." Knob placed his hand on top of the tank to check its temperature, then stirred the hot coals below. "I could use a thermometer."

"You just don't understand, do you?"

"If I had a thermometer, the mash wouldn't burn. And I—"

"The mash ain't gonna burn cuz you ain't letting it," Benoit said. "Dip me a dram."

Knob scurried over to the collection jar and sank a thin metal tube through the neck into the liquid. He withdrew an ounce of clear whiskey, released it into a glass jar, and handed it over. Benoit tipped the jar to his lips and let the fluid spread inside his mouth; vapor filled his nose.

"Not bad. Not good. But not bad. You best have twenty bottles by morning when the corn comes."

"Oh, I will, Mr. B."

"I got me a new runner to the Bella Vista."

"Who?"

"What you needs to know that for?"

"Just curious, boss."

The electric lightbulb flickered, then faded completely, leaving only the orange glow of the fire to illuminate Benoit's face.

"What the hell, Knob? Ain't you running my Delco?"

"No, sir," Knob answered from a shadowed silhouette. "That thing scares me."

"You scairt of most shit, aren't you?" Benoit looked around the clearing for the small electric generator and lead-acid batteries. "Where's it at? Why'd you let my batteries run down?"

"Charging them batteries is not safe. Seen a man with his face eaten off from an explosion."

"Think moonshining's safe? You're more likely to get your face blown apart with a cutoff shotgun, government-style. Get that Delco fired up. I ain't sitting around 'till daybreak in the dark."

Knob felt his way over to the generator, primed the carburetor, and spun the flywheel with a leather belt, kicking the two-stroke into action. Black smoke belched with each cycle. The 20-watt bulb glowed again, and Knob gingerly backed away from the Delco and bank of glass batteries. "Sound will carry at night, you know," Knob said as he picked his way back to the boiler and placed his hand on the steel apron again.

"I told ya, I'm not sitting here in the dark all night."

"Who you got running for ya? I betcha you got that new tenant on Spanker. He ain't making it otherwise."

"No."

"Who then?"

"Not saying." Benoit flicked the butt of his cigarette into the dirt. "If you go running your mouth, someone will put a bullet in it. Might just be my brother."

"I ain't saying nothing, Mr. B."

"Never find your sorry ass after a panther rips the meat off."

"Ain't no *painter* up here," Knob said.

"Believe what you want." Benoit ground the cigarette stub with the toe of his boot. "Corn that's coming tomorrow, you treat it nice. Splendid stuff, sweet. Should be enough for three hundred gallons of mash. Not easy to come by; you treat it nice. I had to scramble to get it."

"I hear ya."

"Stewart, on the other side of the ridge, fucked his load last week. Wood rats done drowned in the pot. The fucker cooked it off anyways, like that; singlings tasted like shit. Never could clear the smell. Ran it three times, he did. Then the *conasse* tried to pass it on. End our goddamn business. Shoulda put a bullet in 'im for it. But you know, Knob, I'm a generous man. I believe in second chances."

The light bulb flickered again.

"Why'd ya get a new runner to the Bell' Vista?" Knob asked. "What happened to Strap?"

"Stupid. That's what happened to Strap. Stupid happened."

"I kinda took to Strap. Not a bad guy. Young."

"Young and stupid," Benoit said. He pinched another wad of tobacco and rolled it in paper.

"I could use a smoke, Mr. B, if you can spare."

Benoit ignored Knob's request, stood, and walked over to the boiler. He pulled a stick from the fire and lit his own cigarette. "Someday, you'll end up like Strap. He wasn't even smart enough to move on. Coulda walked across to *Mizurah,* and my brother woulda stopped at the state line. Stupid ass thought he was too smart."

"I ain't stupid, Mr. B," Knob said.

"If you ain't stupid, you'll do just fine. Too many stupids out there thinking they can make a fast buck. Remember Knob, nothing moves in this county that my brother don't want moved."

"I hear ya." Knob gathered a few split oak logs and nudged them into the fire. He stepped around to the side, wiped a drop of whiskey from the condenser with his forefinger, and tasted it. "This's a good batch, boss. Nobody in the Ozarks makes better hooch than me. I watch the temperature, that's why."

"It's good hooch cuz I give ya good corn. Any half-ass shiner can turn out likker like this with good corn. Don't go stupid on me and think you're something special."

"I'm not saying that, boss man. I like working for you," Knob said. "You're right. It's the corn—sweet and plump."

The Delco generator sputtered and died. The electric light bulb dimmed, flickered, and then went dark.

"*Merde!*" Benoit said. "You top off them batteries lately?"

"No, sir. I told ya they scare me."

"You're the stupidest *fonchock* I've ever known. A l'il coward. Do I have to do that for you, too? What you need is a mama to hold your tender hand. Get on up there and check the level on them batteries and restart the Delco."

Knob fumbled around for a carbide lamp, got it lit, and climbed back up the hill to the light plant. Six rectangular glass boxes held several lead plates, each flooded with sulfuric acid. Insulated wires connected the generator to the batteries in a series. Knob lowered the lamp to gauge their level.

An explosion filled the hollow with orange flame, knocking over the still and snuffing out the fire. The concussion upended barrels of corn and threw Benoit to the ground. Ash debris shot skyward, then drifted down like snow.

Benoit lay among the remains of the tar-paper shack, looking into the dark smoke with an emptiness in his ears. He saw Knob emerge from the haze, stumble down the hill, and collapse with his mouth wide open. He could not hear Knob screaming in pain while tearing at his clothes with fingers melted to the bone.

TEN

"Two revenuers came by Paps's last week, looking for a wild-catter," Jesse said to Silas, who was halfway up a tripod ladder with a wooden-handled pruning saw bitten into a dead limb.

"So."

"So, they had reason to drive all the way up here. Any idea you wanna share with me?" Jesse kicked at the tall grass between the apple trees.

"No," Silas said. He worked the saw back and forth several times before the diseased branch cracked loose. Its cut end pitched into the soft dirt at Jesse's feet. "We shoulda gotten this blight out last winter if we expect to save these trees."

"Listen, Silas, if you're the reason the government is snooping around, I need to know now."

"Now, why do you think I would wanna git messed up with that shit?"

"Cuz we're losing the farm, and you just can't walk away. I wouldn't doubt for a minute you'd git messed up with the Benoits. It ain't gonna work. You need to think of your wife and girls. That's what you needs to do."

Silas dismounted the ladder, pulled its third leg up, and shifted the entire rig to an adjacent tree. "You wanna help?" he asked Jesse.

"It don't matter if you cut out every last twig of blight; we don't have the money to spray, and if the sheriff don't burn the entire farm, the neighbors will."

Silas climbed to another dead branch and pulled the saw blade across its crusty bark. There were only a few diseased limbs on occasional trees, isolated to one corner of the orchard. If left alone, the fire blight would spread, infecting half the trees by winter. Birds and insects would carry the bacteria responsible for the blight from one tree to another and then to the neighboring orchards. Without copper and arsenic sprays, what the blight didn't get, the San Jose scale and cedar-apple rust would finish off.

"I'm making payment to the bank next week. You wait; I'll have sprayers out here by mid-summer," Silas claimed. "What's it matter to you, anyway? You're leaving. You got no goddamn spine."

"I got integrity and enough common sense to know that we're beaten. Running likker for the Benoits is not gonna turn that around." Jesse pulled his shoulders back and took a few steps behind him to view his brother better. "Way I figger, you've been running for the Benoits for several weeks. How else do you explain the picnic dinner with all the fixings? And the Benoits just don't go giving likker out to the likes of Paps for no reason."

"You stay outta my business. And as far as I'm concerned, this whole damn orchard is now my business." Another limb crashed to the ground, and Silas climbed down the ladder to face his brother. "You're the one selling out." Silas dropped the pruning saw to the ground and poked two fingers into Jesse's chest.

"I told you my plans. Don't think I can help you no more."

"Their father will help—Anna Lee's," Silas said.

"No, I talked to the bastard. He ain't moving."

"He ain't moving cuz you didn't stroke his love of money. He'll listen to me. I've got a proposition." Silas moved up into Jesse's face. "And you ain't leaving Paps. You can't do it."

Anger boiled up in Jesse's mind. He knew Silas was going off half-cocked to save the only life he had ever known, to preserve the legacy of their father and grandfather. Jesse looked at his twin's same height, build, hair color, and angular jaw. He was looking at himself—the curve of his shoulder, the rise of his chest with each breath, the tilt of his hips, and the spread of his stance. They were the same, yet separate. How could Silas not see what he saw? They looked through the same eyes. How could he not hear what he heard? They listened through the same ears.

Jesse thought Silas must understand the dismal future of growing apples in Benton County. He must see that getting involved with the Benoits was foolish, risky, and wrong. If they are so much alike—a single seed split in two—why does he not think the same? And, if Silas has such a rotten core, one that suppressed his common sense and duty to live a God-fearing life, could rot be present in both twins? Could they share a streak of wretchedness as well?

Tingling set into Jesse's fingers and toes; his lips quivered, and blood rushed in throbbing beats to his head. Jesse wanted to strike back, pin Silas's arms to the ground, and strangle the air from his lungs. He wanted to dominate, intimidate, and force compliance from his brother like he had never done before. But for Jesse, this would be like the right hand striking the left. They were the same, but two.

Jesse stepped backward when Silas poked him again in the chest with his left hand. He did not see Silas's right hand ball to a fist and deliver a sucker punch to his jaw, knocking his head back and tipping his lifeless frame to the ground like deadwood. Jesse's vacant eyes rolled up in their sockets, disconnected from the last remnants of his consciousness.

"Marybeth, you know it's going to kill Silas if you take Levi with you," Anna Lee said. She sat in a wooden kitchen chair with darning needles and an orphaned sock on her lap. Marybeth sat in a matching chair, patching a knee torn from a pair of overalls. The morning sun shining through the window cast a bright rectangular glow on the pinewood floorboards between the two sisters.

"Then come with us," Marybeth said.

"Can't."

"Come."

"You don't think there's any way to save the land?"

"Jesse says he talked to the bank last week, and they're through with us, sending the sheriff out," Marybeth said.

"When?"

"I don't know."

"How can they do that?"

"I asked the same. Jesse says we got no choice."

"Silas, he's not leaving. He doesn't believe the land is lost. He doesn't think the bank will take it from us."

"If they take it, what are you going to do?" Marybeth asked.

"He won't talk of it."

"We're leaving. We'll wait until you deliver if we can."

"Marybeth, that's kind of you," Anna Lee said. "I don't know what to think. Silas is so hard-headed. This isn't turning out how we'd planned. I thought we'd all be living here, raising the children together, growing fruit, and growing old. It doesn't make sense."

"Nothing does."

"Silas has been talking some hair-brained ideas about making money to pay off the bank. He won't let on exactly. I'm not sure it's law-abiding. Worries me."

"Like what?" Marybeth had suspicions but did not want to tell her sister what she suspected.

"Like something's not right. Like something he shouldn't be doing. He's obsessed. It's a fight for him. Makes me afraid. I wish we could just leave with you."

"Would you leave him and come with us?"

"Can't. Couldn't live with it if I did."

"You're so blinded, Anna Lee. Loyal but blind." Marybeth said. "I commend you for it, but you must consider your girls. If Silas is messed up in something and gets thrown in jail or, worse, shot, where does that leave you? Where do you go when we no longer own the land? Father's? Would you go knocking on Father's door, begging to be let back in?"

"No, I couldn't. I could never go back."

"Then you need to come with us. Make plans."

Anna Lee paused and put her darning into a basket at her side. She stood and smoothed out her dress with both hands. "More tea?"

Marybeth shook her head.

"Do you think Jesse suspects? You know, Levi?" Anna Lee asked.

"No." This was not a topic Marybeth wished to discuss.

Six-year-old Mayel burst through the open front doorway. A calico dress hung limp on her slight frame. "Mom, Vesta's not watching Polly."

"Where's Sussie?" Anna Lee asked her daughter.

"She's there," Mayel said. "Polly's running."

"Tell Sussie to take care of Polly and Vesta and you if she needs to. Now run along. I'm talking to your aunt."

"But Mom. Vesta—"

"Run." Mayel turned for the door, and Anna Lee turned to her sister. "We thought we were doing the right thing."

"Sure."

"Then again, who would have thought the family might split up, and Levi was the only son? I told you Silas won't take well to your leaving."

"Let's not talk about this." Marybeth shifted in her chair and pulled her shoulders back. "Jesse talked to Father."

"When?"

"Last week when he was in town."

"And?"

"He won't help. You know he could. I didn't expect he would." Marybeth said.

"Don't surprise me." Anna Lee sat back down and worked the darning needles through the sock. "Went to town?"

"Yes."

"When was the last time you or I went to town?" Anna Lee asked. "Did Jesse say anything about what they're wearing this summer?"

Marybeth's eyes lit up, and she grinned at her sister. "Pink, yellow, and lavender. He picked this up at the five-and-dime." She slipped her hand into a tote and retrieved the latest edition of *Red Book*.

"What tint of pink?" Anna Lee asked, taking the woman's magazine and letting the pages flip through her fingers.

"Rose."

"Love rose."

"You know I look horrid in rose," Marybeth said. "You could pull it off, though. I don't have your fairness."

"Fairness? I'll trade my fairness for your figure. And you, in lavender, would turn a crick into every man's neck from here to Fayetteville. We've got to find a way to get to town before the summer is over. What about this?" Anna Lee displayed a line drawing of a pencil-thin model in a dropped waist frock over a pleated skirt barely covering the knees.

"Too every day," Marybeth said. "Go to the dog-eared page. That's what you need, a satin dress. Read what it says, 'All silk crepe.' 'Shimmering and lustrous.' It has a *ja-bot* frill."

"*Ja-bot*?"

"Not sure. Might be *ja-bo*, you know, *François*. But just look at the dress. Above the knees. You'd need silk stockings with that one."

"Fourteen seventy-five. I don't think it's going to happen. Not in my lifetime." Anna Lee put the magazine down on her lap.

"Go to the next page. Can you imagine wearing that chiffon dress, silk?" Marybeth stood, held her skirt hem above her knees with one hand on her hip, and sashayed about the kitchen. "We'd be strolling along the veranda of the Park Springs Hotel with something tall and cool to drink in our hand. A little umbrella stuck in a cherry. Just a little tipsy. 'Good day, mister.' 'Not tonight, mister.' 'Oh, thank you for your compliment, but I'm spoken for.' It would be marvelous."

"I'm spoken for," Anna Lee reflected. "How about these knickers?" She showed the next page to her sister. "Shuffleboard at the Bella Vista. Driving golf balls into the lake, just us girls."

Marybeth swung at an imaginary golf ball, spinning herself back into her chair. She scooted forward and faced her sister. "Jesse said Garbo is playing at the Royal Theater."

Anna Lee smiled, then turned away. She looked out the window to see her daughters in the yard, playing an unstructured game of tag around her youngest, sitting in the dirt. Dust caked their sweaty arms and legs. Her gaiety drained. "I'm spoken for, and . . . this is our fate, is it not?"

"It is."

"Do you think it would help to go to Father ourselves?"

"I don't think so. We're dead to him, killed off when we married," Marybeth said. "You can hold on to that magazine if you want for a while. I've seen it." Marybeth folded the jeans she was working on and tucked them into the tote. "I wish we had a brother."

"A brother? For heaven's sake, why?" Anna Lee asked.

"Yeah, a brother."

"What would a brother do?"

"He would be a conduit to Father. Explain things, look after us."

"Why do you think Father would treat a brother any better than he treats us?"

"To a man—hear me out—a son is like the taproot of a tree. You can't just cut it off. He carries your name, your legacy, your entire being. You cut off your roots, and you die yourself."

"Marybeth, you're talking nonsense."

"No, no, listen, I've been thinking about this. Daughters are like the fruit of a tree. Shiny, sweet, desirable. They carry the seed, a part of the father tree, plucked from the family and planted afar. It is easy to be cast out if you're a fruit—"

"Tomatoes are fruits. Are you a tomato?"

"You're not hearing what I'm saying, Anna Lee. If we had a brother, Father couldn't cast him out. We'd have an advocate in the family. That's all."

"Like a turnip?"

"Forget about roots."

"Brother or no brother, I don't think Father will help save the farm," Anna Lee said. "I told you Silas says he has some ideas."

"Not good ones, you implied."

"To make money, to pay the note. Just some ideas. Maybe it'll work out."

"I hope you're careful."

"Oh, Marybeth, this ain't how I thought it would be. Silas is trying. It's not fair. Don't tell Jesse about Silas's ideas, whatever they are." Anna Lee shifted uncomfortably in her chair, then stood and arched her back. "You know we're hoping for a son. Maybe that would make your taking Levi away easier on Silas."

"I'm hoping for a son for you, too."

Marybeth's mind flashed back to Anna Lee's bedroom, a time that felt like yesterday. Filtered light peeked around the drawn curtains from a rain-laden winter sky into the dim room. It was not a joyful day, not a happy time. She was sitting on her sister's bed with bare feet on clean sheets, her knees pulled up to her chest; Anna Lee stood in the doorway. Tremor coursed through her body. She stared at Anna Lee, looking for strength. "You don't think it could be me?"

"No. It's not you," Anna Lee said.

Marybeth faced the plaster wall, two feet from the end of the bed. Alabaster paint peeled from water stains along a diagonal crack. The noise of nothingness filled the chamber.

Anna Lee spoke, "Nobody will ever know," as she closed the door, leaving her alone in the room with Silas. That was eight years ago.

Marybeth focused with moist eyes on her sister holding the *Red Book,* then covered her face with her hands and sobbed. Anna Lee stepped over and pulled her sister's head against her pregnant abdomen with both arms. "It's dead. It never happened. You must forget."

Cheerful children's voices skipped through the open kitchen window while Anna Lee wept with her sister.

An oriole's rich, piping whistle touched Jesse's consciousness; blackness obscured his vision. The bird's song warbled in and out and seemed to move from one ear to the other. Gradually, as if a fire of light burned out from the center, his sight returned, revealing a tangle of black branches with oval-shaped green leaves arching in front of a sky-blue backdrop.

Jesse drew both arms. Placing palms on his chest, he felt the rise and fall of his breathing and the beat of his heart. He lay in the grass on his back for several minutes, unable to move. The oriole continued its song from somewhere nearby. Jesse touched the left side of his face and felt the swelling around his lips and cheek. Running his tongue across a split in his lower lip, he picked up the metallic taste of blood. A pain pulsed from raw tissues between his left eye and jawline. It hurt to open his mouth. It hurt to close.

Disorientation and confusion swirled in his head. Had he fallen off a ladder? Was he struck by a branch? Kicked by a horse? Where was Silas? Piece by piece, the events leading up to the last Jesse could recall came into focus—Silas in his face, an argument with taunting, and the sting of an unexpected blow.

Jesse propped his elbows on the ground and brought himself up to a semi-sitting position, enough to look around. Silas was gone. The tripod ladder stood ten feet away. Several cut limbs littered the space between the tree trunks—their diseased bark split, blackened, and oozed sap. The unsheathed pruning saw lay in the grass by his feet. As his mind cleared, anger grew.

ELEVEN

LEVI LOOKED UP TO see his uncle weave diagonally through the orchard, downhill and toward him. He dropped his gaze and pushed a handled shovel deep into a pile of cow manure on the barn floor. He still felt uneasy after what had happened at the picnic supper the last time he saw him.

Silas waved a friendly hand as he approached and shouted, "Hey, Levi, I come to say I'm sorry. How are you making out?" He stepped into the barn.

"Okay."

"Just okay? You're seven years old. You should be doing great." Silas moved toward Levi and extended his arm.

Levi took a step back and turned the shovel, holding it with both hands in front of his chest. He looked cautiously at his uncle.

"Levi, relax. I just come to apologize for grabbing you the other day. I didn't mean no harm. Didn't intend to give you a startle. Just, I'd had a little to drink, and maybe I didn't act the way I shoulda." Silas leaned against a stall and threw his arm over the top rail. "I said I'm sorry." He glared at Levi. "You're supposed to respond, young man. Show some respect for your elders. Did your mama teach you nothing?"

"I'm okay, Uncle Silas. I accept your word," Levi said. He lowered the shovel to his waist but still stood off.

"Where's your mama?" Silas looked toward the house and then back to Levi.

"With Aunt Anna Lee."

"My house?"

"Yes, sir. All morning."

"All morning? What's she doing?" Silas asked.

"Mending."

Silas stepped forward. "Gimme that." He reached out and took the shovel from Levi. "Are you done with chores when you got this barn cleaned out?"

"Yes, sir. This is my last doing," Levi answered.

"I'll help ya. Okay?" Silas ran the shovel across the floor and lifted a scoopful of hay and manure. He turned the muck over into a wheelbarrow and scooped again. "We'll get this done right fast. You're a good boy. I know you can do this by yourself, but I've got nothing else to do right now." Silas delivered another three loads into the wheelbarrow.

"I'll take it, Uncle Silas," Levi volunteered when the bucket was full. He struggled with the handles, finding balance in the load, and wheeled the manure outside.

Silas watched Levi return with the empty wheelbarrow, silhouetted at first against the brightness in the doorway. His features filled out with depth and color as he entered the barn. A good-looking boy, Silas thought. He was tall for his age; he had his mother's height. Of course, he would also favor Jesse and himself with a sturdy frame. Silas looked at Levi's bare feet and thought they seemed large. It would be hard to keep a boy like this in properly fitting clothes, let alone shoes. Levi was destined to grow into a powerful, handsome young man who could someday run this farm. Someone to carry on the Fitch name in Benton County.

"When we finish here, what you say we look out back for some grunt worms and go fishing?" Silas said, taking the wheelbarrow from Levi and parking it next to the remaining manure.

"I don't know if I can."

"Sure, you can. I just come from the top of the orchard, left your pa cutting blight, and he even mentioned it. Thought you might like to spend some time with your uncle." Silas grabbed the shovel with both hands.

"He said that?"

"Sure, Levi, it's okay that we spend some time together now and then. Like men." Silas mucked the corners of the barn. "We're almost done. It'll be fun."

Levi shifted uneasily. "It don't sound right. I best check with Ma."

"Last week, when I was coming up Spanker, I saw a fellow with a cane pole and a tin bucket sitting on the bank. I stopped the truck and walked over to be friendly and all. Wouldn't you know that boy had a dozen rock bass in his pail? Big googly eyes, all shiny and such. He wanted to sell them to me for a nickel apiece, but I told 'im I could catch as much as I wanted for free. That's when I got the idea, we should spend some time together fishing. Your ma is busy with your aunt right now. No harm in doing a little fishing, now, is there?" Silas grasped Levi's upper arm and pulled him over to address him directly. "You go inside and find some fishing line and a couple of bait hooks. I know your pa's got some. You go get that, and I'll meet you in the garden to find some worms." Silas gave

Levi a gentle but purposeful shove toward the open barn door. "Get some cork if you got it."

Levi emerged from the house with a small tackle box his father seldom used, just as his mother stepped onto the porch.

"Young man," she said, "and just where do you think you are going with that?" She motioned to the box in Levi's hand.

"Uncle Silas—"

"Now you turn around and put that back where it came. Now."

"Ma, Uncle Silas helped me finish my chores, and he really wants to go fishing. I told 'im I didn't think it was right and that I should check with you first. But he said Pa said it was ok."

Marybeth guided her son back into the house. "And where is your uncle right now?"

"Out back, getting worms."

"You stay here. Put your father's stuff away. Stay." She set her sewing tote inside the house and closed the door.

"Silas," Marybeth called to her brother-in-law from the edge of the house, "I would like to have some words with you."

"Marybeth? Sure." Silas dropped a fistful of worms onto the freshly overturned earth and carried the shovel out of the garden to where Marybeth was standing. "I meant no harm. I didn't think you or Jesse would mind me spending some idle time with Levi."

"You ask before you do something like this. Do you understand me?" Marybeth put both hands on her hips to block Silas's path. "I don't know what has gotten into you."

"I didn't touch your son, didn't lay a hand on 'im. I don't especially like the way you're talking to me right now." Silas held the shovel by its collar with the blade in Marybeth's face. "You think you are better than me, don't you? You and Jesse, always riding the high road. Plotting with Anna Lee against me. Well, it ain't happening no more. You'll see. I've got every right to live on this land and be with my family. Nobody is going to take that away from me."

"Silas."

"Don't 'Silas' me. Don't interrupt me. I say what happens to the land. I say what happens to Anna Lee. I say what happens to my children. Do you hear me?"

Marybeth stepped to the side and relaxed her arms, turning her palms outward. "Calm down, now. Nobody is threatening you. Nobody is conspiring against you. We all need to work together on this."

Silas lowered the shovel. "I just wanted to spend time with Levi. I felt bad about how I acted at Sunday dinner. We gotta a lot going on."

"Of course, we all gotta a lot happening right now, but we gotta work together. Anna Lee needs us right now. She needs support. She needs your help. Jesse and I are going to do everything possible to stay until she delivers. After that, we'll see. We are not going to leave her when she needs us the most. But you have to do your part as well."

Silas tossed the shovel into the grass at his side. "Jesse and I used to get along so well when we was younger."

"Come, Silas, sit a spell." Marybeth guided him to the edge of the porch where they could sit. "Water?"

"No, thank you." Silas dusted off his overalls and sat a few feet from Marybeth. "I don't know what has come between us, Jesse and me. We had fun when we was boys. Paps never was much of a father after Mother and Achsah died. I guess he never had the time or energy to give us much mind. But we had each other. Always got along great."

"You still have each other if you both want it," Marybeth said.

"You and Anna Lee are lucky. Nobody expects you to be the same. Sisters, yes, but not identical. That's not true for Jesse and me. Everyone thinks we are one and the same person. Do you know what that is like? It is enough to drive you crazy. People assume if they've told one of us, they've told us both. If Jesse thinks one way, they think we both do. I am not Jesse, and he is not me. Of course, I want to try to be there for Anna Lee. I love her. I've made some mistakes. Jesse, too." Silas turned to Marybeth. "I'm rambling, I know. You're probably thinking I've lost my mind. I don't want to lose the farm. I don't want to lose what we have. Trust me."

Marybeth had heard this banter before. She, Jesse, and Anna Lee had all suffered through his half-truths, deception, hyperbole, and manipulation for years. "Silas, I will trust you when you give me a reason to."

"I'm telling the truth, and . . . Levi and I were going to have some fun this afternoon. You ruined that. Whose side are you on anyway?" Silas said.

"Your side. We are all on your side. Jesse is on your side. We can get through this together. Calm down?"

"Goddamn it, I say. Goddamn it, all of you." Silas jumped up and stood in front of Marybeth. "Goddamn it, I say. You want me to calm down?"

"Please leave."

"Calm down or leave? What is it? Fine. I'll leave before I do something stupid that I'll regret. Or maybe I won't regret it. I don't give a damn anymore." Silas spun on his boot heel and took several steps away from the porch. "I could make you and Jesse's lives miserable. You know that? I don't give a shit anymore." Silas marched through the yard gate and then turned, facing Marybeth again. "Jesse is up at the top of the orchard cutting blight if you are looking for 'im. I left 'im there this morning. He said I wasn't working hard enough and that I could get the hell out if I wanted. So, I left 'im. If he's not back by supper, you'll know where to find 'im."

An odd thing to say, Marybeth thought as she watched Silas enter the orchard and head uphill toward his home. She rose from the porch, opened the door, and called into the house, "Levi, run on up to fetch your pa."

TWELVE

December 1910

"JESSE, YOU AWAKE?" SILAS whispered as he poked his brother sleeping next to him.

"No."

"Let's do something."

"Silas, go back to sleep. It's midnight or later. I don't know. Go back to sleep." Jesse rolled over, pulling the bedcovers with him.

The bedroom next to their father's room was dark and cold. An early December storm had brought a rare dusting of snow, which briefly settled on the window muntins before running down the glass in a slush.

Jesse looked through the door into the hall and kitchen and saw the faint yellow glow of the stove's dying embers, no longer warming their room. He closed his eyes and wished Silas would do the same.

"Let's go," Silas said as he threw his legs off the bed and sat. "Come on." He pulled a sweater and coat over his long underwear, then stepped into a worn pair of canvas pants. Silas then yanked the covers off the bed, leaving his twin exposed on the bare mattress. "I want you to come with me."

Jesse reached for the blankets as Silas tossed them behind a chair. "Okay. Give me a minute. I don't know what has gotten into your noggin this time of night, but it won't be long before sunup."

"Right. Now get dressed."

Moments later, Jesse and Silas padded down the hall past their sleeping father. They eased open the farmhouse front door and stepped into the fresh night air. Both boys slipped on their boots and tracked out into the light snow. Moonlight filtered through the thin clouds that hovered just over the treetops. The boys made their way in the faint illumination to the big barn. Once inside, Silas removed a lighter from his coat pocket and struck the flint, producing a sooty yellow kerosene flare.

"That's Paps's," Jesse said, his face animated by the dancing flame. "He'll kill you if he finds out you have it."

"He won't know now, will he?" Silas held the lighter to scan the tackle hanging from pegs on the inside wall. He selected a short length of braided rope and wrapped it around his hand. "Let's go."

"Silas, I don't know what the heck you're doing. It seems to me no good. I don't want any part of this. I'm going back inside." Jesse turned toward the barn door, but Silas caught him by the arm before he could step away.

"We're just going to have a little fun. Trust me." Silas extinguished the lighter and pulled his brother out of the barn. The two boys headed into the woods, down familiar trails covered in the evening's snow. The black trunks of deciduous oak and chestnut picketed the white forest floor in sharp contrast. Silas and Jesse dropped into a gully, crossed the dry, rocky bed, and climbed the far side. A great horned owl questioned the night with a haunting "Hoo-h'HOO? Who? Who?" but it was unanswered.

The trail led up to a rock outcropping the size of a railroad car. Silas stopped on the downhill side, where an overhead ledge created a small pocket with an exposed dirt floor, just large enough for two boys. Silas sparked the lighter and lit up the shallow walls. "Injuns lived here," he said, scanning the rock sides as if looking for ancient petroglyphs.

"Is this what this is all about?" Jesse asked.

"No. We're just taking a rest. This is not it. I told you we're gonna have some fun."

Jesse questioned why he always let his brother call the shots and lead the way. They were both thirteen, old enough to know right from wrong. Old enough to take responsibility on the farm. Since their mother and sister had died, both boys were called into service to help their father, perhaps at a younger age than most. By and large, they both did their part. But as Jesse called it, Silas had a "streak" in his mind. A streak of independence, rebellion, and hardheadedness. Whatever it was, it was foreign to him. It was the one thing that defined the difference between the identical twins. The one thing that was felt by Jesse but not seen. In their outward appearance, they were indistinguishable. Inside, Jesse always gave in to his brother's ideas, antics, and mischief, and he hated himself for it.

"Come on, time to go." Silas capped the flame and pulled himself up, using Jesse for support. Both boys continued their trek uphill until the forest gave way to a tilled wheat field. The straight rows of overturned clods, dusted in white frost, produced an illusion of an undulating frozen bay receiving the waves of a distant ocean. At the far corner of the mirage, nearly invisible against the dark shadows of another forest, was a barn.

Silas prodded Jesse along as they skirted the field and crept up to the homestead. Ahead was a white two-story farmhouse; its windows were dark and asleep. To the right stood an unpainted wooden barn. A horse or a cow shifted in its stall, sending an eerie creaking sound across the barnyard. Chickens clucked. The boys crouched behind a buckboard. A black cat silently navigated the thin carpet of snow between the house and the barn, shaking its paws after each step.

"I think we should go," Jesse whispered.

"Ah, c'mon. You are such a little girl. Mr. Phelps just got some goats. I saw 'em last week when they were delivered. Goats are fun."

"I don't like this. I think we should go."

"Give me five minutes. You'll be happy you came. You ain't seen nothing like this. Come." Silas crab-walked over to the side of the barn where a newly erected pen stood. He looked at a dozen white and brown goats standing under a low lean-to. "Don't they have the stupidest faces? Stupid standing there, looking at us with stupid eyes and that stupid beard." Silas edged up to the fence and squatted in the dirt.

Jesse knelt next to him. "Waste of money if you'd ast me," Jesse said. "Who in the hell would want a goat when you could have a cow? I hate goat milk."

"I agree with you, brother." Silas unwound the ten-foot length of rope and tied a loop on one end with a slipknot. He laid the other end on the dirt and uncapped the lighter.

Jesse watched Silas pour kerosene from the palm-sized lighter on the last foot of the rope, soaking the cotton braid. "What the hell you doing?" Jesse asked.

"I told you we're having some fun, fun with those stupid goats." Silas fingered a carrot out of his pocket and held it through the pen rails toward the wary animals. The doe goats backed up at the scent of the kerosene but kept a curious eye on the carrot. Eventually, a large nanny goat ventured toward the carrot, gingerly stepping across the half-frozen mud.

Silas broke off a piece of carrot and offered it to the goat in his flattened palm. The goat stretched its neck, snatched the morsel with nimble lips, and retreated two steps. Silas broke another piece and held it just outside the fence to entice the goat to reach between the rails. Again, the goat seized the bit and stepped back. Several others edged forward.

Silas took one end of the rope and handed it to Jesse. "Hold on to this. Better yet, wrap it around the post, then hold on." Silas took the other end of the rope and draped it over the top of the fence, opening the loop between the lower rails. "Watch Mrs. Stupid here," Silas said. He held the rest of the carrot in his left hand and pushed it through the fence and rope loop. As the goat stepped closer, Silas slowly pulled the carrot back, enticing it to stick her head through the loop. At the right moment, Silas jerked on the rope, tightening the noose around the animal's neck. The goat initially lurched forward against the fence, then tipped and wrenched its neck between the rails before pulling its head free. It regained its footing and shot out toward the pen's center, then cartwheeled to the ground when it reached the tether's end.

Not knowing what to do, Jesse handed the rope to his brother. Silas struggled against the goat as the rope slipped on the pole. With one hand, he lit the lighter and touched it to the kerosene-soaked rope. A smart yellow flame shot up from the end, and Silas quickly unwrapped the rope from the post and tossed it into the pen.

At first, terror seized the goat in place, then it shot out across the mud, dragging the flaming rope behind. The other goats bleated and then scattered across the pen. Silas and Jesse ducked out and scurried twenty-five yards across the barnyard to the shadows of the woods. From behind a tree, they watched the dozen panicked goats fly about the enclosure, bawling and bleating. The nanny goat raced around in circles, spinning the herd into a terrifying mess in a futile attempt to escape the flame that followed. The screams of the does sounded like those of a tortured baby: loud, human-like, and unnerving.

Silas slapped Jesse's shoulder and pulled a toothy grin across his face. "See. I told ya we'd have some fun. You ever seen such a sight?"

"This is cruel. This ain't fun. Had I known this was what you were up to, I never would have come."

"But you are here, and you are enjoying it. Right?"

"Ain't nothing to enjoy."

"Ah, c'mon. This is funny." Silas looked over to the pen at the side of the barn and watched the commotion. Goats jumped and darted as the nanny sprinted through their ranks, dragging the flaming rope. A window in the farmhouse lit behind drawn curtains. Another window lit, and the front door flew open, casting yellow light across the barnyard. The silhouette of a man appeared in front of the glow, rifle in hand. He bolted from the house toward the barn and the frenzied screams of the goats. Silas bit his lip to keep from erupting into laughter; he placed his hand over his mouth to muffle a snicker.

The man leaned his gun against a rail, climbed the fence, and jumped into the pen. The nanny goat continued its frantic darting to flee the flaming rope and the man who followed its every move. When the man seemed to corner the goat to grab the rope, the goat leaped over the fence, pulling the flame with it.

Jesse watched in horror as the flame raced around the farmyard, spinning off small fires on the ground that were quickly extinguished in the wet snow. The goat ran behind the barn with the man close behind.

"Now that's funny," Silas whispered. "I'll be laughing into next week."

The inside of the barn then glowed with faint orange light. Then, with a roar, the barn exploded into an inferno. Hay bales erupted. Flame licked out of the gaps in the barn door, searching for oxygen. A horse screamed and splintered planks as it busted its way out of a stall. The barn door opened, releasing the goat and the horse. The man appeared briefly in the opening, retreated into the barn with a pitchfork, and hurled sheaves of burning hay into the snow. Soon, flames shot out of the upper hay door and climbed the shake roof. Within a minute, the entire barn was engulfed in flames.

"We gotta help," Jesse said, stepping out from behind the tree.

Silas grabbed his arm and held him back. "No."

"What do you mean, no?"

"I said no. You weren't here. We weren't here. Got it?"

"The barn—"

"It's gone. Let's get out of here." Silas pulled his brother deep into the darkness of the woods, beyond the glow of the expanding pyre.

The boys raced back through the gully toward their farm. As they approached the house, snow fell, covering their tracks. The tolling of a farm bell echoed across the ravine and through the woods. Panic rang with each swing of the clapper, faster than what was typical to call in workers for dinner or summon the faithful to an impromptu sermon by an itinerant preacher. "Fire! Fire!" spoke the strident peal. Despite the cacophony, their father did not stir as the boys slipped into the house with boots in hand, undressed, and crawled into bed.

Silas whispered to Jesse, "You did this, too. You were there. It took two of us to rope that goat, remember? Keep your mouth shut, or I'll bring you down with me. Do you understand?"

Jesse nodded in the darkness.

Thirteen

"WHAT HAPPENED TO YOUR face?" the agricultural inspector asked.

"Fell," Jesse replied. He set a can of kerosene at his feet. "Cutting blight. Ladder broke. The trees are almost clean." It had been three days since Silas laid him out in the grass under the apple trees.

"You oughta get someone to look at that eye."

"Just swollen. It'll be okay. Give it a few more days."

The inspector reached into his Model T Ford, pulled out a ledger book bound in heavy canvas, and placed it on the runabout's hood. He looked out into the barren Fitch orchard, not the first apple farm he had visited that week with no set fruit. "Frost got you pretty good, huh? South slope?"

"Yeah."

"You know it's a little late to be cutting blight. Neighbors not gonna take kindly to you stirring it up during the growing season," the agent said.

"Silas and me just couldn't git it all done last winter. Been short-handed."

The inspector was a slight man with round wire-rimmed glasses and rosy cheeks on a cherub face. He had gentle, soft-looking hands with clean nails and smooth skin—hands made for holding pencils and turning pages, crafting numbers and letters in straight rows and columns, not the hard labor of working the land, mending barns, packing fruit, or cutting blight. He wore a dark suit coat on his narrow shoulders, wrinkled in the back from sitting on the Ford's bench seat during the long, steamy drive from town.

"Jesse, I've got a whole county to worry about. You can't go maverick on me. You get your pruning done in the winter, or I'll be issuing citations come next spring."

"Yes, sir," Jesse responded.

"I'm gonna need a certificate that you sprayed this season," the inspector said.

"Not yet."

"You're late. Just cuz you ain't got no fruit, don't excuse you from spraying."

"We know. Silas and me are working something out with the bank. We'll be sprayed by month's end."

"You heard what happened to the Wilkes place?" the inspector asked.

"Yes, sir."

"Sheriff had 'em all cut and burned, the whole lot. I know things are tight this year, but I'm just doing my job. Investors back East don't understand."

"Sir, I'll bring our certificate to your office myself just as soon as we spray. Appreciate your understanding."

"Where's Silas?" the inspector asked. "I drove by his house first. The missus wouldn't answer the door."

"Sick, laid up in bed past week, I think."

The agricultural inspector opened his recording book, pulled a tapered finger down the page to the first blank entry, and carefully penciled the details of the day's visit to the Fitch farm. He closed the journal with a snap, tossed it to the seat through the open car door, turned to Jesse, and said, "I've known your pappy a long time. Good man in his younger years. As far as I can tell, he raised himself two fine sons. It's not fair what's happening here. It's not right. The market don't support folks like you anymore."

Jesse dug his hands into the front pockets of his overalls. "We'll git through this okay. You watch."

"You ain't getting through this. You're smart enough to know. I know you ain't keeping the farm. You're not the only one," the inspector said.

"You're underestimating the Fitches, sir."

"Don't bullshit me, Jesse. Cavness says you're through. I've been covering for you boys for the past few months, last year, too. Can't do it no more."

"Not asking you to," Jesse said.

The inspector lowered himself into the driver's seat with one hand on the roof edge and the other on the wheel. He pulled the door closed through the open window. "I don't believe Silas is sick." The little man choked the engine and pushed the starter button, coughing the four-cylinder block to life. "I'll be waiting for your paperwork. You got two weeks."

Jesse watched the two-seater's spindle wheels find the ruts in the dirt, leading the agricultural inspector down the hill, back to Spanker Creek, and perhaps the next orchard up the road. Jesse knew what he had said was a lie; they did not have the money to spray for scale this year—and didn't have it last year, either. He was leaving the farm, saving himself and his family, but it hurt to think of what his father and his sucker-punching brother would go through when they lost their land.

Jesse lifted the can of kerosene and walked the oil to a pile of blackened and dead limbs stacked like an Indian teepee in an open field. Ash from previous fires spread beneath the stack. Jesse doused the branches with fuel and tossed a lit match. Black oil smoke curled from the rick into the waning light of the summer sky. Futile, he thought, and he turned home.

Marybeth replaced the compress on the left side of Jesse's face with another one soaked in chilly water drawn up from the well. With effort, he could open his left eye and reclaim depth in his sight. The bedroom was dark, with curtains pulled across the blackness of the evening. A single tallow candle burned on the nightstand, casting gamboled shadows across the room in the dim yellow light.

"We can leave now. I'm ready to go. It's time," Marybeth whispered to Jesse. She sat on the bed at his side in a light cotton nightshirt.

Jesse lay on the bedcovers, fully dressed except for his boots. He did not respond. He watched the candlelight play off his wife's beautiful face with his working eye. Her lips, made richly hued by the yellow light, puckered into a kiss and gently landed on his forehead. He reached up with both hands and pulled her shoulders to his chest. Her head nestled under his chin, and locks of her brown hair draped over his face. Jesse wrapped his arms around her body and held her tight. Lovemaking entered his mind as he sensed the firm roundness of her breasts pressed up against his chest. He reached one hand down to cup the contour of her thigh and lifted her close.

He knew Marybeth would be hesitant to allow herself pleasure at this moment. She would be afraid of him hurting himself further, being in his condition. Jesse was ready, willing, and wanting, but he would respect his wife tonight and wait for her desire to build. He held her secure as minutes passed.

Perhaps he was wrong, he thought. He forced the right side of his lips together and squeezed off a series of sideways kisses on Marybeth's cheek, working his way to her lips. She responded by tilting her head back to receive his advances. Marybeth ran her fingers through his hair and then unfastened the top buttons of his shirt.

The rumble of an approaching vehicle cut short their efforts. He lifted Marybeth off his chest, sat in bed, and pulled his boots on in one fluid motion. Jesse crossed the room, retrieved a 300 Savage bolt-action rifle from the corner, and pocketed a handful of cartridges. The rifle smelled of gun oil and linseed. He opened the breech and loaded a round into the chamber, driving it home with the bolt.

"Jesse," Marybeth said.

"Nothing good's driving up this time of night," he responded. "You bar the door behind me. Keep Levi in here with the flame out." Jesse opened the bedroom door, moved into the hallway, and fastened his shirt. "Lock the back, too." He lifted the latch on the front door and stepped out into the warm night air, not knowing what he might find.

FOURTEEN

JESSE CUT THROUGH THE orchard with the rifle in his right hand; he held his left across his face to deflect low-hanging branches. He ducked behind a tree trunk when he heard a vehicle emerge from the wooded slope at the bottom of the orchard and turn south toward Silas's place. Jesse tracked the outline of the small truck, picking its way up the bumpy drive with headlights off. He followed the engine noise around the orchard and up to the big barn behind Silas's house. Heavy clouds slate-hued the night sky.

Jesse crept his way to the edge of the orchard and saw the outlines of three men standing in the glow of a torch in the open barn doorway. A tarp covered the contents of the truck bed. One man, whom he recognized as his brother, spoke in hushed tones, negotiating. Another man had soiled bandages covering his right hand and half his face.

Jesse watched the men lift the tarp and carry several wide, flat boxes into the big barn. The torchlight cast huge, almost comical, shadows on the ground, shadows of the men and boxes as they ferried in and out of the barn door. The bandaged man handed Silas a leather fold when the truck bed was empty. Silas peered into it and seemed to take stock of its contents. The three exchanged handshakes, and two men got back into the truck and quietly left under the night's darkness. The entire event concluded in less than five minutes.

Jesse watched Silas extinguish the torch and place a board across the cleats on the door. Silas then walked across the barnyard to his house and entered.

Jesse backtracked into the orchard and worked his way downhill toward his father's cabin. As he approached, the clouds thinned, and a sliver of moonlight fell from the southwestern sky, casting a bluish glow on the front of the house. He noticed his father sitting in a wooden chair under the porch roof, facing the waning moon. Both hands rested on the chair's arms; both feet were firmly planted on the porch boards, straddling a bottle.

"You're out late," Paps said as Jesse entered the space between the cabin and the split-rail fence.

"You, too, Paps."

As Jesse stepped onto the porch and sat, Paps glanced at his son. "Face looks better." He then motioned at the gun. "Hunting bear?"

Jesse propped the Savage rifle against the cabin wall between the chairs. "Paps, I just come from the big barn."

"Wildcatters."

"Yeah, wildcatters. You know about this?" Jesse asked, looking at his father for a read on his answer.

"Yup. Your brother's at least trying to do somepin."

"I thought he might get messed up with the Benoits, but I didn't expect 'im to bring it here. He's got a wife and kids living a stone's throw from that barn. What the hell's he thinking?" Jesse placed both hands on the side of his head. "So, how long have you known? Nobody was gonna tell me that we're moving likker through the farm?" Jesse turned to his father. "Don't you think this concerns me?"

"You'd given up."

"I ain't given up. It's me who went to the bank. It's me who put off the creditors last year. It's me who was looking at every licit way to save the farm. Hell, I even talked to Suggs."

"He's in," Paps said.

"What you mean, he's in?"

"He's in. Suggs's bankrolling the Benoits. Buying corn. Gitting a cut," Paps said. "Silas is making payment to Mr. Cavness tomorrow." Paps reached down, pulled the bottle to his mouth, and took a generous swig.

Jesse stood and walked the length of the porch. He stopped at the edge, stared out into the darkness of the woods shadowed by the overhead canopy, and listened to the tinkle of water in the springhouse. Now, he realized why their wives' father abruptly dismissed his plea for help, why Silas wasn't conceding the farm to the bank, and why the revenuers found a reason to pay them a visit. It was wrong, illegal. But then, weren't they the innocent victims of the times? Times of declining apple prices in the face of insurmountable costs. Theirs wasn't the only struggling orchard in Northwest Arkansas. Others were feeling the same pressure. They might have made it if they had not leveraged the entire orchard, betting on a bountiful harvest this season. Might have survived with enough equity to move from apples to wheat, corn, or even poultry.

Jesse had heard of a man in Washington County named Shelby Ford, a banker lending money for chickens. Up the road in Pea Ridge, Hugh Webb built himself a chicken house for 500 chicks and sold broilers for a dollar apiece in Kansas City. Markets were bound to open back East. Arkansas could supply spring fryers all year long with modern technology—science. The future was chickens if they could only hold on to their land. He crossed back to his father.

"I don't like it," Jesse said. "I don't go with wildcatting likker for the Benoits. Not through this farm. He ain't doing it."

"You got a better plan, except running away?"

"No."

"Then, you best git onboard, son."

"What about chickens?" Jesse asked.

"We know apples. Silas knows apples. He don't know chickens. The running's just to git us through."

"Apples are gone. You ain't gonna make it work next year, either. If we're lucky enough to keep the land, we'll be wise to cut down every one of them Blacks and do something else."

"We're not touching the trees." Paps reached behind and grabbed the rifle, leaning against the wall. He placed it on his lap and fingered the trigger. "No bear around here. I reckon you don't need this no more."

"Listen, Paps. I don't see a way out. Silas don't know what he's doing in Bell' Vista or wherever else he's running. The G-men ain't dumb. Won't take long to throw his ass in jail. Then what're his girls gonna do? You thought about that?"

"Suggs gonna make sure that don't happen," Paps said.

"Mr. Suggs don't give a shit about Silas, Anna Lee, or Marybeth. He don't give a shit about you or me. He'd be happy to buy this land from the bank—"

"Nobody's selling."

"—at a discount with money he skimmed from the Benoits."

"I think it's best that you git on back to Marybeth right now." Paps lifted the rifle, brought the stock to his shoulder, and sighted the moon. He squeezed off a shot; the recoil almost knocked him backward off the chair. Paps worked the bolt action and ejected the spent cartridge onto the porch boards. He reset the bolt and swung the muzzle into Jesse's abdomen. "You let Silas do what you ain't willing."

Jesse took a step back.

Paps pulled an empty click with the trigger. He turned the rifle up and handed it to Jesse. "Unlike you, Silas woulda loaded more than one round in her box."

FIFTEEN

THE SMELL OF COFFEE accompanied Jesse's transition from a dream to wakefulness. It was dark in his bedroom. He reached over to an empty side of the bed, and the day came into focus.

"Good morning," Marybeth said as Jesse stepped into the kitchen barefoot, fastening his suspenders to the front of his trousers.

Jesse welcomed the sounds and scents of breakfast as he planted a quick kiss on his wife's neck. "Morning." He sat at the table among a white dusting of flour.

Marybeth opened the oven door and retrieved a tray of high biscuits, light and fluffy with golden-brown tops and white layered sides. She placed three on a crockery plate and then ladled beef chips in a cream sauce. The sauce formed a thickened crust as it cooled, encasing the biscuits in savory warmth. Marybeth delivered her husband's breakfast to the table with a cup of coffee.

"This must be the last of the canned beef," Jesse said.

"Anna Lee gave us this."

Jesse looked up at his wife. Furls formed on his forehead. "We're not charity, Marybeth. I can provide for my own family," he said in a shaky voice.

"The stores are low. I told you last night that I'm ready if we need to go."

"Anna Lee?"

"I'm not sure we can wait for her to birth," she said.

Jesse had been willing to leave the farm two weeks ago to get to Washington in early summer. It was Marybeth who wanted to wait. Now, it looked like their decision to go would be made for them.

"Silas is running likker," he said.

"I didn't wanna ask."

"Benoit brothers dropped off cases in apple boxes last night. That's where he's gitting the cash. Paps knows."

Marybeth sat across from Jesse to see his face and read his thoughts. "I don't think Anna Lee knows, nothing specific, at least. She'd go to Father if she knew Silas was running up against the law."

"Your father is in on it, too."

Marybeth turned and stared out the window. "How can you be sure?"

"Paps knows the whole game. We're the ones who said we'd bail and leave the land to the bank. Your father had different plans," he said. "Silas is making payment to the bank today. Reckon, we'll hear the flatbed pull out soon—first to the thirsty tourists, then the bank."

Marybeth stood and abruptly paced the room, wringing her hands in her apron. Everything was moving so fast. Decisions she wanted to put off until later were now pressed into action. "Silas doesn't want our Levi to leave," she blurted.

"Of course not."

"No, Levi—"

"That's why he went to your father, why he went to the Benoits. He's crazed in thinking we can all stay and make a living."

"You? You think he's crazy?" she asked.

"I don't know."

"You want to give him a chance?"

"Marybeth, if the revenuers don't git 'im, the Benoits will," Jesse said. "Then again, with a little time, opportunities open up. Chickens, that's the future. But we got debt and apple trees in the way right now."

"You're not going along with Silas, are you?"

"I just don't know what to do. We should just pack up and leave, you, me, and Levi. Just go and say the hell with it all. . . . But then, what does that make me? A coward? Isn't it cowardly to just walk away without fighting for what my grandfather gave me? Is running away the right thing to do? Hell, I know what Silas is up to, up against. The odds ain't good. He's a fool. They're all fools."

Marybeth pulled up a chair across the table and sat again.

"Let's see what he does. I just wanna see," Jesse said. He opened up a biscuit and spooned gravy onto its open face before taking a bite. He looked up at Marybeth. "Woman . . ."

She studied his face for an end to his thought.

"Woman, you brought me a son. You make a wholesome home. God-fearing, beautiful, a damn good cook."

"Jesse, I think I need to tell you something about Silas."

"I know all I need to know. He's a no-good son of a bitch, lazy as a day's long, and if he wasn't married to your sister, I would have disowned 'im years ago."

"He don't want Levi to leave the farm. He has a good reason." Moisture pooled on her lower eyelids and glistened in the lamplight.

"Jealous, he is. Jealous, I've got a son. Well, if we do end up staying, I'm not doing it for 'im. I'm doing it for Paps, for Anna Lee, for you."

"I told you I'm ready to leave. But he doesn't want our Levi to go. It's complicated," Marybeth said as a tear dislodged and raced down her cheek.

The crack of a gunshot broke the air. Another came within seconds of the first. Jesse sprang from the table, grabbed his 300 Savage rifle, loaded five cartridges in the magazine, and darted onto the porch.

Barefoot, he scanned the orchard and edge of the woods. Marybeth appeared with his boots in hand. Another shot rang out from somewhere in the center of the orchard. Half-light filled the humid sky as if the sun rose through frosted glass. Jesse slid into his boots. He headed into the rows of trees with his thumb on the rifle tang, ready to disengage the safety. Three more gunshots broke the morning calm. Jesse moved toward the action.

Lars Jacobsson stood between the trees, reloading his rifle as Jesse approached. Lars pointed the weapon into the air and fired off two more shots.

"What the hell are you doing?" Jesse called out, lowering his own rifle to his side.

"About time you showed up," Lars said.

"I said, what the hell are you doing?"

"I saw your bugs when I dropped off your young'uns the other day. You ain't doing that to me."

"You're some crazy son of a bitch. You can't come wandering over on my land and start shooting off at the mouth, talking to me like that," Jesse said.

"I sure as hell can if it means you're harboring scale. Ja, these trees are full of it. Didn't ya oil spray?"

"I ain't answering you."

"Can't afford to lose no trees this year." Lars pulled down a branch and broke off a twig covered with white scale. "See that? Them's an infestation. I got a hard enough time keeping my own trees clean without having to worry about them critters coming from you."

"We're spraying . . . arsenate. Soon as we can," Jesse said. He swept his outstretched arm to the side. "Whole damn orchard. Soon."

"I'm warning ya. I can't afford to lose no more trees."

"Look like we can? We're gonna do it. Fitches have been farming this land long before your blue-eyed kin slithered to this country, let alone Arkansas. Now git your ass going. Leave us be," Jesse said.

"Slap da horse, would ya? We're all in this together. We are. We gotta watch out for each other now. You think I got apples this year? No. I'm with you. But you can't go spreading pests." Lars pulled his shoulders back, stressing the size of his barrel chest, and slung his rifle over his back. "I'm warning ya, Jesse. You keep up this orchard, or I'm cutting them down myself." He then turned to leave. Several yards off, he said over his shoulder, "You keep an eye on that niece of yours, the eldest."

"Where'd that come from?"

Lars turned but continued to walk. "She's caught the boy's attention at the bottom of the hill. You'd best look out for 'im."

"She ain't none of your business."

"No, none of my business. But them scale is," Lars said.

Jesse watched Lars through the rows of Arkansas Blacks until the foliage in front of the land's upward curve hid his frame. If only to protect his neighbor's trees, Jesse would spray. Razing and burning the orchard would be a better alternative. If he could save the farm from foreclosure and weren't leaving, he would move on to corn, tomatoes, and chickens. If he could only convince Silas.

SIXTEEN

April 1914

MARYBETH TUCKED ONE LEG under her cotton skirt as she sat on the bench swing with Anna Lee. She extended the other leg, pointing her toes to reach the ground, and gave a little push each time the swing fell backward, spinning dust from the dirt.

"When you get a husband, what will he be like?" Marybeth asked her older sister.

"Smart, rich, worldly," Anna Lee answered.

"No, what's he gonna look like? Tall, blond, redhead, dark? What?"

"Short, fat, and bald. What do you think? Stupid," Anna Lee said. "Stop with the pushing. You're making us go catawampus." Anna Lee put down her foot to straighten the swing and smoothed out the body of her dress with her palms.

"I wanna know. You must know what type of men attract you."

"I know what doesn't attract me. I don't know what Mother ever saw in him," Anna Lee said.

"Yeah, I wish she were here now." Marybeth looked across the side yard of their house, across the well-manicured lawn to Southeast A Street with young elm trees planted as sentinels on either side. Light pink native azaleas, transplanted from the forest, surrounded the black oak tree from which the swing was suspended. The green tongues of cast iron plants leapt from the ground at the house's foundation like battle line pickets. The last of the spring's fresh breezes whispered through the overhead canopy, which shaded the girls from the rising sun.

A two-wheeled milk wagon pulled by a chocolate mule made its way along the gravel street from house to house. The young man delivering quart milk bottles was dressed in a short white coat over black trousers.

"What about Randy Stahl?" Marybeth asked when the cart pulled up to their home.

"No." Anna Lee shook her head.

"Randy. Hey, Randy," Marybeth called out, waving her delicate hand and trying to get his attention.

Anna Lee gave her a shove up against the chains. "Shut up," she hissed.

"Hey, Randy. Over here," Marybeth repeated.

Randy Stahl looked up from the concrete path leading to their house. He carried a wire basket of four white bottles and pulled a smile for Marybeth into his red-acned cheeks, but his gaze fell on Anna Lee. Randy left the pathway and cut across the glade to the swing.

"Hi, Anna Lee," he said, standing before the sisters. "Fancy morning to be taking a swing."

"We swing every day," Anna Lee responded. "Don't you have work to do?"

Marybeth giggled, dropped both feet off the seat, and sat up as tall as possible. Still, at fourteen, she was not yet the height of Anna Lee, who had already blossomed with a curvaceous figure Randy Stahl could not overlook.

"I'm not working Saturday." Randy diverted his eyes from the tailored bodice of Anna Lee's dress and carefully measured his thoughts.

"You got me," Anna Lee said. "What are you talking about?"

"I'm off Saturday, and I was meaning to ask you something."

"Ask her," Marybeth interjected. Anna Lee dug her elbow into her sister's ribs and gave Randy a blank stare.

"Would you like to go to the May Day parade with me Saturday?" he asked. "Lots of folks will be there. We can watch it together."

"That's sweet, Randy. But I don't think I can," Anna Lee said.

"Is it me?"

"No, no. Socialists. My father says there are socialists in the parade. He won't let me go," Anna Lee answered.

"They're not socialists."

"Socialists." Anna Lee held her palms upward and shrugged her shoulders like there was nothing she could do about it.

"How about suffragettes? They're marching right after the Confederate Veterans band. Don't you support them?" Randy asked.

"I don't know. I'll have to think about this. Best you get on with your work and leave us be," Anna Lee said. She pulled both legs up onto the bench swing and turned sideways, facing her sister.

"There's a war brewing in Europe. It's best you start paying attention to your civic duties."

Anna Lee waved him off.

"I'll call on you tomorrow if that is okay. G'day Anna Lee," he said, tipping his black-billed cap, "You too, Marybeth," and he turned toward the kitchen door. "Don't let this milk sit in the sun."

"He likes you," Marybeth said, kicking the swing into motion again. "What is a suffragette?"

"It's who."

"Fine, who's a suffragette?" Marybeth watched Randy march stiffly back to his milk cart, climb in, and snap the reins to move the mule to the next house.

"Women who want to vote."

"They can't?"

"Nope, stupid little sister. Women can't vote, just men," Anna Lee said.

"What do you think?"

"I don't know. I guess I would think what my husband wanted me to think."

"Number one, you don't have a husband . . . yet. Number two, you should be able to think what you want and vote if you want."

"It's not that simple. Father is against it," Anna Lee said.

"Anna Lee, you can't be worrying what Father likes or dislikes. You need to be your own woman. Find your own husband. Lead your own life. Father doesn't care half as much for you as I do. You need to be happy. Leave town if you must."

"Marybeth, you know not what you are talking about."

"Take a train to Chicago or New Orleans. See the world. Get yourself an enormous, feathered hat and a lingerie dress. Hold a matching parasol and strut about the Kentucky Derby." Marybeth mimed the sipping of a drink and twirling an umbrella over her shoulder. "You're bound to land a husband there."

"The Derby is next week."

"I know."

"You're talking foolishness, Marybeth. The foolishness of a little girl. You have so much to learn. I'm not about to go far. I don't have the desire, means, or worldliness to do anything you just mentioned."

"You best get on with buying a dress if you are going to Kentucky."

"I'm not going to Kentucky." Anna Lee heard a noise behind her. She turned to look over her shoulder and saw a young girl. "Delilah, what on earth are you doing here? Your mama knows you're out and about?"

"No, ma'am," four-year-old Delilah answered, standing ten feet behind the swing.

"Come here, girl," Marybeth said after she, too, turned to look at the child.

Delilah was barefoot in a simple, patterned dress with long, puffy sleeves. She looked at the grass, then to the street, not knowing what to do.

"Delilah, I said to come around here and talk to us." Anna Lee motioned with her arms for the child to walk around the swing. She did.

"Now," Anna Lee continued, "your mama doesn't know you came. Is that what you just said?"

"Yes, ma'am," Delilah said, facing the sisters.

"Now, why, for heaven's sake, would you walk all the way across town by yourself if your mama doesn't know you're coming?" Anna Lee questioned.

"My mama's here."

"We know your mama's here. She's inside fixing dinner. She's going to give you a whooping if she sees you here. You know that?" Marybeth said.

"Yes, ma'am," Delilah said to Marybeth. "Yes, ma'am." Delilah folded her arms across her chest.

"You think she et today?" Marybeth asked her sister.

"I don't know."

"You et today?" Marybeth asked the little girl.

"No, ma'am." Delilah looked at her feet, not knowing if she was supposed to say what she did.

Anna Lee slid off the swing, stepped forward, and placed both hands on Delilah's shoulders. "You sit here with Marybeth. I'll get you something to eat." Anna Lee lifted Delilah's slight frame and sat her next to Marybeth, saying, "Watch her, she doesn't run off." She crossed the yard to the kitchen door, retrieved the milk bottles, and went in.

Delilah sat quietly on the swing; neither said a word for several seconds.

"You have older brothers or sisters?" Marybeth asked.

"No, ma'am," Delilah answered.

"Father?"

"No, ma'am."

Marybeth turned to look at the child sitting next to her. "Who stays with you while your mamma works here? Who watches you?"

"Uncle Jet."

"Where's Uncle Jet?"

"Working." Delilah spun her neck, looking to the kitchen door. "I sit with him, sometimes."

Anna Lee returned with a package wrapped in a towel and a pint of milk. Delilah's eyes lit up, and she jumped off the swing. Anna Lee spread the towel on the grass, revealing a chunk of white bread with a slab of roast beef stuffed in the center. A fold of waxed paper held sliced and boiled carrots and turnips. Anna Lee handed the milk to Delilah, who upended the jar, drinking half in a running gulp.

"Mercy, little one. Slow down, or you'll make yourself sick," Marybeth said as she sat on the grass beside the towel. "Let me hold the milk so it doesn't tip." She stuck her hand out.

Delilah knelt in the grass, facing away from the sisters, and ate rapidly and warily, unsure of their generosity. After consuming the bread, meat, and boiled vegetables, she tipped the waxed paper, letting the remaining juice roll onto her lips. She left the towel on the grass, stood, looked at the street, and licked her fingers. She did not know to say thank you.

"You done, little girl?" Marybeth asked.

"Yes, ma'am." She straightened out her dress, wiping spittle from her hands simultaneously.

"Nobody's watching her today," Marybeth whispered to her sister.

"She can't stay. Father would have a fit." Anna Lee bent down to speak to Delilah. "You best let us walk you home before your mama sees you here."

"I wanna stay," Delilah said, then looked at Marybeth for permission.

Marybeth stood and grabbed Delilah's tiny arm. "We'll see you home."

With Delilah in the middle, the three girls walked hand in hand down the street and turned left at the livery stable. They knew the neighborhood where their cook lived, the colored section of town on the other side of the rails beyond the whole-root nursery. Once there, they would find someone to take Delilah in until her mother came home.

Delilah's mother returned home that evening—like she would do each evening for the next ten years—after cooking and cleaning for the Suggs family. Until one night, when she trudged home from work, an errant ox cart struck her. Its wooden wheels shattered her lower leg, sending fragments of bone into the dirt. It took three days for gangrene to set in, and she died the next day while her teenage daughter, Delilah, fixed Mr. Sugg's breakfast.

Seventeen

"Going try to forget you'd rabbited me, no warning, nothing," Jesse said to his brother while standing inside the open barn door.

"Deserved it, the way you're talking," Silas said from a dark corner.

Jesse stepped into the big barn and let his eyes adjust to the sudden darkness; slivers of vertical sunlight knifed through gaps in the planking along the southern wall. The air had the familiar sweetness of winter-stored hay, and the rancidness of gear oil dripped into the dirt floor from farm tractors and implements they no longer owned. The Dodge flatbed sat in the middle of the open space. Two-foot square and half as deep, wooden boxes were stacked fifteen feet high along the north wall. Boxes that were to be filled during the fall apple harvest, but not this season, not ever, thought Jesse.

"You left me cold-cocked. Ain't looking for no fight with you. Nothing I done provoked a sucker punch," Jesse said, touching his left cheek, still red and swollen, oozing fluid from *orange-peel* skin.

Silas was down on his haunches, transferring glass bottles from an unmarked box to one with FITCH FARMS stenciled across the side in blue letters. Between each layer of glass, he spread a handful of hay. After twelve bottles, he nailed the wooden lid shut. Silas looked up at his brother. "You coward. You're a goddamn coward. I'm trying to save this farm, and you ain't got the guts to help."

"I got more sense than a fool. Running for the Benoits ain't smart."

"The hell it ain't, make twenty-five bucks a load. I paid Cavness last week."

"Figgered."

"That's why the sheriff ain't been calling."

Silas lifted the wooden box and loaded it onto the truck's bed with several others. He knelt next to another box in the dirt and pried off the lid with a bar. Again, he transferred bottles from one box to another, layering hay.

"You ain't fooling nobody with them apple boxes. Nobody's picking yet, and everyone knows we, like most, don't got no fruit this year."

"Revenuers ain't that smart, now, are they?" Silas asked.

"Agents don't git you, some Yankee's bluenose wife will finger your ass to the sheriff when you start handing the shit out."

"Benoits not gonna let that happen. Keeping those lodgers at the Bell' Vista lit up and happy is how they make money."

"Those bootleggers don't give a shit what happens to you. You guess you're the only one who can transport? You're a bigger fool than I thought," Jesse said.

"Suggs works for them. He'll make sure the sheriff stays clear. Benoits say Suggs is buying corn and padding pockets. We're good, brother."

"I know Suggs is involved. Paps said so. But why?

"Money."

"I know money. But it don't make sense. There are other ways to turn a dollar that don't involve the Benoits. It seems high risk for a man of his stature. Why risk getting wrapped up with bootleggers?"

"He buys corn, sells it for a profit, and spreads a little cash to make everyone happy. I don't git what you're gitting at," Silas said.

"What I'm gitting at is that Suggs is up to something else. I don't know what, but this is the first time he has had any business dealings that even remotely involve our family, and I don't like it."

"You don't have to." Silas climbed onto the truck bed and unfolded a green canvas tarp, letting the edges fall over the side of the stacked boxes. He lashed the tarped load down with a heavy rope. "You could help if you wanted," he said to Jesse.

"I ain't gitting involved. This's your doing."

"Four months, and I'll have the bank put off for a year. Saving the farm single-handed. Plus, you ain't leaving anyways."

"I told you I was leaving," Jesse said.

"Heard ya. Don't believe you will. You ain't leaving Paps. You don't got the guts to even tell 'im. You ain't taking Marybeth from her sister, either."

"She's ready. Told me so this morning. I'll deal with Paps when I's ready."

Silas jumped off the truck and stood a few feet from Jesse. "Listen, I'm doing all I can to save the farm. I don't want you to leave, but then, I don't much care if you do. Next season will be good. You'll see. This is our home. Where we belong. You got no business in Washington or California. That's not you. You're here. Paps wants to stay. He ain't got much time. He should have his sons around. You can't take Levi. He belongs here."

Jesse stepped back, pulled up a milking stool, sat, and leaned up against the rails of a stall. He pushed his hair back and swatted a fly buzzing his face. Silas took a seat on the Dodge's running board, opposite and at eye level with his brother.

"Silas, this just ain't gonna work. Two hundred bucks, what you'll earn this season, not gonna be enough." Jesse picked up a twist of baling wire, straightened it out into a poker, and traced his thoughts on the dirt floor at his feet. "You might hold off Cavness, but we ain't spraying this year. We owe from spraying last year. Can't you see we're through? You need to let this go and come out with us."

"Paps?"

"He can come, too," Jesse said. He smoothed out his scratching in the dust with his foot and began again.

"You're a coward. Got no faith. Paps don't deserve no disrespect from you. He don't deserve to be mule-kicked off his land. At this point, it looks like I'm the only one looking after 'im."

"Ok, what about chickens?" Jesse bent his wire poker in half with both hands.

"We're not doing chickens. You don't know a damn thing about chickens. We know apples," Silas said.

"They're lending for chickens down in Washington County. Three months to profit. We could do it with ten acres. We just put up a grow-out house. They just give you the chicks and feed, and in nine weeks, we have broilers, and they buy 'em back for a dollar apiece. Ain't no risk."

"Not cutting no trees."

"Ten acres' all we need. Profit three months," Jesse pleaded.

"I got profit each week now and don't have to cut any of Paps's trees. You don't know chickens."

"I know chickens ain't gonna land you behind bars like corn mash will."

"Ain't gonna happen. I told ya, Suggs got my back," Silas said. "Think we're done talking. You ain't seeing straight. You don't help out now; I'm not sure how you're gonna pay me back when I own this place. You think about that." Silas stood and climbed into the truck cab. "I got a delivery to make, and you're not standing in my way."

Jesse stood and slung an elbow over the top rail of the stall. "That truck belongs to both of us. Don't reckon you're making any deliveries if I sell my half."

Silas choked the engine and pushed the starter. Black smoke belched from the exhaust pipe. "If it wasn't for me, you'd have half of nothing." He pulled the floor shifter into gear, eased the clutch, and the truck lurched forward and out of the barn.

As Jesse watched lingering exhaust dance within vanes of light, slanting into the barn between vertical planks, he heard a noise behind a barrel. A tuft of blonde hair caught his eye. He crossed over and found his niece crouched low in the shadows. "Vesta, come out here," he said.

Nine-year-old Vesta stood barefoot in overalls with no shirt. Dust coated her face and shoulders.

"What're you doing? Your mama knows you're here?" Jesse asked.

"No, sir. She's off with Nancy."

"Where you supposed to be?"

"Chores, Uncle Jesse. I'm supposed to be doing chores. Garden chores."

Jesse knelt on one knee and held Vesta by the shoulders. "I know what you heard. No need to fret. Now, your papa and me's just talking like brothers sometimes do. Don't mean nothing, you hear?"

Vesta shifted one foot on top of the other and dropped her chin. "We're in trouble?"

"No, little girl. We're not in trouble. We'll work things out. Your papa's gonna work things out for your sisters and mama."

"Why's the sheriff gonna get Papa?" Vesta said, lifting her gaze to her uncle.

"He's not. I said everything's gonna be fine. Now, it would be best if you just keep this all to yourself. You old enough to keep secrets?"

"Yes, sir."

"Good. Your mama, Sussie, and Nancy don't need to hear what you heard. Your papa's gonna work it out. But he's gonna need your help."

Vesta nodded and looked through the open barn door, squinting at the brightness beyond.

"Now, you git on with your routines." Jesse released her, and she sped out of the barn, flaxen hair flowing behind her. He followed, pulling the sliding door closed behind him.

The long walk across the orchard to his own house allowed Jesse time to piece together his thoughts. Silas was reckless, risking his entire family's safety by running liquor for the Benoits. It was a goddamn dream of his to think he could make enough to save the farm. The Benoits weren't anybody you wanted to cross. They'd put a bullet in you if they even thought you were shorting them. Suggs was not going to protect him or the farm. He never got over losing his girls to the country. Perhaps that was his plan: bankrupt the farm to get even. He didn't want Anna Lee and Marybeth to move back to town and didn't much care. He just didn't want Silas and himself to have what he had lost.

There was no future here. Apples were dead, having been dying for years. Nobody was turning a profit anymore from growing apples in Benton County. Why couldn't Silas see this? In trying to save the trees, he was going to kill himself. No profit next year, even with a warm spring and wet summer. The market was gone, gone to the Pacific Northwest.

They could switch to raising broilers, but he could not do it alone. All they needed was a grow-out house. It seemed so clear to him, but so opaque to Silas.

Not knowing why, Jesse changed course and cut downhill toward his father's cabin. The dogtrot came into view through the rows of black-barked apple trees. Perhaps he was looking for approval from his father to leave the farm. Maybe he wanted to gain acceptance for his idea of raising poultry. He did not know. Jesse had always had a good relationship with his father, but they did not think the same. Paps's mind worked like Silas's: narrow, myopic, limited in depth and ideas. Impulsive and hardheaded.

Paps owned the farm but had not had a hand running the place for several years. He usually defaulted to whatever Silas and he came up with. Age and alcohol had dulled his senses and ambition. He was content with frittering his time in the limited world of his cabin and dooryard. A bottle of applejack or corn mash helped.

As Jesse approached the house, he settled on two options: take his family and leave, hoping Silas would do the same, or try his hand at chickens. He still was not sure he could leave his father behind.

The unmistakable smooth sound of a Hudson Super Six Coach coming up the hill, downshifting at the switchbacks, caught Jesse's attention. It was not an extension agent or inspector straining a four-cylinder. The Benoit brothers weren't brazen enough to drive during daylight, plus this was no truck.

The black Hudson with a hardtop and side curtains came around the last curve and into view. No mistake, it was the sheriff. The sedan pulled up on the dirt drive just as Jesse emerged from the orchard. Jesse stood in the middle of the road, blocking the car from progressing farther onto the property.

"Wouldn't bother me none to mow you down, Jesse," Sheriff Ricketts said as he cut the engine and opened the half-door. "Nobody would believe it wasn't an accident. Save me a lot of trouble."

"You looking for Anna Lee?" Jesse asked, resting a boot on the polished chrome bumper.

"No, why would I be looking for Anna Lee?"

"Thought maybe you had some news about Silas."

"Not Silas. I come to serve your father." The sheriff held out a stiff bone-white sheet and waved it at Jesse.

"Whatever you got, we don't want," Jesse said.

"I don't much care what you want, and Judge don't care neither. Where's your father?"

Jesse motioned to the cabin. "I don't know what kind of mind he's in, but if you're wanting 'im, he's in there."

The sheriff shut his car door and pulled on a black ten-gallon Stetson. He lifted the waist of his pants under his dark coat and walked up to Jesse. "This here is an eviction decree," he said, waving the page in front of him. "Sez y'all got to leave the bank's property in two weeks. Generous if you ask me."

"Sheriff Ricketts, you can't do that to us. Silas done paid the bank. We got some money coming. Hell, just this morning, we talked about raising broilers. We'll have enough profit in three months to pay what we owe by the end of the year," Jesse pleaded.

"You done missed your chance."

"Anna Lee's expecting anytime now. She's got nowhere to go. Two months, and we'll be making good with Mr. Cavness."

"Not just the bank, Jesse. You got sour credit all over this county. Time's over," the sheriff said as he moseyed down the path and studied the cabin. "Don't see how nobody can live like this."

"Farm's been in the family a long time. You can't do this to us." Jesse followed.

"I said, I ain't doing it. I don't make the law. Just my job to make sure the law's carried out."

The two men stepped onto the front porch of the dogtrot, and Jesse called out, "Paps, sheriff's calling on you."

There was no answer. Jesse pushed open the kitchen door to find his father sleeping in a chair with his ear resting in the bend of his elbow on the table. His hat sat upside down in front of him.

"Paps, wake now," Jesse said to his father.

Ricketts stepped into the room and took stock of the place. The room had a musty, rodent smell. Loose floorboards creaked as he walked over to the corner. He ladled a cup of water from a standing bucket into his mouth, holding the bowl up to his lips and tasting its wetness. "Long, dry drive up from the Little Sugar." He looked at a clear-glass bottle tipped next to Paps's hat. "A man can git thirsty up here."

The sheriff dipped the ladle into the bucket again. He held the bowl with the palm of his hand, crossed back to where Paps slumped, and splashed water on his face with a quick flick. Paps popped into consciousness, and the sheriff pushed his head onto the table. "Whoa, there, partner. Git ahold of yourself. Jesse is here with me to talk to you."

Paps looked sideways across the room to where his son stood near the door. The sheriff eased up on his temple and pulled him upright.

"Now, Mr. Fitch, it wouldn't be proper for me to serve this decree if you're not sober, would it?" the sheriff said. "Tell me you're sober, or I'll take you in for drunkenness."

"I'm fine now. Who you?" Paps asked. "Jesse?"

"Paps, Sheriff Ricketts's got something you gotta take. Then he'll leave us be. Just take it," Jesse said.

"This here is an eviction." The sheriff slapped the notice on the table in front of Paps. "You got two weeks to vacate. Your sons, too."

Paps looked up at the sheriff and then again at Jesse. "I ain't moving. You can git the hell out of here," he said before dropping his head back onto his arm.

Expecting as much, Ricketts said, "Suit yourself. Be back in two weeks." He stepped past Jesse and exited the open doorway. Jesse watched him climb the path to his car and get in. The six-cylinder fired up and purred as the sheriff turned her around and coasted down the hill.

EIGHTEEN

"COME SIT A SPELL with me. I need to get off my feet," Anna Lee said to her daughter before cautiously lowering herself onto a rock ledge protruding from the hillside.

Nancy set her basket of blackberries in the dirt and joined her mother in the shade of a white oak tree. Mother and daughter sat silently, taking in the sounds of the forest: the repetitive chatter of a Carolina wren, the rustle of a squirrel, the creak of a partially fallen tree trunk against another in the breeze. Anna Lee ran her fingers through Nancy's hair, pulling out wind-born tangles and combing cascading curls into the bulk of it. So much had happened in the past few months: the crop loss, her husband's erratic behavior, threats of foreclosure, possibilities of fracture in the family, and her advancing pregnancy. Coming to the woods with Nancy to pick berries had been her idea, a respite from her woes. But she also had a nagging feeling, a premonition, that she must talk to her daughter soon. Talk to her about the life ahead of her, her dreams. But was it also time to disclose to Nancy the mistakes she had made in her life, her own lost opportunities, and regrets?

Anna Lee shifted her weight to find a more comfortable position on the rock. "Look at these swollen ankles, will you?" She motioned to her legs with her outstretched palm.

Nancy sprang up and knelt at her mother's side, taking her lower legs in her hands. "Fluid, Mother." She sank a depression into the flesh with her thumb. "You are doing too much on your feet. Your boots are tight at the top." She undid the lacing and spread out the gusset and quarters. She did the same for the other boot. "Better?"

Anna Lee nodded and smiled. "Thank you, my dear."

Nancy reclaimed her place on the rock ledge and turned her back so her mother could resume caressing her hair.

"How's that new book Aunt Marybeth lent you?"

"You mean *Anne of Green Gables*?"

"Precisely. Did she tell you that the book belonged to me and that she stole it from me when we were younger?"

"No, not exactly. But she did say it was your favorite book at my age. I can just imagine all the books you had in your home. How wonderful it must have been. But I'm glad she saved this one for me. I just love Prince Edward Island. Don't you? I would love to go there someday."

"That you may—not as an orphan, mind you."

"Of course not. But maybe I'll find a *bosom friend and kindred spirit* like Diana. You do remember Diana?"

"Why, yes. I thought last week you wanted to be a veterinarian."

"That was last week. Now I want to travel the world," Nancy said. "Do you remember Gilbert? Do you think Anne and Gilbert marry in the end?"

"That you will have to find out for yourself. I'm not going to spoil the story for you," Anna Lee said.

"Gilbert is so handsome, but he annoys Anne. I think they marry."

"You must choose your Gilberts carefully, Nancy. You have so much potential. Find someone who will fly with you while you spread your wings. Someone who derives pleasure from your success. Men like that do exist. Find one."

"Now?"

"No, not now. Not now. I'm talking about when you are older. When you are older, you will know when that is. Let your heart lead you to the right man."

"Did you follow your heart?" Nancy asked.

"I was young. But I got you, Sussie, Vesta, Mayel, and Polly, for starters." She patted her pregnant belly. "I guess, in a sense, I followed my heart. Your aunt followed her heart, and it did not disappoint her."

"I am blessed to have you and Aunt Marybeth in my life." Nancy reached into her basket and retrieved a handful of blackberries. She offered some to her mother and ate the rest. "What if I meet someone here, and then we have to move before I get married? Are we moving?" she asked.

"Moving? Oh, honey, where did that come from? Where did you hear that?"

"Talk."

"That's a difficult question to answer." Anna Lee suspected Nancy was much more perceptive than she allowed others to see.

"I heard Papa say that the land was no good no more. He said Uncle Jesse was going to Washington. I shouldn't have listened. I know it was wrong, but I heard from the kitchen door at the picnic dinner, and it caught me by surprise. Uncle Jesse seems quite upset. I didn't know what he meant, but now I can see that we have no apples this year. I can see that. I see you minding every penny. The land is no good, and Uncle Jesse is going to Washington. Sussie thinks the same."

"The land is still good. We'll have apples next year. The frost got the blossoms, that's all. Nobody is leaving right now. Not you worry."

"But we might have to move with Uncle Jesse?"

"Yes, Nancy, we might. But your father is doing his best. Uncle Jesse is a smart man, and he will help as well. We've gotten through tough times before, and this year will be no different."

"Is that why Papa goes to town so often? Why does he do that?"

"Business. He has business in town and must meet with the bank. The bank loaned us money we must pay back. But don't you worry yourself. We'll find the money. You concern yourself with your sisters. Can I count on you? You must keep your chin up and do your best. Think of Anne in the book. Think of all that she goes through and still comes out on top. You can do the same."

"I want to stay here, on the farm."

"Of course you do. We all do." Anna Lee felt a sharp pain in her pelvis. She lifted her abdomen with both hands to shift the baby's weight. She then leaned back, arching her back. "I think we best head back to the house. I'm feeling a little uneasy."

Nancy helped her mother to her feet, guiding her down the slope by her elbow.

"When this baby comes," Anna Lee said, "I will need your help. I can't do it without you. We can't leave before this baby comes, even if we wanted to."

"Yes, I expect to help," Nancy said. "I'll do whatever you want. I'm so looking forward to meeting my baby sister."

"Sister? Now, why do you think it will be a girl?"

"Five sisters and no brothers, I just assumed. Have you and Papa picked out a name? Would you tell me if you had?"

"No names yet. Maybe you can name the baby. What would you choose?"

"Lula Mae."

Nineteen

Silas maneuvered the flatbed down a graded dirt road following Spanker Creek's gentle but circuitous bank. He passed a cottonwood trunk, three feet in diameter with furrowed gray-brown bark, leaning over the river where the erosive wandering of the channel had robbed the tree of its tenuous clutch on the sandy bank. From its massive, canted crown, delta-shaped leaves, spinning between shamrock and mint on long stalks in the afternoon sun, hung just inches from the clear current. Behind the falling riparian giant's unearthed root ball, a saw-toothed hackberry bush claimed the newly open skylight. Messy black willows stretched up and down the bank on nimble roots with multiple leaning trunks and irregular clumps of twigs. On the outside curve of the alluvial bank, all would eventually be lost when the next flood rearranged the water's course. After the deluge, the inside bend's flora would be rewarded with new, nutrient-rich real estate while the losers on the other side washed downstream.

The valley eventually opened up to verdant pastureland bordered with wire fencing. A dozen piebald black and white cows had their snouts on the ground in a lush field, raking sheaves of grass into their mouths with long pink tongues. They hardly seemed to notice Silas's truck rumbling past. Behind the cows, a muddy path led to a dairy barn on a slight rise across the field. The moist bottomland was prime for growing grass to feed cattle, but too poorly drained for fruit.

Silas's truck forded the clear water of Little Sugar Creek at a wide spot on algae-covered stones in the shade of box elder. He ascended the far bank and turned onto County Highway 100, connecting Bentonville to the Missouri state line. As he followed the creek downstream, Lake Bella Vista came into view a mile down the road on the right. Across the lake, Silas saw the thirty-room Bella Vista Lodge on an overlooking bluff. Stilled by a man-made dam, guests with straw hats and parasols navigated colorful prams in the tranquil water. Lively young women in skirted one-piece bathing suits and rubber caps splashed in the shallows of a roped-off swimming area along the far side. Just up from the beach, beyond a willow thicket and the judgmental control of parents, a group of young boys shared a cigarette.

The sun danced off the water's surface to the south as Silas drove across the one-hundred-yard-long weir. He took in the frolic and carefree recreation of the beneficiaries of wealth. As soon as he crossed the lake, he passed a spring-fed swimming pool and a pitched-roof dance pavilion perched on pilings before curling up the hill toward the lodge. A large wooden sign at the top advertised parcels and acreage for sale to build a summer cabin.

Seasonal homes larger than his own had already been built in choice locations close to the lake and lodge. Rich men who made their money elsewhere—oil and gas industrialists from Dallas, cattlemen from Kansas City, financiers from Chicago—erected homes for use only three months a year, from Decoration Day to Labor Day. Men who could afford to bring their families to the Ozarks for the entire summer. Men who couldn't care less about local orchards and farms, suffocating under failed crops, debt, and falling prices. Men who made money even while they vacationed at the Bella Vista.

Silas pulled the Dodge truck around the back of the lodge, then headed uphill again to a storage shed at the rear of the dining hall. He slowed next to a dense pawpaw copse to shield the truck from inquisitive eyes and unload his cargo.

"You're late," the assistant caretaker barked at Silas when his truck came to a stop.

"I don't think so," Silas replied, watching the man place his boot on the truck's running board. "Git your goddamn foot off my truck, or I'll just drive right on out."

The assistant caretaker, a small, tonsured man with sloped shoulders and an unnatural curve to his spine, pulled his foot back. Silas thought his legs were too long for his torso, or his torso was too short. Even though he had been making weekly deliveries to the Bella Vista for two months, and the same man always addressed him, he did not know his name and was not inclined to ask for fear he might have to supply his own.

The assistant caretaker stepped away from the cab and wandered to the rear of the truck. He looked at the tarped load covering only a third of its bed.

"We paid for more," the assistant caretaker said as Silas hopped out of the cab.

"You paid for thirty boxes, and that's what I brung."

"Mr. C ain't gonna be too pleased with you and the Benoits if you can't deliver."

"I told you, you got what you paid for." Silas climbed onto the flatbed and undid the tie-downs, releasing the tarp. The apple boxes stood three high. He lifted the side rail and placed it behind the stack. Hoisting the first box, he said, "Best get some help here to get these off. I got thirty."

"Bust it open. I need to check what you got."

Silas dropped the box on the flatbed, produced a screwdriver from a nearby toolbox, and pried the wooden lid off. He scooped hay from the top, pulled out a glass quart bottle full of clear liquid, and held it out for the assistant caretaker.

"Not that one. I say which."

Silas laid the bottle at the edge of the tarp and rummaged for another in the box. He held out an identical bottle for the bent-back man, who took it from his hands.

The assistant caretaker twisted out the cork and drew a mouthful, savoring the fiery liquid as he let it slide down his throat. "Nice. Real nice," he said, then he slipped the bottle into the generous front pocket of his britches.

"The best in Benton County," Silas said, then he nudged the first bottle under the tarp with his foot. "No, the best this side of the Mississippi and all the way to Kentucky."

"That don't make no sense."

"It's good, huh?"

"The hell with you." The assistant caretaker called into the shed, "Jared."

Two ungainly teenage boys whose limbs were too long for their cotton jeans and loose button-up shirts emerged from the storage shed. The boys set to work, ferrying the boxes from the flatbed to a dark corner of the building without further instruction. The assistant caretaker counted each box and occasionally lifted one to gauge its fill.

"You mind if I look around before I leave?" Silas asked as he rolled his tarp after the boys collected the last box. "You got a nice place here. Might be interested in investing someday."

"It ain't for you. Mr. C don't take kindly to the help wandering around. You best skedaddle and be happy he lets you deliver on the property."

Silas jumped off the flatbed and reset the side rail. He did not care for the arrogant and demeaning tone in the assistant caretaker's voice. "I'm not the help."

"You sure as hell are—produce delivery boy. You'll keep it that way if you wanna keep your job."

Silas climbed into the truck cab and kicked on the engine. "You watch your mouth. You'll be working for me someday." He backed the truck around and coasted down the hill.

Across the dam, Silas turned left toward Bentonville, ten miles away. He intended to stop by the bank and make a payment on the loan. The road widened into a pullout overlooking the lake and resort beyond. Silas eased off the shoulder and parked the truck facing the Bella Vista Lodge.

He hopped out of the truck, retrieved the whiskey bottle from the rolled tarp, slipped the cork out, and drew a long swallow. The bank can wait, he reasoned. Silas climbed back into the cab and took another swig. Through the windshield, he watched the boats spin on the water's surface without purpose. Bathers continued to splash and sun themselves at the beach. Two lissome women in tight bathing suits batted a ball to each other in the sand, naively exposing the curves of their youthful bodies to Silas's lusting eyes. He took another drink and continued to gaze.

Silas watched three men in white linen summer suits, double-breasted and vested, with walking sticks and highball glasses, strolling down the staircase from the lodge. They radiated power and influence, wealth and command. The trio reached the bottom of the hill and sauntered over to the boardwalk overlooking the narrow beach. They, too, took notice of the two young women batting a ball. To Silas, these men looked like they could buy whatever and whomever they wished. The men appeared to share a joke and belly laugh as they scanned the view.

A black-tie waiter appeared with a silver tray of fresh drinks. The men exchanged glasses, sipped, and then continued to stroll. Silas took another swig from his bottle.

TWENTY

JESSE PULLED THE SHED door and propped it open with a splitting stump. Dust sucked in by the sudden sweep settled down on a canvas tarp covering a boxy frame. He lifted and rolled the tarp, revealing a black 1917 Model T Ford. Half of the two-seater's right front fender and the entire right running board were missing.

Jesse walked around the car, looking for tire rot on its wooden-spoke wheels and found none. He reached into the passenger side and lifted the seat. Here, he fingered the petrol filler cap. He dropped a thin wooden stick into the tank. It was half full. Down on his knees, he fumbled under the car and opened the fuel cock, feeding gas to the carburetor.

Jesse reached back inside, set the parking brake, slid the spark advance and throttle levers down a couple of notches on the steering column, flipped the start switch, and pulled the choke. It had been several weeks since he fired up the engine, and he was unsure it would engage. This was his father's first and only car. Brake failure was the stated reason his father left the fender and running board embedded in a roadside tree. Jesse suspected otherwise. There was no money for repair, especially a cosmetic luxury like a fender.

Jesse hopped out of the car and stepped to the front. He engaged a cast-iron starter crank hanging below the radiator between two bug-eyed headlights and gave it a sharp upward pull. Empty popping-off of the cylinder compression sputtered from the exhaust pipe. He pulled several more times until a gas smell told him he had flooded the engine. Jesse raised the cowling and drained the float bowl onto the ground. Next time, with the spin of the handle, the four-cylinder engine sputtered to life. He adjusted the spark advance and dropped the throttle and choke until she ran smoothly.

"What're you doing, Pa?" Levi yelled over the engine noise that drew him out of the house.

"Just testing her out, son."

"Can we take a ride? Can I steer? Can we?" Levi hopped onto the passenger side of the bench seat and put his left hand on the steering wheel.

"Not today." Jesse shut off the engine, which sputtered several times before quitting. "We got work to do. What's Ma doing?"

"Putting up the carrots I pulled."

"Good. I got a job for you," Jesse said. "You take a rag from the hamper and fetch a pail of water, and I'll have you wash her down, and maybe later we'll go riding."

"Yes, sir, Pa." Levi sprang from the seat, searching for a rag and pail.

Jesse walked across the yard and entered the house to speak to his wife.

"We got two weeks. Best we start figgerin out what we gonna take," Jesse said to Marybeth, who was ladling boiling water into Kerr jars filled with carrot spears. The kitchen was hot with steaming water.

"Two weeks?"

"Sheriff served Paps an eviction this morning."

"What's that mean for us? How's that work?" Marybeth asked.

"We no longer own this land. Bank does. We got to go. Silas and them, too."

"They're not leaving. Anna Lee says Silas is not leaving."

"It's not up to them no longer. We got two weeks. You heard me run the Ford. We'll take that as far as it lasts. Not sure it's gonna make it to Washington. I'll take Paps if I have to."

"He's not going anywhere, you know that, Jesse." Marybeth continued to fill a dozen jars, place flat metal seals on top, and then screw on loose metal bands.

"I need to talk to 'im again. Sheriff'll throw 'im in jail, he don't leave."

"Does Silas know about this yet?"

"Not yet."

"How am I to know what to bring?" She set her spoon down and wiped moisture off her arms with her apron.

Jesse looked around the kitchen to the few possessions they owned: a cast-iron stove, various pots, crockery, enameled cups, flatware, a wooden box of linens, a pie safe, nearly barren shelves of canned food, a farm table, and chairs. Not much else was in the room. Only two beds and a bureau occupied the rest of the house. Nothing of much value, nothing to show for the decade they had been a family. A tintype photo of Jesse's mother hung in the hall. A Bible sat on a small reading table in their bedroom. Candles and a few kerosene lamps hung from hooks.

"Anything we take gots to be strapped on the back. You best be careful with your choices," Jesse said.

"What about the flatbed?"

"Silas will need it for his family. I can't take that from 'im and Anna Lee."

Tears welled up in Marybeth's eyes. She dabbed her cheeks with the corner of the cloth. The world she had stitched together was falling apart. This was not how she envisioned her life with Jesse. The four of them—two brothers and two sisters, raising close-knit families, working the land, making memories—would no longer be together. Cousins separated. Siblings separated. The West was an unknown. Unless Silas and Anna Lee came along, an insurmountable chasm would forever divide them. She doubted she would ever see her sister and nieces again. Marybeth trusted Jesse and swore to stand by him in good times and bad. She believed he was making the right decisions for their family. But it was more complicated than he knew. Secrets were kept, and white lies played. All for his benefit, she had told herself for years. All because she loved him. She dabbed her eyes and addressed Jesse, "We can't eat all these carrots in two weeks."

"Sell what you can. We got to travel light. I'm gonna see what I can do to fashion a bed on the back of the Ford. Someone's riding in the back. It's two thousand miles."

Two footfalls on the porch preceded the front door bursting open. Nancy stood in the doorway, trying to catch her breath. "Come, Aunt—" she gasped. "Come."

Marybeth pulled her niece into the house. "What's wrong, sweetie? What's wrong?"

"Mama." Nancy sucked in deep breaths. Sweat matted her hair.

"Sit." Marybeth guided her to the kitchen table.

"Mama's bleeding. The baby's coming," Nancy finally got out.

"Where's your father?" Marybeth asked.

"Town."

"Jesse," Marybeth commanded, "gather some linens. Can we drive?" She closed the air dampers on the stove to starve the fire.

Jesse sprinted into the bedrooms and pulled sheets off the beds, rolling them into a bundle by the door. He ran out to the shed barn, where Levi was sitting on an overturned pail, admiring his work on the car. "Levi, run inside to your mother and see if she needs help. Now!"

"Pa?"

"Run, Aunt Anna Lee's bleeding."

Levi ran. Jesse started up the Ford and pulled it around the front of the house. Marybeth lifted sheets and towels into the cab and sat next to Jesse.

"Levi, you and Nancy come along quickly," Marybeth said as the runabout puttered, then leaped forward on stiff suspension for a rocky ride to the other side of the orchard, leaving the children to join them on foot.

Marybeth charged into the bedroom to find her sister lying on the floor in a pool of bright red blood. Her dress lay crumpled above her pregnant belly. From the corner of her eye, she saw children standing up against the wall, wide-eyed, silent. "Sussie," she said, "take your sisters to the other room. Get some water."

Marybeth leaned down to speak. "Anna Lee, we're here. Everything's going to be all right." She touched her forehead, and Anna Lee opened her eyes. Marybeth turned to her husband, standing in the doorway. "Jesse, help me."

The two lifted Anna Lee into the bed and adjusted a feather pillow under her head.

"Heat some water, warm and hot," Marybeth said to Jesse. "Bring the linens in. Where's your brother?"

Jesse popped into the kitchen and stoked the fire. Sussie entered with a pail of water, pouring it into a kettle. "More," he said, and Sussie spun on her heels.

In the bedroom, Marybeth looked at her sister. She was pale, breathing hard. Her hands were cool despite the summer heat. "Vesta," Marybeth called, "come here."

Vesta trembled. She stood in the doorway, waiting for further instructions.

"Take that blanket and spread it out on the floor. We'll clean up the mess later. Tell me when Levi and Nancy get here."

Vesta did as she was told, then eagerly left the room. Jesse appeared with a glass of water and handed it to Marybeth, sitting on the bed next to her sister's shoulder.

"Here, take some of this." Marybeth tipped the glass to Anna Lee's dry lips.

Anna Lee screamed, then grabbed her abdomen as waves of pain shot through her body. Again, another contraction and screams. More blood soaked the bed under her hips.

Jesse brought a pot of warm water and set it on a small side table. Marybeth lathered soap and washed her hands.

"The baby?" Anna Lee asked.

"Yes, it's coming. I'm going to look." Marybeth spread Anna Lee's legs and wiped away the blood from her thighs. Jesse turned toward the window. Marybeth inserted two fingers into the birth canal, feeling the crown of an infant. "It's coming. Everything's all right.

It's coming." Marybeth washed the blood off her hands, stepped over to Jesse, and whispered, "We need a doctor."

Jesse rushed onto the porch and found Vesta sitting on the edge with Mayel and holding Polly in her lap. Sussie came around the corner with yet another pail of water from the well. "Put that on the stove. We need it hot," Jesse said to her.

Levi came up the drive at a half trot, Nancy following behind. "Levi," Jesse said, "go over to the Jacobssons' and tell 'im to fetch the doctor. Your aunt needs 'im. Go fast." Jesse stepped back into the house with Nancy as Levi ran uphill to the neighbors' farm.

Anna Lee knew she was not due to deliver for another four weeks. The bleeding had begun in the morning, raising some concern but not enough to mention to Silas before he left with the truck. By mid-morning, after her return from picking blackberries with Nancy, her water broke with a gush of blood. Shock clouded her focus between gripping contractions. This labor was unlike her previous five and should have gone smoothly. Something was terribly wrong, she had thought, so she sent Nancy for help.

"Push!" Marybeth coached. "Push, push, push. The baby's coming." Marybeth had both of her hands on Anna Lee's abdomen, feeling the strength of the uterus tightening. "Get some more towels," she said to Nancy, standing beside her. Nancy left, then bounded in with what she could find and placed them at the foot of the bed. Marybeth tried to deliver more water to her sister's lips.

A half-hour passed, the labor progressed, and the bleeding seemed to stop. Anna Lee slipped out of consciousness, only to be brought back with each contraction. Jesse paced the hallway outside the bedroom, trying to think of what he could do. Childbirth and blood did not sit well with him.

"Need anything?" Jesse asked through the cracked-open door into the room.

Nancy came to the door and whispered, "Doctor."

Mrs. Jacobsson arrived with Levi as the sun dipped below the perimeter woods. She was in her fifties, with a thick waist and a gray-haired bun. She walked with purpose, swinging both arms forcefully as she propelled her stocky legs forward against the drape of her Mother Hubbard. Levi held a handbasket she had instructed him to carry.

"Mrs. Jacobsson." Jesse greeted her at the front door. "Come. Come." He guided her to the bedroom.

"Ma'am," Marybeth said when she entered.

"Lars went for the doctor," Mrs. Jacobsson said as she scanned the room, noticing a blood-soaked blanket on the floor, a pile of soiled towels in the corner, blood-tinged water in a pail next to the bed, and Anna Lee's sallow, dry cheeks and slow, deep breaths.

Anna Lee screamed, grimacing and grasping for the bed sheets. She screamed again.

Mrs. Jacobsson yanked at her dress sleeves and washed her arms up to the elbows. She knelt at the foot of the bed and placed her palm on the emerging head. "Slow it down a little bit, honey," she calmly said.

Marybeth placed a cool cloth on Anna Lee's forehead and touched her shoulder, stroking her skin.

Anna Lee panted. Mrs. Jacobsson reached up and pushed down on the top of the womb with one hand as she guided the baby out with the other. A gush of red blood erupted between Anna Lee's legs as Mrs. Jacobsson pulled the baby clear.

"You have a girl," Marybeth spoke into her sister's ear just as the blue infant sucked in her first breath and let loose a high-pitched cry. Anna Lee smiled, taking in the sound of her new daughter.

Mrs. Jacobsson snatched silk thread and a pair of scissors from her basket and tied off the cord. She handed the infant to Nancy, who was ready with a blanket. The baby bawled herself pink as Nancy laid her on their mother's chest.

"We need the doctor!" Mrs. Jacobsson called out to Jesse. "Now."

Jesse, standing right outside, poked his head into the room. "I'm sure he's on his way."

"Light a lantern," Marybeth said. The room had darkened with the setting of the sun.

Jesse touched a struck match to a wick, and the room came to a glow. He placed the lantern near the foot of the bed when Mrs. Jacobsson motioned for more light.

Blood continued to soak the new towels and sheets brought into the room. Mrs. Jacobsson guided Jesse's hands to Anna Lee's still-swollen abdomen. "Push hard. Push like this," she said.

Jesse did as he was told, massaging the uterus from the top as Mrs. Jacobsson pulled on the cord and tried to deliver the afterbirth. Blood coated her arms and the front of her dress. "Push on the side," she barked.

Marybeth stroked her sister's cheek. Her smile was gone, and her eyes were vacant. Her breaths were shallow. "Nancy," Marybeth said, "take the baby into the other room and stay there. Wait for the doctor. Close the door."

Nancy reached down and bundled the baby. She kissed her mother's cheek and stepped into the kitchen with her little finger stroking the roof of the baby's mouth. Jesse and Mrs. Jacobsson struggled to deliver the membranes while Marybeth comforted her sister. The blood flowed.

TWENTY-ONE

A RAP ON THE metal fender woke Silas. Dusk had settled in the valley. Electric lights filled the glass windows of cabins dotting the far side of the lake. The beach was vacant, and all boats were stored. Barn swallows reeled and swooped over the water, gorging on the evening's mayfly hatch. Another rap on the fender brought to his attention the two men standing at the side of the cab.

"Yeah?"

"Are you Silas? Silas Fitch?"

"Yeah."

"Then what business do you have here?" the tall revenue agent asked. His arms were akimbo, and his stance was wide as if to block any thought of Silas fleeing.

"I'm not doing nothing. I'm on public land," Silas responded. "I ain't trespassing."

"We didn't say you was," the other agent said, standing next to the first. "We ast you what business you have here."

"No business. Just taking a rest."

"We don't believe you," the first agent said.

"Dropped off some early peaches and berries I picked up in Garfield and sold to the Bell' Vista. That's all."

"They pay you in liquor?" The first agent gestured to the corked bottle, half-empty and lying on Silas's bench seat.

"It ain't illegal for a man to drink. You know that. Ain't illegal."

"No, it ain't, 'less you're the one transporting."

"I'm a farmer. Been selling produce. That's all," Silas said.

The first agent leaned in and said, "You ain't got no apples. We saw for ourselves the other day when we met your brother."

"I told you I was reselling berries."

"Someone's bringing whiskey down the hill to the Bella Vista. Only a matter of time before we figure out who. Legal or not, having a bottle in your truck makes you suspicious."

The second agent looked out across the lake to the lodge. Shadows turned in front of bright lights beyond large windows. The sounds of music skipped across the water's surface to his ears. The agent crossed in front of the truck and stood on the passenger's side.

"Peaches and berries. Told you." Silas looked at each agent.

"We think that bottle is evidence of a crime, transporting," the first agent said.

Silas turned to put his hand on the bottle at his side, but he was too late; the second agent had seized it and held it outside the cab. The agent uncorked and inverted the bottle, letting the remaining whiskey gurgle onto the ground. "Guess there ain't no more evidence of a crime here." He tossed the bottle onto the floorboard at Silas's feet. "You're free to go."

"Damn you," Silas said.

"We suggest you find your way back to the farm and stay there. Next time we see you at the Bella Vista, we're hauling you in."

"You ain't got no authority. You ain't the sheriff."

"We got all the authority of the federal government. All the authority we need. Don't test us."

The two agents backed up and got into their Chevrolet parked on the shoulder. The one driving gunned the engine. Two lit headlamps cast cones of light down the dirt road. Silas watched the sedan work its way up the river's edge, headlights swinging from side to side.

He picked the empty bottle off the floor and tossed it on the ground. He looked across the lake and saw that the dance pavilion was ablaze with activity. Couples were arriving, arm in arm, and climbing the broad steps to the main floor. Dim light emanated from large windows through drawn curtains. The layered rhythm of a swing band pulsed out of the building each time the door opened. Silas was captivated.

He left his truck and climbed down the bank to the lake's edge. Large, flat limestone rocks rimmed the water. Silas hopped onto a table-sized one and removed his shirt. He knelt at the side and splashed cool water on his face and shoulders, rubbing dust off his arms and neck. At the water's surface, the jazz tunes only seemed more evident, inviting. Like a siren, the music mesmerized him and filled his head with an erotic beat. An image of undulating bodies, driven into a primitive frenzy on a dance floor by an African rhythm, materialized in his mind. He had to go.

Silas snapped the wrinkles out of his white shirt, threaded his arms, and tucked the tails into his trousers. He combed his wet hair straight back and buttoned his sleeves. After climbing the bank, he ambled across the earthen dam toward the music. What was an insipid raised building when he passed it during the day had come alive like a beating heart.

As he drew near, a group of four young ladies, giggling like schoolgirls, arrived from the opposite direction. They wore loose, dropped waist, sleeveless dresses, barely covering their knees. Bobbed hair emphasized their long necks. Silas stepped into the shadows of the building when the ladies paused at the bottom of the steps. One girl produced a silver flask from her purse and twisted the cap. She tipped it to her red lips, then offered it to her companions, who passed it around. The four ladies tittered in the shared defiance of their parents' Victorian norms as they climbed the steps, swinging their hips to the music. Silas followed as if he had no choice.

At the top landing, a man in a dark three-piece suit with baggy pleated pants and white wingtip oxfords stopped him. He held a clipboard and pinched a monocle into his left eye.

"Cabin number, sir?" the man asked.

"I'm visiting. Just arrived today. I followed my little sister and her three friends. They're right in front of me."

"Cabin number?"

"I don't remember." Silas pointed to the lodge, where homes peeked out from the heavily wooded hillside. "Thirty-one, right over there."

"Jacket is required for gentlemen."

"Right. I knew that. My luggage, it got held up at the station. These are traveling clothes. I'm sorry. Tomorrow, I'll have a coat."

The doorman gave Silas a monocular stare, suspicious of his story, then opened the door for him.

A clave rhythm, accented with a bass beat and raspy snare, anchored a seven-piece band set up on the far wall. A trumpet and saxophone battled in improvisation to establish an ever-changing melody, then capitulated to the mellow woodiness of a solo clarinet.

Small tables dotted the perimeter of the dance floor. Each had a single votive candle, giving the room a mysterious, forbidden, and alluring, voodoo-like atmosphere.

Sweaty couples plied on the parquet with twists and turns, driven by the beat. Silas recognized the ordered touch and step, forward and back, of the Charleston. He backed up to a wall where he could survey the entire room. Handbags and coats claimed most of the unoccupied tables. He noticed the four girls he had followed congregating around a small table in the room's opposite corner, leaning in and giggling. A well-dressed man about his age wove across the room and approached the young ladies. Silas saw him extend his hand to each of them, only to be met with downcast eyes and a subtle head shake. The man then stiffened his spine, threw his hands in his pockets, and turned back toward his buddies, who were bowled over in laughter at another table.

A caller stepped to the microphone. "Ladies only. Gentleman, have a seat." Half the dance floor cleared. The band quickened the tempo. "Remember, when you mooch, shuffle forward with both feet. Hips go first, then feet. Ready to do the *Black Bottom*?

"Hop down front, then doodle back.

Mooch to your left, then mooch to the right.

Hands on your hips and do the mess around.

Break a leg until you're near the ground."

Silas watched a dozen young women gyrate and hop about the dance floor, high-stepping and flailing bare arms in the air. A cheeky brunette in a tight apricot-colored spangled dress smiled at him, spun to the right, and slapped her ass with her hand. Silas smiled back while his feet followed in an abbreviated step.

"Excuse me," Silas said to a man standing by his side in a dark-brown suit. "Where can a fellow get a drink?"

The man in his late forties had deep acne scars on his cheeks. He turned to Silas. "Not here. Management don't allow it."

"Figgered the same. But a good time like this calls for a nip. People's getting it."

"Don't know nothing about that."

"The hell you don't."

The music faded, and the dancers wandered back to their dates. After finishing their first set, the band announced a quick break. The musicians stepped behind the stage and exited through the back door.

"Where they come from? Play here often?" Silas asked the man.

"Not often. We normally have a college group from the university. Hornblower's from the Delta, Itta Bena. Rest of the fellas come from Little Rock. They got this gig only a week. Haven't seen you here before."

"Just got here today. My sister invited me down."

"She here?" The man looked around the room.

"Oh, no. She's not of this type. Don't much take to dancing. Me, I've got different ideas. I just come in from Kansas City. Heard Duke Ellington up there when he first got started," Silas concocted. "A man could get a drink up there if he was thirsty. You've got prettier women down here, though."

"Heifers. Texan heifers. Most folks here're from Dallas, and they're protective of their women. Best you watch your step."

"Yes, of course, that's what my sister said. No, not me. I'm just looking for a little whiskey," Silas said.

"I don't believe a word you say. I know most folks here, and I would've heard about a brother from Kansas City coming to visit. Now, I don't much care who you are, but this here is a private club, and perhaps you need to get along."

Silas stepped from the wall and extended his hand. "I don't mean no trouble. I'll be on my way."

The man took his hand and pulled him close. "You seem like a decent chap. You walk up the road to the left of the lodge, round back the hill. You'll come to a path leading into the woods. Tell 'em Clarence said it was okay. They'll fix you up if you have a few coins in your pocket."

"Proud to have known you," Silas said, then broke off and left the pavilion just as the music spun up.

Steep wooded hills muffled the jazz beat when he turned the corner into the draw. A canopy of tall trees obscured the night sky, and the road was dark. Silas saw a wooden pole with an electric wire crossing the road before spying the small dirt path leading toward the base of a limestone cliff. Dim slivers of light leaked from a wooden wall and a door facing the rock. Silas stepped up and tried the latch. The door was locked.

"Yeah?" a voice asked from inside.

"Clarence sent me."

"Don't know no Clarence." The voice sounded.

"Clarence said it's okay," Silas repeated.

The scraping sounds of a wooden slat lifting off its cleats preceded a slight door opening. The crack spilled smoke and white light on Silas's face.

"A Walking Liberty will get you started," a tall, burly man said. His thick, calloused hand shot out.

Silas knew this hand could ball into a fist and knock out a few of his teeth should he not behave. He rummaged in his pocket and retrieved a small drawstring purse. Silas turned his back to the door and fingered out a silver half dollar. "This better be enough to treat me right for the evening." He handed over the coin.

Silas side-stepped through the doorway into a vast limestone cavern carved from the hillside over the millennia by rainwater. The damp smell of mildew and bat guano mixed with the sweet aroma of cigar smoke. A single electric bulb hung from a bolt in the stone ceiling and lit up only a tiny fraction of the space. Several men nursing highball glasses of whiskey huddled around overturned barrels fitted with simple tabletops. To the left was a wooden bar fashioned from a shipping crate. A small man with a shiny bald head stood behind the counter, wiping glasses with a tattered and discolored rag.

"Double," Silas called out to the bartender.

The little man looked up, irritated, as if he had been interrupted. He flipped the glass in his hand and set it on the bar. "That's all you paid for, don't expect more." He splashed clear liquid to the rim.

Silas poured it down his throat. Not as firm and sweet as the bottle of Benoit whiskey he worked on earlier in the day, but passable. "Another," Silas said as he set the glass down and slid another half-dollar coin next to it.

The shiny-headed man filled the glass again and then put the bottle down, out of sight. Silas sipped his second measure, savoring its hot, earthy taste. Low, hushed voices from the other men in the cave seemed to vanish into the mountain with the light. Silas had never been in a cavern as enormous. The small wooden floor surrounding the bar dropped off at the edge to a pile of rubble, hiding the far corners of the space.

"You don't talk much, do you?" Silas said to the barkeep as he wiped the dust from the counter.

The man ignored Silas's question and kept up with his task.

"I said you don't talk much." Silas looked at the ceiling. "All that dust must come from the rock. Who the hell would think that it was a good idea to sell likker in a rock?"

The barkeeper slid a rag in front of Silas and leaned into his face. "I got nothing to say to you. In fact, I got nothing to say to any man who comes in here acting like a cock. You best swallow what you paid for and leave."

"I don't mean nothing, no trouble." Silas nursed his drink, taking nips while looking at the man. "Say, you got any Carib rum back there? You can get it in Little Rock, I hear."

"Whiskey," the man mumbled.

Silas pulled a wad of rolled bills from his front pocket and flipped through them until he came to a single, which he placed on the bar. The bartender filled two more glasses while Silas drained his second. Silas looked around the room while he stuffed the cash back where it came from. He lifted both glasses and walked to an empty chair by the door. "Mind if I sit?" he asked three men parked around a table.

"We was saving that chair for the women," one man said.

Silas placed his two drinks on the tabletop.

Another man said, "You might think twice before sitting. We's pretty lonely."

Silas pulled up a chair and sat. "Women can sit on my lap when they come."

"Haven't seen you here before. Best watch yourself flashing your wad."

"I can take care of myself," Silas said, padding the bills in his pocket.

"Just saying."

Silas glanced at the three men sharing his barrel table. They looked working-class like he, tanned on the back of their neck and hands—men acquainted with hard labor.

"I hear management don't allow no drinking at the dance club down the hill. You know anything about that?" Silas asked the group.

"Don't know nothing about that. Them aren't my type," said the man sitting to Silas's right.

"I was just wondering where them Texans wet their whistle," Silas said.

The man across the table leaned in. "Wondering too much can get a man killed."

Silas brought his glass to his lips and filled his mouth. "I heard the Benoits deliver to the lodge where they have better shit. Where do you get this?" Silas raised his glass against the light.

"Don't mention the Benoits here," the man on the left whispered, then glanced around the room to see whose ear might turn to their conversation. "Ain't polite and could get a bullet between your eyes."

"Just asking," Silas said.

"Sheriff looks the other way 'long as there ain't no trouble. Same as here. There ain't gonna be no trouble," the man on the right said.

"Just asking." Silas finished his third glass and started his fourth. "So, where's this place get its booze?"

"I told you not to ask no questions. Only two types come in here asking questions: dumbasses and G-men. Way you're flashing cash, I'd say you were a dumbass," the man on the right said, then he looked at his companions.

"Whoa, fellas," Silas said. "I'm in the business, just looking for opportunity."

"You're dumber than I first reckoned you were." The man on the right signaled to the doorman with a subtle nod.

"We got a problem here?" the beast of a man said as he lumbered over from his perch by the door.

"No, we're just talking," Silas said.

The man on the left looked at Silas. "He said he was just leaving and ast to be shown the door."

The doorman lifted Silas by his arms until his boots hung above the floor. He dropped him down on wobbly legs, facing the exit. Silas stumbled, then caught himself on the rock wall of the cave. The doorman grabbed an arm again, leading him out the door and into the night air.

"I'll break both arms if I ever see you coming around here again," the doorman said as he squeezed and torqued Silas's upper arm, sending him to his knees. The man released him and then kicked him over with his boot.

Silas scrambled to his feet and then lurched down the path. At the road, he turned left, uphill, away from his truck. He had not walked twenty yards when he heard the cave door open and excited voices descend the path behind him. Silas fell to his knees and rolled into a ditch, hiding in the brush at the road's edge. He followed the voices down the hill. Several minutes later, two men he had not recognized before climbed up the road. One had a baseball bat slung over his shoulder; the other carried a leather blackjack in his hand.

"Find 'im?" a third man said from the path.

"Nah, sucker's quick," the bat-wielding man said.

All three men reentered the cave while Silas lay face down in the dirt. Thirty minutes passed before he scurried down the road across the dam and climbed into his truck.

TWENTY-TWO

THE MORNING SUN FILTERED through an ancient white oak; pinnate lobes casually spun on their stalks in gentle puffs of air, not quite a breeze, casting shadows alive with motion on the ground. A red-tailed hawk, looking for night vermin not yet burrowed in for the day, circled against a backdrop of blue over a small field separating the cemetery from the apple trees. Jesse and Lars worked the rocky bottom of a rectangular pit with a pointed shovel and a digging bar.

"Doc said it was the membranes. Something like 'grown across the canal' or 'came loose from the womb.' Nothing nobody could do. God's plan," Jesse said as he rested on his shovel for a moment.

"I don't believe it was her time to go," Lars said.

"What do you mean? Who are you to second-guess the will of God? Doc said it was 'God's plan.'"

"I'm not second-guessing nobody. It just don't make no sense to me." Lars plunged his bar behind a melon-size stone and pried it free from the bottom of the hole.

"You think Anna Lee was a bad person, deserving this?" Jesse asked.

"No, course not. But why would God take her now? What purpose would that serve? I know people the world would be better off without—not her."

"I got to agree with you on that. Hell, I don't know. The membranes grew wrong, nothing nobody could do."

The two men then worked silently for several minutes, dropping the hole below knee level and piling the tailings on the uphill side.

"Anyhoo, what's Silas gonna do with six girls?" Lars asked.

"Don't know. Think he's got a choice?"

"Some men, ya know, they just can't handle something like this. Too much pain. They go crazy-cucumber. I knew a fella up Nort' just walked out into the snow, leaving his kids in a cabin with his dead wife. Didn't even bury her. Just walked out into the snow. Presbyterians found 'im naked and stiff in the woods, a day's walk away. Took off all his clothes while he walked. They just followed his trail. Church buried them both in the churchyard. They felt sorry for them children. Buried those parents in the churchyard even though they never set foot there."

"What happened to the young'uns?"

"There weren't no kin around," Lars said. "Some of them Presbyterians wanted to send 'em downstate to a home for orphans. Them women would have none of that. There was four little'uns and a boy old enough to apprentice out. They split the little'uns among families and raised 'em like cousins. The boy worked livery until he moved on." Lars lifted another stone to his waist and rolled it out of the hole. "You and Marybeth taking them in?"

"Don't know. We've not had a chance to discuss it. Reckon we'll do what we can. But we're leaving. You heard that? Can't make this work no more. I'm surprised you ain't talking the same."

"We is."

"We was leaving for Washington State soon as we could pick up. Now I don't know what we're doing," Jesse said. "What're you thinking?"

"Oklahoma. There's still good land out there for wheat if I could sell my place. Get me a tractor and a hundred acres for what my land is worth. Let some other suckers worry about trying to grow apples. Missus got kin between Enid and the Cimarron. They're making a killing in cotton. Needs a tractor," Lars said. "Washington's long way. Must be two thousand miles."

"Something like that. Columbia River valley's got apples. I'll do what I can to git started. Ever heard of We-nat-chee?"

"Nope. Sounds like an Injun." Lars said.

"They grow apples in We-nat-chee. Saw it in a handbill looking for labor. Ain't got no disease out West. Ship 'em anywheres in the States by rail, reefer car."

"Washington, huh? Tell ya a story about a guy I knew from Cave Springs, drove all the way out there with his family and every possession he still owned to work the fields. Was going to pick oranges."

"They ain't got no oranges in Washington," Jesse said.

"Maybe California. Well, when he got there, he finds out that they got Chinamen and Mexicans picking for half-wages. Couldn't support his family on that. Wrote his brother for Western Union money just to eat. I think it was California; you're right. Didn't hear nothing about no apples."

Jesse and Lars climbed out of the grave, now waist-deep, with straight sides and a flat bottom.

"Preacher be proud of us if Silas can find one," Jesse said. He sat with Lars on the pile of dirt to admire their doings.

"I just feel for those kids. It ain't right, losing their mama."

"Marybeth's not gonna let them be unattended. I just don't know what we're gonna do."

"Stay," Lars said. He took off his gloves and lifted a tin canteen to his lips. "Want some?" He held the container out to Jesse.

Jesse shook his head. "Bank's evicting us, two weeks. We gotta go."

"*Lort*—What about Silas?"

"Everybody. They say we owe more than the land is worth. I just don't know what we're gonna do."

"Surely, they give you some time with what's happened to Anna Lee. That ain't right. No God-fearing man would do that to another." Lars picked up a clod and flicked it to the other side of the hole, where it dusted in the grass. "I dug one of these by myself once."

"Sure, you did."

"No, I dug one of these all by myself. Only me."

"I don't know what you're gitting at. Who hasn't dug a grave?"

Lars stared into the woods, beyond the white oak and chinkapin, into the deep shadows of the deciduous forest. "I killed a man."

Jesse turned his shoulders slightly to face Lars.

"I killed 'im. . . . I had to. You know the missus and me never could have no children of our own. But we took care of a niece, Freja. Young, beautiful thing belonged to my wife's sister. Thick blonde hair she kept up in a braid. She'd come stay with us when her mama drew on hard times. That's when I killed 'im."

"You got me all confused."

"Dumb son of a bitch. When Freja came to our farm, he showed up all young and stupid and such. He was fifteen years older than her, twice her age. I warned 'im to stay away. I warned 'im. That's why we left Wisconsin—had to. That's why we came here. I trust my secret is safe with you. We being friends and all, I figure you deserve to know."

"Lars, I really don't need to know. Get this off your chest if you want. I ain't the judging type. Say what you want, but not for me," Jesse said.

"I dug his grave all by myself after I put a bullet in his brain. I had no choice. She was an innocent. Came from a farm even farther out than ours. That boy wouldn't give her no peace from the moment she came to stay with us. I shot over his head more than once to chase 'im off. He'd go lurk in the woods for an hour or two and come slithering back. It was ceaseless. The missus and me had to keep a constant eye out for 'im."

"Why'd you shoot the man?"

"Didn't want to. He gave me no choice. Like I said, he was always prowling around, crazed, like he had nothing else to do. Freja liked the attention, but she didn't understand. She didn't know what this man wanted. Never crossed her mind. The missus tried to explain it to her, but she couldn't understand, couldn't believe it. He finally got to her. Pinned her down in the barn with her dress pulled up and stuffed in her mouth so she couldn't scream. She had not come in for supper, and I went looking for her with my Remington. Dumb son of a bitch came after me with a pitchfork."

Jesse thought about his niece, Nancy, who was not as old as Freja was then. Could he have done the same?

"We had to leave. The law was not on my side. Sent Freja back to her mama's and came south. What was that, ten years ago? Heard tell that she met the right man and has children of her own now. Her mama's passed on. I'd like to go up and pay her a visit, but I can't."

"How's it feel to kill a man?" Jesse asked.

"Rotten. Makes you feel rotten even when you got no choice."

"No choice."

"Yeah, no choice. He done it to hisself. Dumb son of a bitch. But you know it still makes you feel rotten. I hope God judges me kindly," Lars said.

"He will. You said you had no choice."

Lars shook his head.

A rumble of the Dodge flatbed grew, announcing it was coming up the hill and around the orchard. Jesse and Lars watched the truck cross the last stretch of the meadow before halting just yards from them. Silas slung himself out of the cab with one hand on the frame.

"Appreciate what you done for me," Silas said as he walked up to peer into the hole. He then looked out across the graveyard. "Our mother's over there next to our sister, Achsah." Silas gestured to Lars with his chin. "They both died of consumption the same year. We got a grandfather here somewheres." He scanned the rest of the small family plot.

Jesse said, "I don't 'member where he's at. They never did put up a stone. I was 'little afraid we'd come across bones where we're digging, but it's all clean dirt. Anna Lee will have it all to herself. How are you hanging in, brother?"

"Ain't had much time to give it much thought. Couldn't find no preacher, went all the way to town," Silas said. He removed his hat and wiped his brow on his shirt sleeve.

"Did you tell her daddy?" Jesse asked.

"Stopped by. Seemed like that son of a bitch didn't care a lick. No emotion, nothing. Told 'im we're having a burial this afternoon. That's all. Son of a bitch," Silas murmured.

Lars spoke, "I can say some words if ya can't get no preacher. Done it before. Lutheran's all I know. What're you, *Babtiss*?"

"Lutheran's fine," Silas said.

"I'm not meaning no disrespect or nothing. All I know is Lutheran," Lars said. "I think it's the same God and Jesus and all. Missus and I got the King James Bible. It's not in Danish or nothing."

"I said it's fine," Silas repeated.

"I could say a few words. She deserves a few words before we shovel the dirt." Lars looked at Jesse for confirmation.

Jesse said, "Lars, that would be fine. You say a few words from the Bible."

"That's okay if I say a few words before we shovel the dirt?" Lars looked at Silas.

"Lars, I said it's fine."

"The missus and I feel real bad about what happened to Anna Lee. I'm sorry I couldn't get the doctor sooner. Jesse said it was the membranes, and there wasn't nothing nobody could do. I don't know about membranes."

"Nothing."

Lars picked up a clod of dirt and crumbled it in his hands. "It just don't seem right. Right, Jesse?"

"Don't."

"I'll be on my way now." Lars stood and patted the dust off his pant legs. "You want me to bring a shovel back when I come?"

"Not necessary. Just bring the missus and your Bible," Jesse said.

Lars looked to Silas, standing at the foot of the grave and lost in his thoughts. "I'm going to say a few words, Silas, from the Bible if you can't find no preacher." Lars grabbed his canteen by the neck and nodded to Jesse before walking into the adjacent woods separating their farms.

Jesse watched his brother stare silently into the hole for several minutes while he turned over options and possibilities on how their lives could move forward from this point. "You know, Marybeth's gonna take care of the baby and girls. She ain't leaving them now," Jesse said. "We'll do what we needs to."

Silas neither spoke nor looked up. His hair was matted, and his eyes were red and puffy from a long night of drunken rage and remorse after he eventually returned from the Bella Vista hours after the doctor left.

Silas had arrived after midnight to find Anna Lee's cool and stiff body covered with a sheet in their bed. Her blood-soaked linens were immersed in a galvanized tub of warm water in the room's corner, awaiting the morning. Silas threw off the sheet. He grabbed an arm and leg, then pitched his wife's corpse onto the floor. "Who did this?" he screamed. "Who let this happen?"

Marybeth had rushed to comfort Silas and put her arms around his shoulders. He pushed her off and turned to face Jesse in the center of the room.

"Anyone else?" Silas said. "Anyone else? What the hell is going on here? You killed my wife, and now you want to touch me. You can all just go to hell." Silas bent down and tried unsuccessfully to lift Anna Lee's body back onto the bed.

Jesse and Lars had to pull Silas off the floor and wrestle him out of the house before they could shake any sense into him. Pinned up against the barn, he finally came to his wits and accepted that nobody was to blame. Jesse suggested he "walk it off," let the night air sober him up, and they would make plans in the morning. Silas pushed the two men off, staggered into the barn, and shut the doors. Jesse and Lars had left to attend to their wives in the house; a long night lay ahead.

Silas looked up from the grave. "Appreciate you and Lars helping out and digging this hole."

"You already said that."

"I don't know what I'm gonna do. Heard from Mr. Suggs that the bank's foreclosing. How'd he know? Seemed to know all about it."

"He say if he was coming up this afternoon?" Jesse asked.

"No," Silas said. "I ain't letting the bank take my land."

"Ain't got no choice, Silas."

"It ain't right. Where's a man to go with six childrens and no mama, huh? Where's a man to go?" Silas reached up and, with his shirtsleeve, wiped his eyes, smearing moist dust across his cheeks.

Jesse pushed himself up on his shovel handle and stood facing Silas from the other side of the grave. "We gotta take care of Anna Lee first. We'll do that first and then start a worrying about what happens next. You let Marybeth and me help git things settled today—taken care of—then we'll git on with the rest. Anna Lee deserves our attention today. Do that for your girls, too."

Silas looked over to the rest of the graveyard and the only two headstones standing, Achsah's and their mother's. Mature trees and dense summer brush bound the small clearing and threatened to overtake the gravesites. Until recently, Paps had maintained the family plot. Then Jesse and Silas took over, clipping small saplings and shoots at ground level.

"You think Grandy's wife is here somewheres?" Silas asked.

"Don't know. I don't think Paps even knows where she's at."

"I think she's here. Probably next to Grandy, wherever he's at." Silas stepped over to Achsah's marker, where he could read the inscription. "When we're gone, who's gonna keep the woods from taking over? Who does that? Nancy? Levi? Who's gonna keep the ground clear? When the bank takes your land, who does that?"

"I don't know. I think they leave the graveyards alone."

Silas looked up at his brother. "I'm staying. I'm raising the girls right here where their mother is. I'm tending to the graves. When I'm gone, they're doing the same. Lula Mae, that's what Anna Lee was gonna name the baby if she was a girl. Nancy told me last night. Never did pick out a boy name. I guess she just knew. If you take Levi, Lula Mae's gonna be the last of the Fitches to tend to these graves. It ain't right."

"Come on, let's go git ready. We're done here for now," Jesse said. "Mrs. Jacobsson told that she was bringing over dinner after the burial. Let's go git cleaned up." Jesse walked back to the truck, climbed into the driver's side, pumped the accelerator, and fired up the engine. Sheet metal panels rattled on loose rivets and bolts. "You coming?" he called out.

"No. You go on. I'll walk back." Silas continued to stare into the hole.

TWENTY-THREE

"KIND OF YOU," SILAS said to Mr. Suggs as Delilah handed him a tall glass of iced tea. "Shore is a swelter today." He leaned forward in a wing chair and took a cool sip of tea. "Can't imagine what you wanna see me for today."

Suggs squeezed a lemon slice into his glass and stirred the rind into the tea. He looked at his son-in-law, then watched Delilah leave the room.

"Surprised to be called for. I wasn't shore we was on speaking terms when you didn't show up for the burial last week."

"I never tire of watching her ass swing that skirt from side to side."

"I'm sorry?"

"Delilah. Love that high ass, always have. Just like her mother's." Suggs turned to Silas. "You looking at skirts yet?"

"Mr. Suggs, your daughter died ten days ago. This ain't nothing I feel comfortable talking about with you right now," Silas said. He put the empty iced tea glass down on a lace doily covering a small side table and fidgeted in his seat.

"Silas, we've not been the closest these past several years. Maybe I just didn't have much use for country farmers. In a sense, I just let you and Anna Lee be, make your own life. Didn't have much use for either her or Marybeth once they abandoned all that I had given 'em. Didn't see much use for country farmers."

"Anna Lee was a good wife, fine mother. Marybeth, too." Silas was struck by Suggs's callous observations.

"One of these days, I'll make a drive up your way and pay my respects to Anna Lee. You're probably right. Those girls made good wives. Took after their mama." Suggs leaned back, propping his elbows on the chair's sidearms, and brought his fingertips together as if to create a basket to hold his thoughts. He fixed his gaze on Silas, dropping his brow to convey authority. "We have business to discuss."

"Yes, sir."

"The guests at the Bella Vista seem satisfied with the Benoits' product. They're powerful men. Chicago, Dallas, St. Louis. When they come here with their lovely wives for the summer, they don't want their throats to get dry. High-quality likker is what they're expecting. Anyone who can spend the entire summer on holiday ain't settling for less. You hear what I'm saying?"

Silas nodded, then slid his hands under his thighs, not knowing what else to do with them.

"You may have thought you're working for the Benoit brothers. You're not. You're working for me. The Benoits work for me. The Benoits have 'shiners working for them who, in turn, work for me. Do you understand what I'm saying?"

"Yes, sir."

"I sent the Benoits to give your pappy a few bottles just to ease the way."

It was all making sense to Silas how easy it was to run whiskey for the Benoits. A week before the picnic, a green Model T stake bed pulled alongside him as he walked the road to Pea Ridge. Silas had never met the Benoit brothers before, and he was not confident he was speaking to them then. Ten dollars in silver convinced him they were serious about doing business. All he had to do was accept a load that night in his barn and drive it down to some cripple at the Bella Vista the next day. Do it, and he would get another fifteen. Paps was already onboard. Almost too easy to pass up.

"The sheriff works for me. Do you know what that means?" Suggs asked.

"Ricketts?"

"Sheriff Ricketts."

"No, sir. I'm not shore," Silas said.

"It means I got nothing to fear. I got nothing to fear. As long as the Benoits are working for me, they've got nothing to fear. The sheriff works for me."

"Why do you need me?"

"I don't need you. Anyone would do. I need your barn. I need another layer between me and the government. Agents don't know nothing about you. They're on to the Benoits; why they ain't making deliveries. You see, I need a country farmer, delivering produce to all them Yankees and Texan oilmen with dry whistles. I got plans for the whole county," Suggs said. He intertwined his fingers, sealing his thoughts.

Silas felt the small compliment made by his father-in-law, the first he could remember. He considered disclosing his Bella Vista encounter with the revenue agents to Suggs but then thought it would only jeopardize his position. He straightened his back and looked around the room to the quartz fireplace and heavy curtains pulled open. He looked at an oil painting of a middle-aged couple standing next to an ornate chair. Gilded wood framed the portrait, sooted by many lanterns. Silas pulled his hands from his seat and placed them confidently on the chair arms. "May I have some more tea with ice?"

"No," Suggs said. "You're going to drive over to the Park Springs. Ask for a fella named LeRoy at the hotel, and he's going to tell ya when they take deliveries and where to bring 'em. I'm expanding my operation."

"That's kinda close to town."

"You let me worry about how close to town I do business. You will be handsomely rewarded. Unless you think I should find another farm boy with a truck," Suggs said.

"No, I can do it," Silas said. "Jesse and I, as you probably heard, have a little difficulty with the bank right now. The sheriff came by last week with an eviction decree. Signed by the judge, according to Jesse. We're to be out in four days. I told Jesse I ain't quitting. Jesse don't know what to do on account of Anna Lee. I was planning on paying off Mr. Cavness before it came—"

"Shut up. You listen," Suggs said. "I made a deal with Cavness yesterday. You and Jesse, all of you, can stay. You can stay. Stay on your pappy's land. Nobody's evicting you now."

"I don't understand, Mr. Suggs."

"Told ya, I need a farm boy with a truck and a barn. You all can stay as long as you're the farm boy."

"Thank you. Thank you for speaking to Cavness. I don't know what to say. I'll be putting everything from this here job on that note. You watch; I'll have the debt paid off in no time. You wouldn't think unkindly of me if I someday take another wife? I could do that if I was turning income. I'll be selling apples come next year. Them trees are good. You watch."

"You do what you want. You want another wife to raise them young'uns of yours, fine by me. You want to grow apples on the side, have at it. Now, as far as paying off the bank, you don't need to do that. The bank doesn't own your property no more."

Silas caught his breath on an inhale.

"I own the farm. I told ya I need a barn," Suggs said calmly.

"Don't understand."

"I bought your land, fair price. You can live on it as long as you're working for me. I guess I'm in the apple business now." Suggs chortled unnaturally and pulled a narrow smile.

Silas felt the hair on the back of his neck bristle. "I'll pay you instead. I'll pay off the land."

"It's not for sale."

"But Mr. Suggs, you can't do that. Can't do that to me—us."

"Looks like I already have. You best get on down to Park Springs."

"Okay, Mr. Suggs. I'll work with you on this. I don't much like what you done, but I'll work with you. Damn."

"Park Springs?"

"Yeah, yeah." Silas scooted to the edge of his chair, leaned forward, cleared his throat, and studied Suggs for several seconds.

"Something else you want to say?"

"Yeah," Silas fiddled nervously with his cuffs.

"Silas, get it out, boy. You want to speak, be quick."

"Before I go, I've got one more thing about Marybeth and her son you need to hear."

"It best be important, worth my time."

"Oh, it is, Mr. Suggs. Oh, it is."

TWENTY-FOUR

THE REAR WHEELS OF the Dodge flatbed hopped and skipped on loose pebbles and dirt, trying to gain traction as Silas maneuvered the truck up the hill from Spanker Creek. He thought the truck always did better with a load in the back. At the top, he spun the steering left and halted in front of Paps's dogtrot cabin. He saw his father grinding a rocking chair on the porch like it was his job. Silas slid out of the cab and approached.

"You seen Jesse?" Silas asked.

"Went back home a bit ago. Said he was gonna bring somepin by for supper. Think he'll be along soon," Paps responded. "What's eating at ya?"

"We needs to talk. Got some figgerin to do."

"Talk right now if ya want." Paps continued a forced seesaw in his chair, the porch boards protesting with each arc. "If this involves that eviction notice someone left on my table, then you and me best put our heads together before we bring Jesse in. You know he's got no spine."

"I agree with ya, but he's also got no horse-sense. 'Sides, we need 'im if we're gonna pull this off."

"Pull what off?"

"Save the farm, Paps. I got some ideas." Silas sat in another chair to watch the road leading down from Jesse's place. "I'll wait." Silas fiddled with his hat, then asked, "Got anything to eat?"

"I told ya Jesse is bringing supper . . . for me."

A few moments later, Jesse appeared where the road wrapped around the perimeter woods. He carried a basket covered in a red cloth in the crook of his elbow.

"Look like a goddamn Little Red Riding Hood with that basket of yours," Silas called out to his brother. "Come see the Big Bad Wolf."

"Let it go, Silas," Jesse said when he got close. "These fixings ain't for you. Marybeth sent them for Paps."

"She's probably making something for me back at the house. You got yourself a fine cook," Silas said.

Jesse ignored the comment and walked into the kitchen room with the basket. "It'll need heating if you're gonna enjoy it," he called out to his father. Jesse left the food on the table and returned to the porch.

"You best sit. We got something to talk over," Silas said.

Jesse pulled up a box where he could see Silas and Paps. "Heard ya went to town this morn'. Marybeth keeps me informed. What business you got in town?"

"Listen, Jesse, I been doing some thinking about working for the Benoits. You're right. I could git myself wrapped up like a jackrabbit in a briar bush. Wouldn't be right for the girls. You're right. I got more responsibility now that Anna Lee done passed. It lays heavy on a man's mind."

"I hear ya. It's just bad luck. Ain't nobody's fault. We're all here to help. Do what we can." Jesse looked to Paps for confirmation. "Marybeth ain't giving up them girls."

"Appreciate that. Is she watching them? I kinda left this morning in a hurry."

Jesse nodded.

"Good." Silas slid forward in his chair. "Been thinking about what you said about chickens. Been down talking to Mr. Suggs—real sorry he missed the burial, and he's planning on calling on us to pay a visit to Anna Lee's grave. Well, I got to talking to 'im on chickens, and he's willing to hold off the bank three months until we're selling broilers."

"I don't believe a word of your shit. Suggs is a cold-hearted SOB. He don't do nothing out of charity, and we're charity," Jesse said.

Paps listened to the exchange without opening his mouth. It was best if Silas made his own pitch, he thought. He slowed his rocking to match his breathing.

"Oh, no, he'll want a small cut, I'm sure," Silas said. "I think he's doing this for Marybeth. Feeling sorry and everything. We got to talking, and if we took up three rows at the top, stumps and all, there's enough room for a five-hundred-chick grow house. We'll start with less just to git the learning out of the way."

Paps looked at Silas, trying to process what he had just heard.

"You're not moving likker no more?" Jesse asked.

"No, no, no. I told Suggs all about it, and he thought that was a bad idea. Not working with the Benoits no more. Done buying corn for those horse thieves. He's looking after his granddaughters now."

Paps stopped his rocking and started to speak, "Hell—"

"Half them girls he's never met," Jesse said. What his brother was saying was difficult for him to believe. But then, this was the solution he had proffered before Anna Lee died. Taking out a few rows of apples for a growing house might let them keep the farm and get back on their feet next year. He still had a tough time believing anything Silas was saying. A month ago, Suggs told him to go to hell when he asked for help. But then, Anna Lee's death may have changed things. Perhaps her father had a soft spot deep inside his hard shell. "Not running no more?" he asked Silas.

"Nope, don't need to."

Jesse looked at Paps. "What do you think? Shall we cut down a few trees to make room for chickens? We'd still have plenty left."

"Hell no. I planted those damn Arkansas Blacks, every single last one of them. You might as well be pissing on my grave if you cut 'em. Every single one I planted. I gots me a three hundred Savage that sez no banker's taking my land, and no son of mine is cutting my trees."

"No, you don't, Paps," Jesse said, referring to the rifle he kept at his home. "We got to do something, and Silas seems to have a plan."

"Paps," Silas said, "we got no income this year. Three months with chickens, we can sell 'em for a dollar apiece in Little Rock and Kansas City."

Paps did not quite grasp the gravity of their debt, but he recognized it was time to trust his sons to manage the farm. His father, J. R., had reached the same conclusion years ago when Paps planted the Arkansas Blacks. It was time to trust his sons. "Ah, hell. Okay, you boys, do what you want." Paps rose stiffly from the chair and moved toward the kitchen. "I'm eating my goddamn supper."

"You want me to help heat it up?" Jesse asked.

"No, but I needs my rifle back just case you fuck it all up." Paps stepped into the kitchen and shut the door.

Silas said, "That's easy as—"

"Ain't nothing easy about it. I don't entirely believe your story. But I'm going along with you for now. I'll help you clear the land and raise the chicken shed. The way I figger, we can't leave right now anyways. But I'll be watching you. This might buy us some time if you're right, and Suggs can hold off the bank, but I don't trust that son of a bitch. I'm not sure I trust you. Kind of feel like you got me over a barrel. You know I can't take Marybeth and Levi and go right now. You know that. Goddamn it."

"What I was doing with the Benoits was stupid. I wasn't thinking. Things are different now." Silas leaned back in his chair and crossed an ankle over his knee. "I was looking for an easy buck. You can trust me on this. I've got six girls to think about now."

"I'm not giving you a second chance on this. I'm ready to start clearing tomorrow if you are." Jesse stuck out his palm.

Silas reached over, gripped his hand, and held on. "You're my brother. You're all I got left, and Paps is one step out of his mind. We gotta stick together. You watch. Like you said, chickens where it's at. We'll start tomorrow." Silas gave one last squeeze before releasing Jesse.

"Tomorrow."

TWENTY-FIVE

"YOU KNOW, MARYBETH COULDN'T have no children for a while," Jesse said to Lars. "Wanted to tell you when you told me the story of your niece Freja and you not having a family and all."

"But she had one," Lars said as he walked up to Jesse and surveyed the toppled apple trees all around him. The freshly severed stumps oozed clear liquid from their concentric rings surrounding a formative sapling core that was almost as old as Jesse.

"One." Jesse wiped the sweat from his forehead with a handkerchief and reset his canvas hat to shade the sun. "The Lord blessed us with only one."

"One." Lars kicked a root. "You want me to help pull these stumps? I can chain 'em while you run the truck. How many you taking?"

"Top two rows, enough for a single-wide grow house," Jesse said. "Silas gots the truck right now." Jesse lowered himself with the axe handle, sat in the grass, and leaned against a fallen trunk. The tree's finely serrated green leaves on the outermost twigs were cast to the ground and wilted in defeat. Black flies spinning around Jesse's face seemed undeterred by his swatting.

"I see." Lars stood over Jesse and scanned the top edge of the orchard. "Ja, the missus never could have no children, barren. Really pulled her down for the first years we was together. She even told me to go find someone else and released me from my obligations. She wasn't built right, the doctor said. She had a closed womb. He blamed it on too much work."

Jesse swung his arm over the trunk so he could turn and look at Lars. "Have a seat, will you? Rest your dogs for a spell."

Lars bent down, put his hand on the fallen trunk, then eased his hefty frame onto the lush grass next to Jesse and leaned back.

"Missus grew up on a farm, only child, and had to do all the things brothers, if she'd any, done. Worked hard. She's strong as any man. Doctor said all that work done scarred the womb, holds it up too high."

"You believe that?" Jesse asked.

"No other explanation. We done tried. You know what I mean?"

"Yeah. Took us three years to have Levi. I know how it's when the wife can't have you a child. Really tore up Marybeth. She never saw no doctor or nothing. Didn't help that her sister was popping 'em out like a rabbit."

Lars fiddled with a stalk of wheatgrass at his side. "She give you permission to get another wife?"

"No," Jesse said. "I wouldn't want another, barren or not."

"Me, neither."

Jesse lifted the axe from his side and rested the head on his knee. "Funny how the doctor told her she was barren cuz she done too much work. That don't make a lick of sense to me. You'd think it worked the other way."

"We tried. She laid up for near a year. Hung her heels in the air. Didn't work."

"She spent a year in bed?" Jesse asked.

"Pretty darn much. She didn't do no labor. Got soft. Wasn't good for her constitution. Lying around just let her think about her condition more. Laid up is not natural, not good for nobody."

Jesse hiked his hip and pulled a metal file out of his back pocket. "Marybeth didn't lay up, but when she was raised, she didn't do no labor, 'less you think practicing your letters and recitation is work. Her father always had help in the house, never made the girls lift a finger. So, you'd think she'd be as fertile as her sister. Raised the same."

"She done labors now," Lars said.

"Has to. Of course. She knew that when we married. She don't shy away from a day's work." Jesse drew the file against the axe edge, which protested with a strident sigh and exposed a band of fresh steel glistening in the sunlight.

"I knew a guy up in Waupaca was married to the same dame for twenty years before they had their first. They done tried everything like me and the missus to have children. They worried and fretted about it. Finally, the wife turned forty, and they just gave up worrying themselves. Wouldn't you know she got pregnant the same month they gave up? Had a little girl, sweet as pie. They lived down the road a bit from our farm. The missus used to help her sometimes. They were a lot older than us. Gave the missus hope. Me, too. I wanted a boy. You're lucky to have a boy."

"Reckon so."

"Levi's a good kid. You're lucky to have him," Lars said. "They was a lot older than us, past childbearing. Odd to me." Lars broke off the wheatgrass and wrapped the stalk around his two fingers. "Ya know Abraham and Sarah? From the Bible? They was old, a hundred, when they had their first, Issac. God does miracles, ya know?"

"He does. All children are miracles."

"That couple in Wisconsin, they had another when the little girl was two. This one was a boy, but not normal. He was born *mongol*. Just not right. Happy little boy but dumb."

"Mongol?"

"Ja. Didn't live long, five or six years. They loved that little boy, the missus, too. God couldn't have created a happier child. We was all torn up when he died. That was right before Freja came to visit for the last time, and then we left."

Jesse flipped the axe blade and drew the file across the other side. "I'm sorry for you and Mrs. Jacobsson that you never had no children."

"God's will, I reckon." Lars wove the wheatgrass stalk into a circle. "We're gonna name our first Isak, with a *k*, if we was ever blessed with a son. Never did pick out a little girl's name. You had a girl, what would you name her?"

"Mary, I think. That was Marybeth's mother. Sweet lady, I was told, though, I never had the pleasure to know the woman. Why a *k*?"

"*Dansk*, Danish, ya know. They spell it with a *k*."

"I guess you can do whatever you want."

Lars reached out, pulled another grass stalk out, and wrapped it around his fingers again. He swatted at a fly circling his head. "Where's Silas? I'd expect him to be helping ya out in this clearing."

"Was here this morning. I don't know what's got into 'im. He keeps coming up with excuses. Said he had to get on back to town for something. That was five hours ago."

"He's going to be a grieving, he is. You best give him some slack."

"I am."

"Ya think he's being stupid?"

"I worry that he is. Not thinking right. You know the sheriff done served us with an eviction decree?"

"I heard. We all heard."

"We're trying to get some quick cash together to hold off the bank long enough for us to git chickens going. We don't have much time," Jesse said. "I'm over a barrel, hog-tied. I can't leave on account of Anna Lee's girls and the baby, and I can't stay cuz we might lose everything. If we can get something going long enough to sell chickens, I think the bank will let us stay. They don't want this land, can't sell it themselves for what they lent us."

"Want I bring my truck down to help ya pull stumps this afternoon?" Lars asked. "I ain't got much going on for the next few days. I got me a chain."

"Mighty kind of you, but I think Silas will be back soon. I could accept and appreciate your help. Don't think Silas would take to it. He wants to do it all hisself. Don't wanna feel like he owes nobody nothing."

"He owes the bank."

"That's different. He'd steal from the bank if he thought he could get away with it. He don't wanna look weak to his family, owe his neighbors."

"He's weak."

"I know." Jesse stood, leaned on the axe handle, and pulled Lars up with his other hand. "You're welcome to swing this blade if you really got nothing else to do." Jesse bent down to pick up a crosscut saw, then handed the axe to Lars.

TWENTY-SIX

"Nancy, please hold the baby," Marybeth said, handing Lula Mae to her in Silas's kitchen. "Where's Polly?"

"With Mayel in the mudroom," Nancy responded, pointing to the back of the house.

Marybeth smoothed out her apron and pulled her long brown hair back again with a black ribbon. "Check those loaves in about five minutes and pull 'em out if they look done. Did you all get cleaned up yesterday?"

"Yes, ma'am. I helped Vesta and Mayel. Don't know about Sussie," Nancy said. She held the infant in a light cotton blanket in her left arm and a small glass bottle of sweetened milk with a rubber teat in her other. She rotated her shoulders on her hips from side to side, gently rocking; the baby worked the nipple. Nancy felt proud to accept the added responsibilities of womanhood pressed upon her. No longer was she a child.

Sussie appeared in the kitchen doorway in a soiled shift with tears running down her face. Straw tangled in her hair.

"Come here, child," Marybeth said, and she extended her arms.

Sussie darted across the room and buried her face in her aunt's apron, wrapping her freckled arms around her waist. "I want Mama."

"Course you do. We all do." Marybeth held Sussie tight against her abdomen. "For heaven's sake, where have you been?" she said, picking hay out of her hair.

"Barn with Vesta. She says Mama's coming back. I know she's not. Vesta says she is." Sussie looked up at Marybeth. "I told the truth, and she pushed me over."

"Where's Vesta," Marybeth asked.

"Hay."

"Did you tussle?"

"I had to push her back. She shoved me for telling the truth. I told the truth. I didn't hit her. She's not going to say I hit her. I jumped on her, but I didn't hit her."

"Come with me," Marybeth said. "Nancy, I'll be right back. Listen for Polly." Marybeth led Sussie by the hand out of the house and across the dooryard to the big barn. They found Vesta curled up on loose straw in the corner with her eyes tightly closed. Marybeth reached down and touched her bare shoulder. Her skin was moist and warm. Her dress, heavy with sweat, clung to her slight frame. "Vesta, my dear."

Marybeth sat down next to Vesta and pulled Sussie in on her other side. She put her arms around both girls and drew them close. Vesta choked out near-silent sniffles, her chest shuddering. Nothing needed to be said for several minutes. Marybeth pulled a handkerchief out of her sleeve and dabbed Vesta's eyes when she finally opened them. Sussie took the hankie and wiped her own cheeks. Summer katydids drummed in the air. A slight breeze found its way into the barn, carrying the sweet smell of grass. Silas's cow shifted in her stall, then made smacking sounds with her mouth. Flies buzzed from the cow to the girls and back again.

"Come with me," Marybeth said to the girls. "Let's run a brush through that hair of yours and get you cleaned up. I need some help with hanging the laundry. I think you two are big enough. Get you a stool."

Marybeth led her nieces from the barn to a small shed on the side of the house. A two-handled basket of wet clothes sat on a wooden pallet under a tin roof. Sussie and Vesta wrestled the load over to the south side of the house. Marybeth brought a short wooden box for the girls to stand on, and she ran a boar-bristle brush through their hair.

"Come to the kitchen when you're done. Don't let the laundry fall to the dirt, or you'll be washing 'em again." She kissed each girl on the forehead before leaving them to their task at the clothesline.

Marybeth stepped into the mudroom, lifting her black skirt over the threshold. Six-year-old Mayel held Polly's shoulders as she balanced her on a homemade swing horse. Suspended from a crude frame with leather straps, the horse rocked back and forth with Mayel's help. Both girls were quiet as if they were just biding their time. Marybeth had never seen either of them not squealing with laughter while riding the cockhorse.

"Aunt Marybeth, Polly's hungry, me too," Mayel said, looking up at her aunt.

"Here." Marybeth reached down, lifted Polly off the wooden horse, and planted her on her hip. "Let's see what we can find." She held Mayel's hand and led her into the kitchen. "Nancy, did you check the bread?"

"Yes, ma'am. A couple more minutes," Nancy responded, still rocking Lula Mae.

Marybeth let go of Mayel and opened the pantry door. "Let's see." She selected a can of store-bought Crowley Ridge peaches in a heavy syrup, one of the last items on the shelf. She set Polly to stand on a chair at the table and took the tin over to a wall-mounted Dazey opener. Viscus syrup spilled over the can's side as she cut the top. She dumped the peaches into a bowl on the table, wiping her hands on a dishcloth. Marybeth crossed over to the wood-burning stove and opened the side oven door. She retrieved two iron pans of risen bread, brown on the top, and knocked them onto a cooling rack. The smell of yeast bread filled the room, watering the mouths of the children.

Marybeth let the loaves cool before making five thick, spongy slices. She placed each on an enameled plate and spooned sliced peaches and syrup on top. "Now you wait for Sussie and Vesta," she said, gently slapping Mayel's hand from a plate.

"Sussie, hurry up," Mayel screamed through the back door. "We got peaches."

Marybeth took the baby from Nancy. The five girls dove into the warm bread and sweetened fruit, letting the juices run down their chins. "Now, don't you go telling your papa what we just et when he gets home," Marybeth said as she continued to coax the baby to drink from the bottle. "You best take your plates outside. You'll have your mama's kitchen crawling with ants and—" Marybeth then seized on her words.

Nancy and Vesta paused their eating and stared at their aunt. The mention of their mother immediately shattered their enjoyment of the moment, a short-lived respite from sorrow.

"Run along, girls. I'll get on with supper." Marybeth herded the four younger ones outside. "Nancy, you stay here." She handed the baby back.

Fireflies sparked at the edge of the woods along the dirt track leading to Silas's house. Jesse thought, *Silas's house, not Anna Lee and Silas's house,* as he climbed the hill in the waning daylight. Several paces behind, Levi kicked at the clumps of grass growing between the ruts.

"Levi, keep up. Ma's bound to got supper on the stove," Jesse said without looking back. He stopped momentarily to let his son catch up.

"I ain't hungry."

"Course you are. You haven't et since morning. Do you good to see your cousins."

"They're different now, orphans."

"They ain't orphans. Orphans got no mama or papa. Uncle Silas's still their papa. He's working hard to care for 'em," Jesse said. "Ma's helping. She'll come home soon. Lula Mae's little. She needs a mama."

"Is she gonna be my sister?" Levi asked.

"Them your cousins. Always be your cousins." Jesse put his arm around Levi's shoulder and fell into a short step with him. "They need your mama now."

"Nancy'll care for 'em."

"She'll help but can't do it alone. She's not old enough to be a mama."

"I thought we're leaving for Washington," Levi said.

Jesse stopped and turned to face his son. He knelt on one knee and held Levi's shoulders with both hands. "We was, Levi; we is. We was leaving this week, but things have changed. Uncle Silas needs us here right now."

"Grandpaps said the bank was taking our land. Told me yesterday."

"Uncle Silas has things worked out for us to stay. We're staying. Everything's gonna be all right. Uncle Silas has things worked out with the bank. We're gonna be okay. Not you worry." Jesse let go of Levi and stood still. "Race you to the house." He then swatted Levi on his bottom and took off up the hill. Levi quickly overcame him and did not stop until he reached the front door.

"For heaven's sake, son. What's got into you?" Marybeth asked when Levi bolted into the kitchen, breathless. "Where's your pa?"

"Coming."

Lula Mae, lying in a bassinet, burst into a wail. Marybeth stooped to pick her up. "Supper will be ready soon. Go wash up. Tell your girl cousins to do the same." She turned to Nancy at the stove. "Dish those beans out so they'll cool."

"What about Papa?" she asked.

"I don't know when to expect your papa. Your uncle, Jesse, will be along shortly."

Nancy dished the red beans and laid a slice of bread on top. "Get your own water," Nancy said to Vesta as she entered the kitchen. "Mayel, come here and set these out on the table," she called into the hallway.

Sussie, Vesta, and Mayel sat on a bench at the wooden table in the kitchen center. Levi sat opposite. Nancy sat on a chair at the end with Polly on her lap, spooning mashed beans into her mouth. A kerosene lantern flickered from a hook on the wall, casting an undulating glow across the room.

Marybeth stepped outside on the front porch with the baby in her arms. She watched night stars appear in groups in the east, marching westward, revealing their fire as if the setting sun was pulling a dark curtain across the sky.

Jesse eventually arrived at the house, stepped into the kitchen, and returned to the porch with his supper in hand. He joined Marybeth and Lula Mae on a short bench and leaned against the wall. While shoveling beans into his mouth, he asked his wife, "Have you et?"

"Later. I'll get something later." She bobbled the baby on her chest.

Jesse scraped his empty bowl with a slice of bread. He looked past the yard to the big barn, silhouetted against the darkening sky. "I talked to Silas again today," Jesse said. "He helped clear a few trees this morning, then left. Said he had business in town. This ain't gonna work. Last night, he was all about chickens. We was gonna git started today."

"You think he's serious?"

"No. I don't know what to think. Sez he ain't dealing with the Benoits no more. I don't believe 'im. He knows he's in a bind. We all are. I think he's stalling. Hell, I don't know what to do."

"Give him some time. He's grieving bad, needs some space. I'll do what I can for the girls. I feel bad about you and Levi."

"We're managing just fine. You stay here where you're needed," Jesse said. He placed the empty bowl and spoon at his feet.

"I saw bottles in the barn today, hidden in the back," she said.

"I know."

Marybeth stood to walk the length of the porch with the baby. Mayel appeared in the doorway. "You girls finish up the pot, split it with Levi," Marybeth said to her. Mayel turned back inside. Marybeth stopped in front of Jesse. "I don't like this."

"Reckon we've not much choice in this matter," Jesse said. "We can't just take his girls and leave."

"Why not?"

"Why not? 'Cause, that's kidnapping, that's why."

"He's abandoned those kids. Hasn't been around all week. When he does come back, he's been drinking. That ain't no way to treat your children. It's like he don't care. He scares me." Marybeth sat back down on the bench with Jesse. He pulled her in close to him.

"You wanna come back home with Levi and me tonight? Bring Polly and the baby?" Jesse asked. "I think Nancy can handle the other three."

"Maybe tomorrow."

The snapping of the screen door against its frame woke Marybeth. She figured it was Silas coming home from wherever he had been all night. Marybeth pulled the thin sheet over her and Vesta in their shared bed. Lula Mae slept in a nest of blankets on the floor while Nancy, Sussie, Mayel, and Polly bedded in the attic room.

Marybeth listened to Silas rattle about the house as if he did not know where to go. She heard him open the other bedroom door and enter the room he had shared with Anna Lee. Boots, free from feet, clamored to the floorboards. A belt buckle followed shortly after with a clink. Marybeth studied the sounds, imagining Silas struggling to undress. Vesta stirred, and Marybeth stroked her shoulder until her breath deepened and slowed.

Footsteps padded down the hall, and the front door whined on its hinges. Again, the slap of the fly screen. The slap and whine repeated a minute later, and Silas was back inside. Marybeth concluded Silas did not go far and must have urinated off the porch. Her ear followed his movement about the house by tell-tell sounds: the lid tap of the tin breadbox, the thump of a bottle on the heavy kitchen table, the bang of pantry doors, the creak of floorboards outside her bedroom door.

The inside lever handle dropped, unlatching the door. A sliver of light from the kitchen violated the darkness of her room. Silas's silhouette came into full view as he opened the door farther. Marybeth pulled the sheet over her face and held her breath.

"Marybeth, I know you're not sleeping," Silas slurred. "I needs somepin to eat. Git up, woman, and fix your man somepin to eat."

Marybeth pulled the sheet down to her nose and saw Silas, wearing only a short, sleeveless union suit, unbuttoned to the waist, leaning against the door frame with a bottle in one hand.

He raised his voice, "I said, git up and fix me somepin to eat."

Marybeth slid out of bed, leaving Vesta undisturbed and Lula Mae on the floor. She pulled a robe over her nightgown and walked toward Silas, taking his arm and guiding him out of the room. "Shh. Children are asleep. You'll wake 'em," she said. "I'll make you some breakfast. But I'm not your woman."

Marybeth stepped into the kitchen and donned an apron. She busied herself by stoking the stove and frying down fatback.

Silas pulled up a chair and stared at Marybeth from behind. He took another swig from the bottle, then carefully balanced it on the table with both hands. The crackling of fat in the hot cast-iron skillet and the smell of fried pork brought moisture to his mouth.

Marybeth folded three eggs into the crisp morsels of side meat and cooked them until firm. She sensed she was being watched and felt uneasy.

"Here's your breakfast," Marybeth said as she dropped the plate and a wood-handled fork on the table in front of Silas and turned to leave.

He reached up, grabbed her arm with one of his, and pulled her onto his lap. "Sit with me. I needs some company."

Marybeth struggled to stand, but he overpowered her. Screaming would only awaken the children and produce an uncomfortable situation for their father and her. "Silas," she said calmly, "please let me go. You're drunk. You don't know what you're doing."

"I know what I's doing. I'm gitting what I want. Been waiting a long time for this."

"Silas, you best let me go, now," she raised her voice for emphasis. "You got six girls to think about. Hard losing Anna Lee, but you've got to leave me alone."

"Been thinking about when we had Levi. You liked it, didn't you? Something you wanted, huh?" He tightened his grip around her waist with his left hand and grabbed her apron front with his right.

"You don't want to do this," Marybeth said, clutching his wrist as his hands rummaged over her chest.

"Oh, yeah, I do."

"Silas, you're drunk. You leave me alone. Stop right now, and I'll pretend this never happened."

"Jesse's not here, is he? He left you here. You know why? 'Cause, he ain't man enough to father his own children. That's why." Silas spun her around by her shoulders to face him. He reached forward to kiss her neck. "You needs a man like me."

Marybeth recoiled, pushing his face with her palms. "Silas, leave me be," she said. "You've been drinking. You're not in your right head." She turned away, but he held her firmly on his lap. Her robe fell open, exposing a fine-print cotton nightgown. Silas reached down and slid his hand up her leg, cradling the inside of her thigh.

"I don't remember you being so feisty," he said, then he tried to kiss her neck again. "Quite a little filly, I got here. Might need a firm hand."

Marybeth reached for the bottle on the table and swung it by its neck across her chest into the side of Silas's head. Blood gushed from his brow and streamed down his face.

"Goddamn it, woman," he yelled. He wrestled the bottle from her hand, and it fell to the floor. Marybeth struggled to free herself. The plate of eggs flew off the table when she tried to brace, spinning the fork in place. Silas watched liquor dribble from the bottle's neck. She grabbed the fork by its wooden handle with a freed hand, lifted it high over her shoulder, and then plunged it deep into the side of Silas's thigh, making bone.

Silas shrieked and released her. He stared, unbelievingly, at the fork planted in his leg. Marybeth sprang up, ran to the kitchen doorway, and stopped. Silas reached down with one hand and pulled the utensil out as blood pooled at the puncture and trickled down his leg. He looked at Marybeth, confused, and then bent down to salvage what was left of his whiskey. Holding the bottle upright with one hand, he pushed himself up from the chair with his elbow.

"You bitch," he said to Marybeth, then stumbled through the mudroom and out the back door.

Marybeth heard him land with a thud in the dirt at the bottom of the steps, and she sprinted across the kitchen and barred the door. She then went to the front door and did the same. When she turned, she noticed Nancy standing in the hallway with a wailing baby in her arms.

"She woke up," Nancy said.

Marybeth calmly stepped over to Nancy and took the baby from her. "Your papa was drunk. He meant nothing he said." She embraced Nancy's shoulders. "Tomorrow, everything's gonna be all right."

Nancy buried her cheek in Marybeth's bosom. "I miss her."

"We all do. We all do. Tomorrow's gonna be better. Each day, better," Marybeth said. "Go warm up some top milk, and we'll try to get this l'il tyke back to sleep."

TWENTY-SEVEN

FIST-POUNDING ON THE FRONT door startled Marybeth. She had dozed off in a rocking chair in the kitchen corner with Lula Mae in her arms. Now, she was awake, focusing on what she had just heard. Slices of dawn cast through the window, giving the room a bluish tint.

The pounding resumed, panicked and loud.

"Marybeth," Jesse called out from the other side of the door. "Marybeth, open the damn door."

She cradled the baby in her left elbow and unbarred the front door.

Jesse entered, bewildered. "What is going on?" He stepped into the hallway and then looked at the open bedroom door. "Where's Silas?" Jesse had seen the truck parked in front of the big barn and expected to find him inside. Discovering the front door locked and barred disturbed him. "Where's Silas?"

"I don't know. He came home drunk, middle of the night. He left," she said.

"He left? Didn't go to bed but left?" Jesse sensed Marybeth was stalling with her story. "Tell me what happened?"

"I stuck him with a fork."

"You stuck 'im?"

"I did. He was making advances. He left." This was not the time, Marybeth reasoned, to unveil the past. It was not the time to make things more complicated than they already were. "Silas was drunk. He mistook me for Anna Lee. All's innocent."

Jesse hit the wall with the heel of his fist.

"Quiet. The children," Marybeth whispered. "He didn't know what he was doing. Didn't harm me. I'm fine."

"That son of a bitch." Jesse paced across the narrow hallway, almost spinning in circles. "Goddamn son of a bitch. Where's he at?"

"It's okay, Jesse. No harm done. He was drunk. He was going to 'waken the girls. The fork convinced him to leave. You might find him somewhere outside. I doubt he went far, as drunk as he was."

Jesse stepped out of the house and walked to the side. He found his brother curled up in the dirt at the bottom of the steps with a ribbon of dried blood across his forehead. Piss-soaked mud stained the bottom half of his short one-piece underclothes, unbuttoned at the top. Dark blood caked his thigh and lower leg. Rage burned within Jesse as he watched his brother stir, heave several times, and drift back to an unconscious stupor. Jesse turned away.

"Come," Jesse said to Marybeth when he reentered the house, "we're gitting you out of here. The girls, too. We'll load the truck and be gone."

Marybeth had the stove stoked and the coffee ready to boil. "Where are you taking us? Did you forget we got five little girls and a two-week-old infant?" she said.

"Our place. We'll all go to our place. That son of a bitch comes close, I'm gonna blow his brains out. Then we're leaving for Washington."

"Jesse, he was drunk. He meant no harm. We can't travel with this baby. We'll have no milk. This is all too much for the girls. They've got to have some steadiness in their lives right now. I'm sure if we talk to Silas, he'll understand. He can stay with Paps, and I could come home with Lula Mae and Polly. Nancy can handle the others at night, like you said. Or we could all stay here, and Silas can have our place. Jesse, we can't just drive off right now. We can't do it."

Jesse fingered his hat, then sat at the kitchen table. "Give me the baby." He reached out and took the infant in his arms. She was so small, fragile, he thought, delicate. Barely a couple of ears of corn wrapped in a blanket. Marybeth was right. "I'll speak to Silas when he dries out. These are his kids. He should have a say in the matter."

Silas lay on an old mule blanket on the barn floor where Jesse had dragged him. Black flies spun about his face, landing momentarily at the corners of his eyes and mouth to scavenge for salt, moisture, and dead skin.

Jesse stood at his brother's feet and watched the flies buzz, land, dart about on his face in short bursts, then take off again. They also worked the wound on his leg, looking for a place to lay their eggs. He watched for several minutes. It was time to get to the truth. It was time to agree on how to proceed. He would pay another visit to Suggs himself if he had to. He would deal with Paps.

Silas opened his eyes, squinting at the sunlight coming through the door. "Shit," he said. "Goddamn shit." He noticed Jesse standing at the edge of the blanket. "Shit." Silas propped himself up on one elbow and looked at his thigh. "What the hell?" he said, then looked back at Jesse. "What you looking at?"

"I'm gonna give you a chance to clean up, and then we're gonna take a stroll, you and me. Marybeth done brought some clothes out for you." Jesse motioned to the garments draped over a stall. "She don't want the girls seeing you in your condition. You can clean up here. There's a bucket of water by the door. I'll be outside." Jesse stepped out the barn door and closed it behind him. He sat on a bench and leaned against the wall.

He could look across the orchard from the barnyard, over the canopy of Arkansas Blacks, to the woods where his house sat on the other side of a low rise. He had left Levi home to attend to chores: milking the cow, gathering eggs from the coop, and slopping food scraps for the pig. In an hour, Levi would wonder where his father was. He would mosey up to the top edge of the orchard where they had been cutting trees the day before. Jesse was unsure what Levi would do when he failed to find his father and uncle. Would he visit Paps or look for his mother at Silas's house? Jesse needed to get Silas away soon to settle their differences in private.

Silas stepped out of the barn, dressed in fresh clothes. "I needs a drink," he said to Jesse. "Throat's dry as burlap. I needs to git some water first." Silas limped over to the well and drew a bucket. Water spilled over his shirt as he drank.

"Let's go. You'll sober up when you git moving." Jesse guided Silas by the arm and headed up the perimeter trail toward the graveyard, a private place.

The dirt track followed the orchard's edge, with mature apple trees on the left and deep woods of oak and chestnut on the right. Bright green grass grew ankle high below the black apple branches, reaching outward from the trunk for sunlight. Jesse and Silas sighted a deer and its fawn on the road ahead. With a hazelnut coat, black-marble eyes, and erect, black-tipped ears, she froze protectively over her spotted baby. The brothers stopped. The doe stared unblinkingly at them.

"Wish I had me a gun," Silas said, looking at the deer. "We'd be eating good tonight."

"What are you talking about? You can't just shoot the mama and leave the baby."

"I'd shoot 'em both. You gots to git the mama first; that little'un won't go far. They're easy to drop once you git the mama."

"Crazy shit," Jesse said. Then he raised his arms and shouted. The deer bounded into the brush, gone.

"I'm jesting with you. Where's your humor?" Silas asked. "So serious. 'Silas got stuck with a fork by my wife,' serious. 'I'm gonna talk some sense into 'im,' serious. You think I touched Marybeth? You're wrong. I didn't lay a hand on her. I was a little drunk, I admit, making noisy trouble. She asked me to leave. I guess I didn't take too well to being kicked out of my own damn house. It got me a fork in the leg." Silas reached down to feel his thigh. "Let's go."

The brothers arrived at the cemetery just as sunlight cut above Elkhorn Mountain and filtered through the surrounding trees. They stopped at Anna Lee's grave. The mounded dirt had settled. Fresh weeds and grass sprouted where the wind had blown seeds, and the rains had soaked the earth. Jesse sat on a fallen tree trunk at the graveyard's edge and looked at her grave.

"Ain't nothing nobody could do. That's what the doctor told," Jesse said. He looked up at Silas.

Silas continued to stand near the fresh dirt, looking down. "We need to git a stone set up."

"A stone would be good."

"I guess I should put up a cross 'til we git a stone." Silas walked over to the log and sat near Jesse. "Would you make sure she gets a stone before you leave?"

"I don't know what you mean. You can put up a stone."

"If I can't, would you before you leave?" Silas asked.

"I'll make sure Anna Lee gets a stone." Jesse pulled a stray wheat-grass stalk apart, stuck the end in his mouth, and chewed on its sweetness. "Silas, I know this has been hard on you. Been hard on all of us. Marybeth wants to help out with the girls, me too. But you got to do your part. You got to be honest with us. What happened to you yesterday when we was gonna clear trees together?"

"Had business in town."

"Your business is here on the farm. Your business is to take care of your young'uns and not bob up drunk in the middle of the night. Your business is to tell the truth to the only person who gives a shit about you."

Silas's head was not completely clear from the night before. But he was sober enough to realize he needed to measure his words carefully. "I took my last load to the Bell' Vista. I had to. The Benoits already paid me for it. I told them I'm done, couldn't do it no more. Don't need to do it no more. We got Suggs helping. I'm done."

"I wish I could believe you. I wish you was honest. Don't know why I keep giving you chances. Been doing it all my life, letting you slide by. Well, I'm through. I don't know what to believe about Suggs and the farm. I expect the sheriff to come by any day and push us off with the barrel end of a gun. You can't keep doing this to me," Jesse said. He tossed the grass stalk and pulled another one.

"Jesse, we're doing chickens. I'm all in with you. This afternoon, I'll fell the rest of the trees we talked about. Tomorrow, we can pull stumps with the truck. No time at all, we'll have chicks running around looking like little silver dollars. This afternoon, we'll git started again, promise. I'll sharpen my axe."

"You're gonna stay with Paps from now on. I ain't having you walking in on my wife in the middle of the night. I'd move your whole brood to my place if I had space. Might do it anyways."

"Trust me, Jesse. Ain't doing that no more."

"You're staying with Paps. Am I clear?" Jesse said.

"Clear. Marybeth and the girls can stay. You can stay too, if you want. Have my bed. I haven't slept in it since Anna Lee died. I'll move in with Paps. He could use a little company, to boot."

"I'll be watching you," Jesse said. "Giving you another chance. Next time, I'm packing the Ford and leaving with Marybeth and Levi. Leaving in the middle of the night. Leaving for Washington. I'll be done with you. You can take them girls down to Suggs's house, let their grandfather raise 'em in town. I ain't putting up with your deceit no more." Jesse knew he could not follow through with his threats; Silas knew it, too.

"We need to git a stone," Silas said. Then he rose and started down the hill, back toward the barn. Several paces off, he turned to Jesse. "I'll git an axe."

TWENTY-EIGHT

LULA MAE WORKED THE rubber nipple on an upturned bottle in Marybeth's hand. The other children were asleep. Marybeth sat in the kitchen, expecting Jesse to come over for a late supper after another day of pulling stumps with the truck. She turned down the lantern wick to dim the room as the baby's eyes closed and her suckling sounds paused. Marybeth thought about their uncertain future. Jesse had reassured her they were safe on the farm for now. It had been a month since the sheriff gave Paps a two-week notice, and nothing had happened. Perhaps Silas had everything worked out with her father. It was still hard for her to believe Father would be so generous.

She and her sister had a warm bond with their mother when they grew up in the same house their father still occupied on Southeast A Street. Their mother was refined and well-schooled, bringing financial security to their family. She was attentive, loving, and supportive of the girls, always encouraging their best. Their relationship with their father was completely different. Marybeth remembered him when she was a little girl as distant, cold. *Brass tacks and all business*, their mother used to say.

Marybeth was eleven when their mother died of typhoid fever. "It was the water," she remembered her sister telling her. Their mother had traveled to Little Rock with a brother to visit an ailing uncle. "Unclean water." One of the saddest days of her life—a turning point in the Suggs household—was her mother's burial in the Bentonville Cemetery, a day when dark rain clouds filled the sky. Afterward, their father's callous disregard for Anna Lee and Marybeth only intensified, casting the girls into a loveless corner of his life when they needed love the most.

Four years later, at eighteen, Anna Lee escaped their father's uncaring rigidness and readily accepted a teaching position near Pea Ridge and the hand of matrimony. Two years later, Marybeth married Jesse without their father's consent. The quiet farm was a needed respite from their hollowed family life after their mother's death.

Anna Lee and Silas welcomed three girls into their family within the first three years of marriage—three beautiful babies whom Anna Lee adored. She was a wonderful mother and provided a warm, lively home filled with joyful sounds of children. Marybeth and Jesse had tried to begin a family without immediate success.

Lula Mae stirred in Marybeth's arms. Her little closed eyelids fluttered, and she smiled as if in a dream. Marybeth wondered what dreams an infant would have and what world occupied their mind when their eyes were closed. She was delighted to believe Lula Mae's world was happy for the moment, unconnected to the tragedy of her mother's death, the drunken rage of her father, and the tension on the farm. She would learn these things when she was older but could sleep in sweetness for now.

The rumble of a truck caught Marybeth's attention. Someone was coming up the drive to Silas's house. She snuffed the lantern, rendering the kitchen pitch-black. The engine stopped outside near the big barn. She stood and walked to the window. From her darkened viewpoint, she saw two men get out of a pickup truck and pull open the barn door. Someone lit a lantern inside the barn, and the two men unloaded boxes from the truck bed and carried them toward the light. Was there a third man inside the barn? She could not tell. Only shadows moved about in the lantern's glow. Within minutes, someone quenched the light, and the two men returned to the truck and left.

"They delivered booze tonight," Marybeth said to Jesse when he arrived at the house later. "A truck and two men. I'm sure."

"When?"

"Hour ago."

"Have you seen Silas?"

"Perhaps he was with them. I couldn't be sure. I had the house dark like we were all asleep," Marybeth said. "Silas didn't come in, if that is what you mean. I haven't talked to him all day."

"Stay here." Jesse grabbed a lantern, darted across the barn-yard, and pushed a bar off the door cleats. Long shadows from the Dodge truck, roof posts, and stalls danced about the dark space as if choreographed by the singular light. In the corner was a freshly tossed mound of hay, partially covering a dozen boxes. Jesse had no doubt they held whiskey.

"I thought he told you he was no longer working for the Benoits," Marybeth said when he returned to the kitchen and extinguished the lantern.

"He said that. I didn't completely believe 'im then," Jesse said. "I should just get the rifle and shoot the hell out of that stash. Blow the shit away."

"Curb your language in this house, will you? There are children here," she whispered.

"I can't stand by and watch this happen."

"Destroying Silas's load is not going to end well for anyone. You know the Benoits will retaliate. Might just come after you and me. But I'm not living here in this house if there's moonshine still running through the farm. I'm not raising Levi with that. I'm not going to expose the girls to that. Something else needs to be done."

"Marybeth, what do you propose we do? We don't own anything here no more. Should we just gather Levi and leave like we was planning?"

"I don't know." Marybeth put Lula Mae down in a bassinet, stood, and closed the door to the kitchen. She reached out and embraced her husband, resting the side of her face against his chest. "I don't know what to do."

Jesse pulled her in tight.

"I can't leave the girls. They got nowhere to go," she said.

"Then we'll take them with us."

"How is that even possible?

"The flatbed Dodge is half mine. We'll load it at night and leave. Take all the children."

Marybeth pushed herself away from Jesse to see his face. "What about your father? What are you going to do? He won't go."

"I don't know. I don't know what to do about 'im. He and Silas still think they can make a go with apples. They don't understand that the market is gone and is not returning. I thought Silas would go along with raising chickens, but I have my doubts. We was supposed to pull stumps together and clear a plot for the grow house. His heart was not in it. I could tell. This is a game he's playing to buy time for hisself and perhaps your father. I don't know. It's not all adding up. Paps don't understand, and he don't wanna leave."

"When can we go? I'm ready," she said.

"Soon. We'll go west. I'll get me some day labor in Oklahoma and enough money to get out to Washington. We'll be there by the end of the summer."

"I would like that. Can we get a little house along the Columbia?"

"It's gonna have to be a big house, Marybeth. You'll be raising seven. I hope I can feed seven in Washington. I know I can't here, not by myself."

"We can't leave soon enough." Marybeth left Jesse's embrace and walked over to the pantry. She opened the doors to reveal near-empty shelves. "I'll gather from this house what we need. I've got to get the girls' clothes together."

"Gather them, and I'll bring 'em over to our place. In a few days, we'll leave from there."

"What are you going to say to Silas?"

"Nothing," Jesse said. "He don't deserve to know. Best if he don't know. We leave at night. Do you feel the need to talk to your father? Do you wanna tell 'im where you're going?"

"No, he don't deserve to know either. He couldn't care less that Anna Lee died. Barely even acknowledged when she did. As far as I'm concerned, he's dead to me," she said. "What are you going to tell Paps?"

"I don't know."

TWENTY-NINE

"AUNT MARYBETH, A CAR'S coming," Sussie said as she ran into the kitchen from the dooryard. "Big one."

Marybeth removed a pan of cornbread from the stove and wiped her hands on her apron. She followed Sussie to the front door and saw a large, teal-green car lumber up the road toward the house. "Step back inside," she directed Sussie. "Tell your sisters to stay inside. Tell Nancy to come here."

A four-door Packard Six sedan navigated the ruts in the dirt road as it approached in the mid-afternoon sun. Marybeth recognized her father, seated in the back. A colored man was at the wheel.

Nancy appeared next to Marybeth just as the car arrived at the house. Marybeth put her arm around Nancy, watching the vehicle slow but not stop. Her father continued to stare forward over the shiny chrome "Goddess of Speed" hood ornament, apparently without recognizing his daughter or oldest granddaughter. The sedan cruised past the house and bumped up the hill toward the graveyard.

"I'll be damned," Marybeth whispered as the car passed.

"Who was that?" Nancy asked.

"Your grandfather."

Nancy had rarely heard anything about her grandfather. His name was never mentioned. She knew he must live in Bentonville, where she had only visited occasionally. Nancy knew nothing of his wife, her grandmother. She was old enough to understand that what was unspoken in the family was not for her to know. What was hidden was undesirable. This hidden man must be that.

"Is he coming back? Will he stop?"

"I don't know, my dear." Marybeth guided Nancy back inside. "Go get your sisters cleaned up just in case he does."

Her father's arrival on the farm forced Marybeth to draw lines in her mind, compartmentalizing what she would reveal to him and what she would not. Should she tell him she suspects he was protecting them from the bank? Should she speak of her plan to leave at night, taking all his grandchildren west? Would she ask for money to get the farm through another year? She was not prepared for this visit if it happened.

Ten minutes later, the Packard bounced down the perimeter road toward Silas's house. Marybeth still stood in the open doorway. The sedan cruised up, stopping halfway between the big barn and the farmhouse. A swirling cloud of reddish dust caught up with the automobile and temporarily engulfed it, drifting off with a breeze. The driver, dressed in a dark suit, emerged from an open door. He was a small man with an angular face and short-cropped black hair under a billed cap band. Engorged veins snaked along the back of his dark hands and stood like pipes on either side of his neck.

"Afternoon, ma'am," the driver said as he tipped his hat and approached the doorway. He cupped his hands together in front of his waist.

"Good afternoon to you," Marybeth said, her hands wrapped in a dishrag. She stood in the doorway, judging the messenger and the message her father was sending.

"Mr. Suggs would like to have a word with you, ma'am."

"He's welcome in the home."

"Mr. Suggs prefers that you accompany him in the coach." The driver gestured for her to follow him.

Marybeth hesitated. She turned to Nancy, standing behind her, handed her the rag, and said, "Take the girls inside and wait. I'll be right back." She followed the driver to the car, and he swung the rear door for her.

"Please sit, Marybeth," her father said from the other side of the bench seat. Suggs perched on the rich mahogany leather with his knees touching and his black polished shoes positioned neatly on the floorboard. His gray, lightly pinstriped suit draped his thin frame under generous shoulder pads, making his arms resemble a marionette's. He held his felt hat on his lap with manicured, delicate fingers.

Marybeth stood at the open car door. "Father, I would rather you step out and speak to me if you've something to say."

"Just get in the damn car."

"What's this about?"

"Anna Lee. I want to speak about Anna Lee," he said.

Marybeth lifted the hem of her skirt and turned to sit in the back. The driver guided her shoulders, gently shut the door, then ambled off toward the shade of the big barn, rolling a wad of tobacco in papers.

Suggs watched Marybeth sit, then directed his unfocused gaze forward and out the front windshield. "I'm sorry about your sister. I know you've always been close. I'm sorry I missed the burial."

"You could have sent word," she said.

"I said, I'm sorry. I think about Silas and the children. How many children?"

"Six. Your newest granddaughter is Lula Mae."

If this was all her father wanted to say, Marybeth was done. She was ready to leave the car, leave her miserable father to himself, and leave Benton County for good. His concern for Anna Lee and her family seemed so shallow and impenitent. Marybeth grabbed the door handle. "Is that all?"

"No. I understand Jesse and Silas are having financial difficulties with the farm. No market for apples these past few years, huh? Frost got ya this year? Jesse told me all about it. I told him I ain't interested in investing in apples. I told him apples are dead. I think he knew. He knew. Not sure why he was coming to me in the first place. But after Anna Lee, I guess I had a change of heart. I think I can work with Jesse and Silas. Silas has some ideas. I can work with that."

"His ideas are corrupt," Marybeth blurted out.

"Are you not trying to save the farm?"

"Don't know," she said. "Jesse and I have plans."

"Did Silas tell you that I own your farm now?"

She felt her face flush with the next beat of her heart. She knew her father could do this, but it surprised her that he would be so brazen. "No."

"Well, I do. Y'all are living on my property, at my pleasure, now."

Marybeth reached for the door handle again and turned to her father. "I don't have to listen to this. I don't have to."

"Now, Marybeth, calm down. Nobody's kicking your family off the land. I'm willing to work with Jesse and Silas. Chickens are good, and Jesse might be on to something. Washington County is getting all into chickens, and Benton County, too. Might be the future. I could invest in chickens."

"But we own nothing. We have nothing here. Jesse and I are leaving soon, taking the girls with us."

"I don't think that's a good idea," he said.

"I don't care what you think."

"It would be best if you and Jesse just stay put. I'll get you through this year. You want to grow apples? Fine. I don't care. I need you to run this here farm. I need a barn. I need produce trucks a coming and a going. Chicken trucks are fine. Silas can't run this operation by hisself. I need Jesse on board."

"I told you we're leaving," Marybeth said.

Suggs reached down and opened a leather valise at his feet. He pulled out a large paper envelope and unwound its string clasp, removing a tan certificate printed on parchment paper. He showed it to Marybeth. "This is yours."

She had never seen the document before. "What is it?"

"Stock. Stock your mother bought for you when you were a child. Union Pacific Railroad."

"I don't understand." Marybeth reached for the paper, but her father pulled it back.

"Twenty-five shares bought in '04 for fifty dollars apiece, now worth four times that."

"You say this belongs to me?"

"Has your name on it, right here." Suggs pointed out her maiden name in a flowing script on the certificate. "Enough stock to buy this farm twice."

"Then it's mine?"

"It has your name on it, but you're going to give it to me. Sign it over to my name. You see, your mother left this for you in case something ever happened to me. But it was I who raised you, paid for your food and clothing, put a roof over your head. Sent you to school. All at my expense. Did the same for your sister."

"And if I don't sign it over to you?"

"You will," he said.

"You must have one for Anna Lee. Where's her stock?"

Suggs glanced to his right and faced five barefoot girls dressed in loose-fitting cotton shifts, standing in the house doorway with the youngest out front. He turned back to Marybeth. "She signed it over to me several years ago."

"But why?"

"She had the same as you. She made the same mistakes as you. You and I both know she was with family when Silas came to me asking for her hand. I didn't much care for him then, lying with my unwed daughter. Was going to send her to N' Orleans, let the nuns take care of her rather than have her carry that bastard child around my town." He looked again at the girls, this time focusing on Nancy. "We worked a deal."

"She never said of this."

"Never would. You see, I promised to let her marry Silas and live out here in the country, deliver her bastard baby, and we would both never speak of this again. For my part, she signed over the stock."

"I hate you."

"Oh, you will hate me more in a minute."

"Keep your damn worthless certificate. I ain't signing a thing." Marybeth turned again for the side door.

"I know all about your own little bastard boy."

Marybeth arched her back and grabbed the front edge of the seat with her hands, digging her fingers into the leather. "You know not what you're talking about." She glared at her father.

"Oh, I do. And so will Levi if you don't cooperate. You just sign this over to me." He placed the stock certificate face-up on the seat between them and produced a fountain pen from his breast pocket. "Here, let me load this for you." He opened an inkwell and dipped the quill.

Marybeth felt trapped, manipulated, and robbed. Their mother had apparently left a small treasure when she died, a fortune their father had hidden from them for years. He could not get access to the money without their consent. He blackmailed Anna Lee for her share and was doing the same to her. How did he know about Levi? Only three people knew. Anna Lee would never have spoken of this. "Silas told you, didn't he?"

Suggs nodded. "He didn't want you to leave. I need Silas to stay on the farm, and he needs you and Jesse to do the same. He told me, hoping I could convince you. Silas doesn't know about the stock, only you and me."

"If I don't give you the money?"

"Levi finds out who his daddy is. Simple. I figure you would eventually tell Jesse, but never Levi. How's that little bastard going to feel when he finds out who his real father is? By the way, if y'all leave, he finds out as well." Suggs tapped the document with his finger and extended the pen to Marybeth.

Anna Lee, Silas, and she had agreed that the truth should never come out. It was simply not fair to Levi. There was no need to ever speak of it. Anna Lee and Marybeth had timed it right, and she became pregnant with Levi after her first, and only, planned encounter with Silas. They were all supposed to forget it. "Jesse was Levi's father," they vowed to repeat as often and for as long as it took to be true.

Marybeth took the pen with her right hand and turned her hips toward the center of the seat. She signed her name, then stabbed the certificate with the quill, piercing the parchment and bleeding black ink onto the leather seat. "You're a goddamn son of a bitch." She flicked the pen onto her father's tailored suit. "I hope your miserable carcass rots in hell."

Suggs fumbled with the pen and salvaged the stock certificate from the spreading pool of ink. He tucked both into his case. Marybeth's door opened; the driver stood obediently at her side. She pulled herself out, brushed off any help, and stood. She straightened out the folds of her skirt, leaned into the car, and said, "I hate you. I wish it was you who died instead of Mother." She spat on the ground and locked her eyes on her father's face. "You owe me this much." Her voice quivered. "Why did you treat Anna Lee and me like this when we were growing up? Why so cold and hateful? What did we ever do to deserve this from you? What?"

Suggs stared into the windshield with an expression devoid of emotion. At first, Marybeth thought he was ignoring her question.

"What did we do to you?"

"I never wanted children, especially little girls. It was your mother who wanted you and loved you. I hated her for it. When she died, you and your sister became my burden. A burden I never asked for, never wanted. I thought I would hate you, too. But I don't hate you like I hated your mother. You see, I don't feel anything."

Tears ran down Marybeth's cheeks.

Suggs turned to his daughter and said, "You know, I thought I was going to be happy when you and Anna Lee left. Let someone else take the burden. But you know, I didn't feel happiness or sadness. Just a void. The same hollowness I've felt my entire life. I wish I could hate you, but I don't. I don't blame you for your hatred of me and your miserable childhood. Anna Lee, neither. I probably would have felt the same if I were you." Suggs patted his valise with open palms. "There, there, you have it, the truth for you. The truth Anna Lee died not knowing." He looked at his driver and said, "We're done here."

Marybeth stepped away from the car as the driver gently closed the door. She scrambled around the back of the car and into the house, embracing Sussie, Mayel, and Vesta. Nancy followed her with Polly and Lula Mae.

From behind the barn, Silas heard the Packard Six engine release a muscular growl as it sped up and descended the hill.

THIRTY

"WHAT DID HE WANT?" Silas called into his house through the open doorway.

Marybeth emerged from the kitchen to look at her brother-in-law. "Please leave."

"This is my damn house. I'll stay if I wanna. What did he want?"

"To pay his respects," Marybeth answered.

"I know that. What did he want with you? I seen ya sitting in the car. I seen ya spitting in the dirt. What did he want?"

"Nothing. He wants us to stay." Fury burned in her heart when she thought of Silas spilling family secrets to her father.

"Are ya?

"Silas, you uphold your end, and I think Jesse will stay."

"Jesse is a goddamn coward. He don't have the guts to do what it takes to save the farm. I do," Silas said, lurching into the house.

"Leave, Silas. Now," Marybeth said. She turned down the hallway. "Girls, get in the back. Shut the door."

"I said this here is my house. I'll come in if I want," Silas said. He stumbled a little and caught his shoulder against the wall.

Marybeth stepped forward and pushed Silas with both hands. Again, he stumbled, then grabbed Marybeth for support.

"I said this is my house. Those are my childrens." He then pushed her up against the wall and held her shoulders back, overpowering her with his size. Sweat matted his hair, and his eyes were bloodshot.

She smelled it when he was close to her—rotting citrus, whiskey, or both. It was an unusual and unpleasant odor. Distinct and overwhelming. "You've been drinking," she said.

"You and Jesse's making me. Anna Lee and me manage just fine." He then called out, "Anna Lee?"

"Anna Lee's dead. She ain't here."

"Anna Lee, get those children out here to pay some respect to their father," he slurred. He turned to Marybeth. "I'm burning up."

"Silas, let go of me. Come." She wiggled free from his hands and moved behind him. "Into the kitchen."

Silas staggered, limped to the kitchen, and collapsed into a chair. "I needs some water. I'm burning."

Marybeth fetched a cup and filled it from a pail. She brought water to his lips and helped him drink. "You're with fever," she said when she put her hand on his forehead.

"Didn't ya hear me? I'm burning up. Leg's killing." He called out, "Nancy, get your mother in here. Achsah, more water."

"Silas, I'm Marybeth. Anna Lee and Achsah are not here."

"You. You stuck me," he said with a sudden, clear focus on Marybeth.

"Let me look at your leg. Stand. I need to look at your leg." Marybeth grabbed a towel and put it on the table. She reached down to help Silas up. "I need to look."

"I ain't standing for you, not nobody."

Marybeth snatched a pair of shears from Anna Lee's sewing basket on the floor, knelt in front of Silas, and ripped the hem of his right pant leg at the inside seam. She split the pants up to the crotch and folded the fabric back. A swollen wound on the outside of his thigh drained thin brown pus with the pungent, sweet smell of gas bubbling out of the skin. Streaks of redness coursed up and down his leg. Marybeth recoiled and covered her face with the towel. The sight and smell of rotting flesh were overwhelming.

"You need a doctor," she said from behind the towel.

"You did this to me," Silas said.

"I need to get you to a doctor."

"What I needs is some likker."

"You're not in your right mind. The fever's got you confused. Let me think." She walked over to the pail and splashed water on her face. "Stay put," she said to Silas. Marybeth stepped into the hallway and opened the back bedroom door. "Nancy, your father is ill. Run to Uncle Jesse—at the top of the orchard—and tell him to get a doctor. He needs a doctor."

Marybeth turned to see Silas behind her in the hallway, bracing himself against the wall.

"Come lay down," Marybeth said, guiding him into his bedroom. "Nancy's going to get a doctor."

Silas lifted his left hand and brought his palm squarely across Marybeth's face, knocking her backward. "Nobody's telling me what to do in my own house. Let's go, Nancy. Get the girls. We're leaving."

He took a step toward his daughter. Marybeth pushed him off.

"Papa," Nancy screamed.

Silas took another swing at Marybeth but missed.

"Nancy," Marybeth yelled, "get back and lock the door." She shoved Nancy behind her.

Silas stood in the hall facing Marybeth with his back to the front door. "I ain't taking this shit. I ain't waiting around for no doctor. You can all go to hell." Silas turned and limped out of the house, using the wall for support. His pant leg flapped open as he dragged his right leg forward. "You ain't having to worry yourself with me no more." Silas hitched down the dirt track toward Paps's cabin.

Marybeth closed and barred the door. She touched her cheek and felt a sting.

"Girls, now listen to me," Marybeth said to the four oldest who had emerged from the bedroom. "Pack a bag. Get your clothes and only those things you can carry." She knelt to look at Vesta and patted her face with her palms. "Everything will be okay. We just have to move." Tears streamed down Vesta's cheeks, and Marybeth pulled her into her arms. "Everything's going to be all right. I'm not leaving you."

Nancy had Lula Mae cupped in her elbow, gently rocking her. "Auntie, what's wrong with Papa?"

"He's sick, needs a doctor."

"Is he gonna be okay?" Nancy asked.

"Yes, yes, yes. I told you everything is okay." Marybeth stood and extended her arms toward the baby. "Give her to me, and you get busy packing. Help Polly."

The girls retreated to the back bedroom and attic to rummage through their meager assortment of clothes and possessions. Marybeth collected two small cases and three cloth sacks from the mudroom and placed them in the hall. She filled a gunnysack with several cans of sweetened milk, five pounds of cornmeal, a pound of flour, and a lard tin. Outside on the line, she pulled off several nappies and two cotton gowns for the baby and put these in the sack as well. She wrapped two glass bottles with rubber nipples in a dishcloth and stuffed them on top.

Polly appeared in the kitchen doorway. "Papa scairt me."

Marybeth paused for a moment. She set Lula Mae in the bassinet and picked Polly up, mounting her on a cocked hip. She did not know what to say that a two-year-old would understand. Things were moving so fast in her mind—her father's revelation of thousands of dollars in stock, his blackmail and seizure of the money, losing the farm, and Silas's fever and unstable behavior. "Your daddy's strong. When he's better, we'll see him again."

"I don't wanna go," Polly said.

"We must. We must go. Everything's all right. Now run along and get your stuff. Bring you a doll." She sat Polly down and guided her out of the kitchen.

Marybeth took one last look around the house. The girls were all assembled in the dooryard with their cases and sacks. A small silver-framed photograph of her and her sister as teenagers dressed for a summer ball was on a side table. Marybeth lifted the photo and studied it for a minute. She slipped the frame into her blouse, picked up the baby in her arms, lifted the gunnysack over her shoulder, and left the house.

The late-afternoon sun beat down on the parched dirt. A light breeze kicked up dust in a small swirl that danced a pirouette for a moment, then vanished as if it never were. Marybeth handed the baby back to Nancy. "You got her?" she asked, looking at Nancy's case in the other arm.

Nancy nodded.

"Let's go." Marybeth picked up Polly, balanced her on her hip with one arm, tucked the gunnysack under the other, and set off toward the orchard. She turned to see the other three girls following with what they could carry.

Marybeth cut through the apple trees, the shortest route to her house, avoiding Paps's cabin and Silas. The summer grass was already dry where the sunlight found its way between the trees. Next to the trunks, the grass still grew tall and green. The limbs should be heavy with green globes this time of the year, bowing toward the ground. In a typical season, tractor wheels and spray machines would have worn paths between the trees, and Silas and Jesse would have studied the crop, tested the soil, and looked for infestation and blight. The children would have cleaned the ground of deadfall fruit so as not to lure vermin and swine.

But the orchard was fallow, unattended, and neglected. The tops of the trees were thinning, dropping yellow leaves infected with cedar-apple rust. Entire branches, leaves and all, especially water shoots and recent growth, had turned brown as if struck with lightning. Sap oozed from cankers in the cracked bark. Small white scale clung to the twigs like barnacles on a post, sucking fluid from under the thin bark. The trees were weak, vulnerable, and sickly. There was not even fruit to harbor apple maggots or the coddling moth. This was not how Marybeth wished to remember the orchard.

Levi greeted them in front of their house. "Ma, what's happening?" he asked, trying to size up what he saw.

"I'll explain in a little bit. Where's your father? Come help with this." She handed him her sack.

"He's pulling stumps up yonder. Sent me back."

"He's got the truck?"

"Yes, ma'am."

Marybeth sat on the porch and put Lula May on her lap. "Girls, go on in. Nancy put Polly's stuff in our room. You, Vesta, Sussie, and Mayel go to Levi's. Levi, I'll fix you a spot later."

"Ma," Levi protested.

"Levi, just for now until we figger things out."

"What is Uncle Silas gonna say?" he asked.

"I don't know. Now you listen. Go help with the girls and get them settled." She called into the house, "Nancy, don't you go unpacking. Just find a place to put your belongings. Levi, on second thought, run, go get your pa."

The sun cast long shadows behind the Dodge flatbed as Jesse bumped it down the two-track. Levi rode next to him on the bench seat. The truck came to a halt directly in front of the house. Marybeth stood. Jesse jumped out and ran to his wife. "Levi," he called back, "run on in."

"Jesse," Marybeth said, "it's Silas. He needs a doctor but won't go. He's drunk. His leg's infected—gangrene. Went to Paps's last I saw."

"You got the girls?"

"Yes, all of them. I got their things, too."

Jesse looked at her and noticed a red mark on her cheek and a slight bruise under her eye. "He did this? He struck you?"

"He's drunk and with fever. Not in his right mind."

Jesse stepped back and pounded a roof post with his fist. He turned to Marybeth. "Git our things together. Just git what we need. I'm going down to talk to Silas." Jesse set out toward Paps's cabin in a trot.

Marybeth set to work, gathering the essentials. She contemplated telling Jesse about her father's visit to the farm earlier in the day. What could she say? He wanted to see the grave. He wanted to tell her he owned the land and made her sign over a fortune she previously knew nothing about. No, this was not the time; it would raise too many tough questions. It did not matter at this point.

Darkness fell before Jesse came back home. "He ain't there. Paps never seen 'im today. I looked back at his house and in the big barn, but I ain't seen no sign of 'im," Jesse said.

"What are we going to do?"

"Pack up and leave."

"You talk to Paps about that?" Marybeth asked.

"Yeah, he told me to stay. I can't. I can't leave 'im, either. Pack. We'll pack now and figger this out later."

Marybeth pointed to a wooden crate. "This goes, and so does that other one." She pointed to another.

Jesse and Levi packed the truck's bed with crates and boxes, heavy things, along the bottom between the wooden side slats. Jesse removed the iron grate from the stove for cooking over a campfire and lashed a freshwater barrel to the running boards on each side. Levi stuffed cases and bags of clothes between the boxes, anywhere they would fit.

"What do we do with the cow?" Levi asked his father.

"Turn her loose. She won't wander far. We got no room for the chickens. Fill their water and dump some corn in. Someone will come by for them. We got to milk her first. Help me with the mattresses before you go. Leave the pigs penned."

"What about the Ford?"

"It belongs to Paps. Not my concern or yours either."

Jesse handed up three mattresses to Levi, standing on their load. They arranged the mattresses across the top and covered them with a tarp, lashing the canvas down to the truck's sides with a sisal rope.

Marybeth stood next to the truck. The reality of their decision to leave lay heavily on her. "It don't feel right about Silas."

Jesse hopped off the back. Then he tightened a knot, taking the slack out of the rope. "We have no choice but to leave. We're doing this for the girls. There ain't nothing left for us here."

"He's sick."

"He's a drunk like his father."

"He's sick because of me. I stuck him. I made him sick."

Jesse continued to secure the truck. "Silas didn't get no infection from your fork. He got it from wallowing around drunk on the ground in the barnyard. He done this to hisself. You're more concerned about 'im than he is." He turned to Marybeth. "Woman, git hold of yourself and see this for what it is. Silas don't care about you. He don't care about Nancy, Vesta, Sussie, Mayel, or Polly. Hell, he don't even know who Lula Mae is. Has he ever held her? If he cared about the farm, he wouldn't have gotten mixed up with the Benoits like he's done. He wouldn't take to the bottle as he did if he cared. He wandered off somewhere in his condition. Does that sound like someone who frets about hisself? He's beyond my control. I've tried. I've done what I can. He's in God's hands now."

"Without a doctor, he could die," Marybeth said.

"We stay here, we'll die."

THIRTY-ONE

"YA DOING IT, JESSE. Done moving out, are ya?" Lars asked as he emerged from the dark forest into the dooryard and the circular glow of a lantern. He propped his rifle against his shoulder.

"We're leaving. You're right. Leaving right soon," Jesse responded as he tossed a small bag into the truck cab.

"Didn't expect ya to rush off like you're doing."

"We gotta go. What brung you down here this time of night?" Jesse asked.

"Silas. I seen him cross my field at dusk. Limping real bad. Wouldn't stop to talk. I figured something was going on. He okay?"

"Naw. He ain't okay."

"He looked rabid. That's what he looked like, rabid like a dog. I seen a man like that before. Bit by a skunk that never sprayed him. You know there's something wrong with a skunk that don't lift its tail. Three days later, he was having fever and getting all edgy."

"Silas ain't rabid. He's got gangrene. Fever is making 'im crazy. Marybeth seen his leg."

"Gangrene, huh? Well, this guy I knew died rabid, but not before turning on his family with a pick handle. Near killed his wife."

"He ain't rabid," Jesse repeated.

"You said that already. He didn't look too good, a limping and everything. Couldn't get his damn attention. Thought I'd come down to see what was going on."

"We're leaving, Lars."

"You taking everything? Can't fit everything on that truck."

"Come back tomorrow. You can have what we left. Take the cow tonight if you wants. I don't care."

"He don't look good. Needs a doctor."

"Course, he needs a doctor. Take 'im to a doctor if you want, if you can find 'im. I'm tar'd, done all I can." Jesse picked up the lantern and walked around to the other side of the truck to check the tires. He ran his fingers over the thin tread and kicked the sidewalls to gauge the pressure.

Lars followed him around. "Ya going through Enid? Told ya I got kin outside Enid. They're going to have cotton coming in soon. I betcha they need pickers if you're going through Enid. Vestergaard, Jorgen Vestergaard. That's who you ask for, my cousin. Bolls as big as your fist. Easy money if ya need it. You mention my name. Not sure it will help ya any."

"Keep'n mind." Jesse lifted the lantern and held it high to inspect the canvas covering his load on the flatbed.

"You taking them children? Looks like ya got enough room for 'em."

"Got room for you and the missus, you wants to come," Jesse said.

"Mighty kind of ya, but I got to try and sell my place first. Can't leave without trying. Who knows, you still in Oklahoma come fall, we might see ya."

"Be in Washington come fall. Got to git there when the apples come off the trees so I can git settled. Marybeth wants a little house by the river."

"Jesse, I wish ya luck. Don't blame ya none leaving like ya's doing. Did I tell ya about a fella drove all the way to California, straight? Never stopped for nothing except gas. Took him three days. Made it in three days, all by himself. Got there and just plumb turned around and drove back."

"We ain't coming back."

"Didn't reckon ya would. Good luck, my friend." Lars extended his hand, and Jesse took it.

"Them three laying chickens are yours if you want. Thanks for all you've done."

Lars cradled his rifle in his right arm and marched back into the woods toward his place. Jesse watched for a moment as the Dane's solid frame dimmed and vanished in the dark. Jesse stepped back into his house, carrying the lantern.

"Here, eat something," Marybeth said as Jesse entered the kitchen, bare except for the table and stove body, items too large to pack. She handed him a half-dozen pones she had fried up earlier in the evening. "You need to eat. The children have et and are ready to go."

"You et?" Jesse asked.

"I'm not hungry."

Jesse took half of the pones and held them out for his wife. "These the last?"

She nodded.

"Eat." He handed her the three corn dumplings. "We'll leave in a minute." Jesse sat on a milking stool brought in from the barn. "I'm gonna have to stop by and tell Paps we're going. He won't believe me 'til he sees the truck all packed and everything. Could come if he wants. Maybe I should just git 'im a good and drunk and just throw 'im in the back. Be in Oklahoma before he comes around. Maybe I should do that. If I leave 'im here, he'll be dead in a month. Silas don't care. I'll throw Paps in the back. Don't care no more."

"He told you to stay, told you tonight. I don't think he would take kindly to being hauled off his land."

"He don't own the land no more. Don't own nothing except that junk Model T. You think the bank's gonna let 'im stay if we're gone?"

"I think they'll let him stay," she said, knowing her husband knew nothing about her father's acquisition of their farm.

"You gonna send word to your daddy?"

"No." Marybeth bit into the last of the pones and reflected on the gravity of their decision. It was final, definitive, and a reflection point from which she saw no return. Tomorrow, Benton County would be a place in her past. A place of happy memories, wickedness, and the sad graves of people she loved. Jesse was sure to feel the same.

The scuff of a boot on the front porch caught her attention. "Jesse," she whispered.

Another footfall confirmed a visitor. Jesse rose and opened the door. Silas stood lopsided in the light emanating from the kitchen, leaning against a roof post. His slit pants dangled behind his extended right leg. Brown liquid dripped from his swollen thigh and ran down the back of his knee and into his boot. His eyes were searching but vacant. His scratched and marred face hung blankly from his forehead and tangled hairline. Jesse stopped at the doorframe.

"Seen the truck," Silas slurred.

"Then you know we're leaving. Leaving tonight," Jesse responded.

"You're not going. You're not leaving Paps. Ain't got the guts."

"I sure as hell will."

"I just got done telling him all about how I was attacked by your wife. Told 'im the truth. Told 'im you were interfering with me raising my family and keeping the land. He's on my side now, always has been. You had to know that. Didn't ya? Didn't ya?' Silas wiped spittle off his jaw with the back of his hand. "He likes me more. I'm the one who would never leave 'im."

"Silas, it's time for you to leave us alone."

"I'm not going anywhere. In fact, I'll make sure you ain't either and stay here on the farm. I will. We're raising chickens. Come on, Jesse."

"What's it to you? What do you want us to stay for? 'Cause you need cover to run moonshine? Is that it? Well, I ain't believing you no more. Never did."

Silas stepped toward the door and tried to enter. "You ain't taking Levi off the farm."

Jesse pushed him back with both hands. "You have no say in where I take my own son. You don't even care about your own daughters."

"He ain't your son."

"The hell he is." Jesse balled his fist and struck his brother in the jaw.

Silas recoiled but caught his balance again with his good leg. Fire now raged in his eyes. "He's my son. You're not taking 'im."

"Get out of my yard, you son of a bitch." Jesse raised his fist again.

"I'm the father. You ask Marybeth. I'm his father. You're as sterile as a gelding." Silas stepped forward again. "Marybeth. Oh, Marybeth?" he called into the house, trying to look around his brother. "Marybeth, didn't you never tell your man how's you come to have a son?"

"You're talking crazy. Now git away." Jesse cocked his fist again but hesitated.

"She liked it; she did. Had a real man," he said to Jesse. "Nobody's to know. 'Our little secret'—Anna Lee, Marybeth, and me. It was Anna Lee's idea, us being Siamese and all. Who would've known? Did you a good deed, I did. But now you ain't taking my son from me."

Jesse let loose another slug to Silas's face. This one glanced off the side of his ear and landed on hard bone. Silas barely flinched. Jesse pulled back for another.

"Marybeth'll tell you the truth. Ask her. She'll tell ya we did it just once. Anna Lee's idea—stood right outside the door. Yup, a fine woman you have there, nice gams. I enjoyed my time between those long legs. I was a hoping she'd want more children. More than happy to oblige if she'd wanted."

"Shut your goddamn mouth," Jesse said, not believing what he was hearing.

"Didn't ya wonder why it took her three years to have your first, and never again? Oh, Marybeth was beside herself that you couldn't have you a child of your own. She wanted you to be a happy, proud father. I was the perfect fix for your seedless cods. Who would have been the wiser?"

The blow to Silas's stomach from Jesse's fist caught him off guard, expelling the air from his lungs and doubling him over. Silas stumbled on his bad leg and found the wall with his shoulder. He coughed and wheezed, craving air to continue tormenting his brother. "Levi—" Silas coughed. "Levi, he ain't yourn."

Silas turned, still bent over, and hobbled off the porch. Jesse watched his decrepit frame lurch forward into the darkness and disappear. Shocked at what he had just heard, Jesse was speechless. Indeed, it was not true. It couldn't be true. The fiery blood of rage drained from his head, leaving doubt in its place.

"Silas spoke the truth," Marybeth whispered behind him.

Jesse turned to look at his wife. "No."

"It is true. For you, for my love of you."

Jesse collapsed to his knees on the porch and brought his hands to his face. Marybeth hesitated, then knelt and draped her arm over his shoulder. She rested her cheek on the back of his neck.

He brushed her off. Moments ago, he had a wife and a son; now, he was unsure who he had. Four months ago, he had a brother and a farm; now, he had neither. Anna Lee was dead. Paps lost his will to live. The rock, which was his family, had shattered. "I don't know what I have left," he mumbled.

"I'm sorry. Please forgive me."

"What do I have? What do I have left?"

"I'm so sorry. I was naïve and selfish. I meant no harm. I didn't understand. My wish to give you a child clouded my good judgment." She placed her hand on his shoulder and squeezed. "Forgive me. God forgive me." Her sobbing tears burst forth as her emotional foundation crumbled.

Jesse rolled his hips and sat, leaning his back against the outside wall. "What do I have?" Avoiding his wife, he looked straight out into a void.

"Me, if you'll still have me," Marybeth sobbed.

Jesse turned to his wife, and their eyes met. He pulled her in and embraced her with both arms. Her shoulders and back were moist and warm with perspiration. Her chest shuddered with halting breaths. Jesse looked over her shoulder, across the yard, and over the split-rail fence and perimeter road to the apple trees. Massive, mature Arkansas Blacks in the prime of their life, struck down by the casual fickleness of nature. Marybeth remained silent except for her trailing sobs, diminishing and blending into the night sounds of the woods—an animal rustled dry leaves, and owls called and answered. Katydids spun out a din from the deciduous canopy. A child peeped inside the house, then the muffled tones of Nancy's voice briefly sang out.

Clarity emerged where confusion had just been. Jesse stood and brought Marybeth up with him, holding her at arm's length. "You gave your husband a son. You've done nothing wrong that warrants forgiveness from me." He bent down and placed his lips on hers, feeling the warm quivering of her kiss and tasting the saltiness of her tears. "Let's go. It's a long way to Washington. We gotta family to attend to."

THIRTY-TWO

POLLY SAT ON THE kitchen table with Mayel, her gaze fixed on the flickering yellow flame of the lantern beside her. She reached over to finger the wick knob. Sussie slapped her hand away.

"It's late, and we'll be leaving soon. Remember what I told you?" Marybeth said to the children. "We're gonna go in the truck, drive a ways tonight. When your father is feeling better, perhaps he'll join us. We can't stay." Lula Mae fussed in Marybeth's arms. She stroked the roof of the baby's mouth with her little finger.

"I'm hungry," Mayel said.

"I got some pears you can split once we get going," Marybeth said. "Nancy, Vesta, Sussie, and Mayel, you're riding up top in the back with Levi. Polly will sit with the baby and me up front. Soon as your uncle gets back, we're ready. Y'all can sleep when we get going."

"Where did he go?" Vesta asked?

"To the shed barn. He's got a few things to attend to. He'll be back soon."

"I'm scairt Papa will be mad at us," Sussie said to her aunt.

"Uncle Jesse will tell him what good children you were. He's not gonna be mad at you."

"Papa scairt me tonight," Sussie said. Her eyes puffed, and tears formed on the lower lids. "He scairt me."

Marybeth stroked Sussie's blonde hair. "When your uncle, Jesse, gets back, everything's gonna be all right. He'll be right back, just ran out for a minute. He'll be right back."

Nancy stepped into the kitchen from the mudroom. She held out an egg in each hand. "This is it," she said.

The sound of splintering wood breached the quietness of the house. Vesta and Sussie screamed. Nancy cowered behind the table and pulled Polly off. Marybeth rushed to the hall door and slammed it closed, throwing the latch.

"Go," Marybeth said with authority. "Go, get in the room." She pushed all the children into the mudroom. "Lock the outside door. Quiet. Be very quiet." She put her finger to her lips and handed Nancy the baby. "Silent." Marybeth closed the mudroom's door and stood in front of it, facing the opposite side of the kitchen.

"Jesse?" Silas called from the hallway. "Jesse?"

Marybeth reached for an iron poker near the stove and held it out.

"I just wanna talk, Jesse."

The sounds of Silas's boots, in a limp, clicked down the hall toward the back bedroom. A mirror shattered, and glass clinked on the floor. Marybeth snuffed out the lamp. The sudden darkness made her world go black.

"Jesse? Marybeth? I know you got my children."

The kitchen door rattled. "Open up, Marybeth."

Marybeth stood behind the table with the poker held high as her eyes adjusted to the dark shape of the door.

An axe blade sliced through the top panel with a crack, sending splinters into the room. Silas torqued the handle to free the axe head and swung again, shattering the lock rail. He kicked the edge of the door, and it flung open.

"Silas!" Marybeth screamed.

"Looking for you, I was," he said. "Where's Jesse? I seen the truck."

"Coming right now. Leave."

"I went looking for my girls. Looking for my girls. I know you got 'em. Cleaned out my house, you bitch. Went to the house looking for my girls, and they ain't there. You gots my girls."

Marybeth shook the poker in her hands, keeping the wooden table between them. "You ain't got no right to be here."

"Oh, I've got every right to take what's mine. I've got every right. You see, Marybeth, I got the law on my side. Kidnapping, that's what you've done. Kidnapping. I'm fixing to git what's mine." Silas lurched into the kitchen on his bad leg and caught himself on the table's edge. "I'm tar'd of talking. Git me those kids." He raised the axe head to his shoulder with his right hand and planted his other hand on the tabletop for support. "I come for my childrens."

"Can't have them. We made our minds up. Can't have them."

The Dodge engine block sputtered and caught. Jesse advanced the spark and accelerator to a smooth idle, then switched the headlights, illuminating the front of the house and the busted front door. Startled, he reached under the seat, lifted his 300 Savage, and hopped out of the cab.

Silas, drawn out by the sound of the truck, appeared in the doorway with his axe in hand. "Just talking with the missus, Jesse, about my childrens. Come to git what's mine," Silas shouted over the engine rumble. "You didn't tell me you had my childrens when I came by earlier."

Jesse leveled the rifle at Silas's chest. "Git." He loaded a cartridge into the breech with the bolt action and stared at his brother.

Silas lowered the axe handle to the ground, holding the iron head at his side. "We're good here, brother. Just talking, that's what we're doing. Just talking. Right?"

Silas stepped out onto the porch. His right leg buckled, and he caught his balance on a roof post. He crutched his gait using the axe handle and limped into the yard. Jesse followed him with the muzzle of his gun.

"Just talking, Jesse," Silas said as he approached.

"You can talk from there. Hear you fine."

Silas stopped and leaned on the handle. "Afternoon didn't much take to being sucker-punched when I'm sick. All I said was the truth. I'm sure Marybeth backed me up."

"We're taking them. Ain't no place to raise children. You're in no shape to raise your daughters. They deserve better," Jesse said.

"I decide what they deserve."

"Best if you just turn around now and head home. I'll send a doctor to look at that leg in the morning."

Silas took another step forward and lifted the blade to his waist, gripping the handle's shoulder and throat.

"Put it down."

"We're just talking, Jesse." Silas pitched forward, dragging his bad leg behind. Six feet separated the two men.

"I'll shoot." Jesse brought the rifle sight up to his right eye and pushed the butt into his shoulder.

"Ain't got the balls to shoot. You can't do it." Silas lifted the axe head higher. The sharp blade glistened in the truck's headlights.

Jesse stepped back against the truck. "I said stop." The fender vibrated on the back of his legs. Silas lurched forward and swung.

The axe blade fell across the rifle barrel, knocking the gun from Jesse's grasp. Silas pulled back the axe and lifted it again. Jesse leaned back against the engine hood with both hands out front.

"Told ya you couldn't shoot me. Told ya."

Jesse's eyes darted to the rifle at his feet. He then fixed his glare on his brother, his doppelgänger. One face, one body, two minds. Opposite poles of a magnet, oil and water, fire and ice. They could not live together yet could not live apart. Jesse always knew this moment would come when their connected lives would be cleaved, and one would die. Their world was not big enough to thrive together.

As Silas lifted the blade overhead to swing again, a rifle's report cracked in the air. The axe blade fell backward over Silas's shoulder, and he spun to the left. Jesse looked at the edge of the woods. A white muzzle flash lit the surrounding brush, instantaneously followed by another report. He turned to Silas and watched him crumple on the dirt before him. Blood filled a small red dot on his temple and trickled into his ear. Jesse retrieved his rifle and slid behind the truck's hood. He trained his weapon on the tree line where the flash had come, still burning in his sight.

"Who's there?" Jesse called into the woods.

"It's me, my friend. Lars."

THIRTY-THREE

JESSE BOUNDED INTO THE house, pushing the splintered door aside. He searched the two bedrooms and the kitchen for his wife and family. All were empty. "Marybeth," he called. The mudroom door was closed, and he forced it open. Empty. The outside door was ajar, and he stepped outside into the night again.

"Lars, I can't find 'em," Jesse gasped as he sprinted from the back of the house to Silas's body, lying in the dooryard.

Lars sat on the truck's running board and stared at the ground. "I did right. Tell me I did right," he said. His rifle rested across his knees, and he caressed the gunstock. "What was I to do?"

"You, done right. Ain't nothing nobody could do for 'im. You, done right." Jesse paced nervously about the yard, not knowing where Marybeth and the children were or what they saw or heard.

"They're at your father's place, I bet. That's where I would've gone. Slipped out the back. They're down there. You best go," Lars said. "I had no choice."

"No choice." In the dim light of the truck, Jesse looked again at his brother's body. A dark blot had formed in the dirt under his head and shoulders. The axe lay nearby. "I don't know what to do."

"Go to your father's. Take the truck. Leave."

"It don't feel right." Jesse stopped in front of Lars. "You gonna be okay?" He looked at Lars, then again at his brother. "Silas?"

Lars stood facing Jesse. "I'll take care of him. You go."

"It don't feel right just leaving 'im like this," Jesse said.

"Go." Lars stood and shouldered his rifle.

"What do I say to the girls? What do I tell Marybeth? Paps?"

"You will know what to say when the time is right," Lars said. He reached down, pulled Silas's limp legs out straight, and then rolled the body onto its back. "I'll take care of what needs to be done."

"You, done right. You had no choice."

"Right, I had no choice. Go."

"Lantern's in the kitchen." Jesse stowed his rifle under the seat of the cab and climbed in. He increased the throttle and advanced the spark to power the engine. He leaned out of the truck. "Where's you gonna put 'im?"

"Not far. Edge of the woods," Lars said. He gestured into the darkness. "That okay?"

"Edge of the woods is fine." Jesse looked again at his brother's body. "Can you say some words? Just what you can remember. He wasn't all bad. If it was me you're burying, I would want some words."

"I can do that."

"Say, there's a cow up in the big barn. Can you tend to it as well? You can keep both if you want. Some pigs, too."

Lars nodded and then looked away from Jesse to stem a well-spring of emotion.

"Appreciate all you done. I'm proud to have known you." Jesse double-clutched the truck, pulled it into low gear, and inched forward with his heavy load. After a few feet, he stopped and looked back at Lars. "Can you do me another favor?"

Lars refocused on his friend.

"I promised Silas I'd put a stone on Anna Lee's grave. Can you do that for me? I'll send some money when I can. Can you put up a stone?"

"Ja, I'll mark her good in case ya ever return. Now go."

Jesse turned the truck and headed downhill in the dark, leaving Lars standing over Silas's body.

THIRTY-FOUR

MARYBETH BOLTED TOWARD THE truck when she recognized Jesse driving up. He killed the engine and hopped out to embrace her.

"I didn't know," she said. "I didn't know what to do." She pushed his head up to look at him. "Are you all right?"

"All right."

"We left you. I didn't know what to do."

"You did right." Jesse pulled her tightly again. "Silas is dead."

"Dead?" Marybeth pushed herself away again and held Jesse's head with both hands. "I heard the shots. I was so worried."

"I killed 'im."

Marybeth looked at his face to read what she had just heard.

"Killed 'im with the gun. I had no choice."

"Oh, Jesse. Jesse," she sobbed. "Dead?"

"I had to do it. He was not in his mind." Jesse held Marybeth by her shoulders. "It happened so fast. I had to do it. I killed 'im. Lars came when he heard the shots. He said he would take care of things." Jesse looked toward the cabin. "The girls and Levi, what do they know? Did they hear the shots?"

"Of course, we all heard them. They're scared, Jesse. Got them inside with Paps."

"Did Paps say anything about the shots?"

"No."

"Did he hear 'em, too?"

"He heard them."

Jesse saw the curtains part in a dimly lit window. A little face looked back at him from just above the sill. He guessed it was Mayel or Vesta; he couldn't tell. The face in the window continued to stare with unflinching eyes. Orphans, they all were. Orphans so young. Innocent children who were dealt the most unfair blow by fate. Or was this somehow God's plan? How could this be His plan?

"Jesse," Marybeth said. "Jesse, we must go."

He looked at her with sad eyes; she had also seen the child in the window. Questions would be answered later. They would build and nurture a family, and hopefully, the horrors of this night would diminish in their memories, a nightmare cast away by the new dawn.

Paps appeared in the breezeway between the rooms, cautiously walked across the porch, and stepped down into the dirt. He tottered over to the truck and steadied himself with an outstretched hand on the fender. Jesse looked at his father and knew he could see right through him. Jesse knew he was transparent. He always had been. It was Silas who could deceive.

"Jesse, come here," Paps said from the side of the truck.

Jesse obeyed.

"Say not a word to me," Paps said. "Say not a word. Listen."

Jesse saw his father had clear eyes, like he had not seen for several years. Paps looked knowingly at him and placed his hand on his shoulder. Jesse felt the weight of his beefy hand—a hand shaped and built by the land on which they stood.

"Son, you will do what you needs to do. You're wise. You'll take these childrens and raise 'em in a better spot."

"Paps," Jesse said.

"Listen. You'll raise 'em and make a fambly." Paps squeezed his son's shoulder.

"Do you understand—"

"Shh." Paps put a finger to his lips. "Listen, I said. . . . You will leave tonight. Right now, and never turn back. Do you hear me?"

Of course, Jesse heard what his father was saying, but nothing made sense. It was all moving too fast. Silas coming at him with the axe, Lars, the look on a child's face, Marybeth's fright, meltdown, and finally, strength—Levi. The scenes played over one another in his mind with a cacophony of sounds and a jumble of emotions.

"Jesse," Paps said, "you don't need it, but you have my permission to leave."

Jesse blinked and shook his head, trying to clear his thoughts. "You'll come?"

"No."

"Can't leave you here alone."

"I'm old. Where you're going, I don't belong. This is my home."

"You'll die."

"Right. I'll die and lie here with your mother and sister . . . and Silas." Paps pulled his hand off Jesse's shoulder. "Leave now."

"Don't you wanna know what happened to Silas?"

"I know what happened to my son, your brother. Your eyes told me. Remember, you're of one seed, growing and reaching for the same sunlight like two trees planted too close to each other. Your face tells me you're free. No more fighting."

Jesse fought back the tears pooling in his lower lids and turned to Marybeth. "Gather them children. Time's come." He wiped his cheeks before greeting Nancy and taking the baby from her arms. He handed Lula Mae to Paps. "Hold your granddaughter," he said.

Jesse lifted the gate off the truck's back and helped Mayel and Sussie climb onto the tarp, covering the soft mattresses.

Marybeth appeared with a blanket and handed it to the girls. "Take this comfort if you get a chill," she said.

Nancy climbed onto the back of the truck with Levi, finding a spot up against the cab. "Put Vesta here," she called down to her aunt.

Levi pulled Vesta up with his hand. He helped her over to Nancy, then sat down at the back with his legs dangling over the load.

"Get up, so we can git this on," Jesse said, holding the back gate. Levi helped his father set the gate posts into cleats at the back, and he sat down with his arm draped over the top rail.

The faces of the children showed confusion and despair. It was well after midnight, and exhaustion was overcoming them. Marybeth had told them what to do. They trusted her. Questions and answers would come later; that is what she had said.

Paps stood, balancing in the soft glow leaking out of the cabin from the lanterns inside. He held Lula Mae with both hands and looked at her cherub face. Her eyes were closed. The corners of her mouth pulled back momentarily, giving him a flutter in his heart. Her arm fell loose from the swaddle, revealing her walnut-sized hand's pink, translucent skin. Little fingers, resting with a slight curl as if holding an invisible marble, twitched as Paps stroked her palm with the tip of his thumb. She yawned, arched her back, craned her neck, and shuddered. Paps re-wrapped the blanket and tucked her into his elbow. Secure, protected, safe.

Jesse picked up Polly and placed her in the cab at the center of the bench. He pumped the gas pedal and pushed the starter to engage the engine. The truck vibrated with each thrust of its pistons. He got out of the truck and helped Marybeth climb in from the passenger side, lifting the hem of her skirt. He turned to his father, who seemed lost in amazement, looking at his granddaughter.

"It's time," Jesse said.

Paps gently extended Lula Mae, and Jesse took her in his hands. He looked at his father. For the first time in his life, Jesse felt understood by him, and everything would be all right. This was how he wished to remember him. With time, he also hoped his memory of Silas's tragic death would fade, replaced by some of the goodness and sweetness he was sure his brother possessed under his tough skin. Characteristics, perhaps, he carried in his seed.

Jesse handed the baby to Marybeth and climbed into the cab. Without looking back, he eased the truck down the hill toward Spanker Creek and beyond.

AUTHOR'S NOTE

"With an apple, I will astonish Paris."

—Paul Cézanne

IN THE EARLY TWENTIETH-CENTURY, the nation knew Northwest Arkansas as the "Land of the Big Red Apple." Two million apple trees grew in Washington and Benton Counties, more than any other two counties in America. Large tracts on the Springfield Plain grew common Southern varieties such as Ben Davis, Missouri Pippin, Jonathon, and Winesap. Local cultivars with names like Arkansas Red, Lady Pippin, Wilson June, Aston Bitter, Wandering Spy, and, most famously, Arkansas Black anchored "kitchen" and commercial orchards throughout the area. The apple blossom was Arkansas's "Official State Flower." Many upstate farmers believed apple growing was the fastest route to riches. By 1919, Arkansas produced a record five and a half million bushels of apples annually. But "Southern apple mania" would last only two decades.

The decline began in the early 1920s with waves of disease and pest infestation striking entire regions, jumping from orchard to orchard, pitting farmers against neighbors, and rocketing the cost of cultivation. The primary culprits were fire blight, the codling moth, the San Jose scale, apple scab, and cedar-apple rust. Costly treatment was only partially effective: pruning infected limbs, wrapping trunks with burlap, and spraying oil, lead arsenate, and copper sulfate. Pesticide residue demanded an acid wash before shipping, which hastened the ripening and spoiling of the fruit. In 1925, the codling moth alone caused two million dollars of damage to the Arkansas apple industry. In 1930, fire blight destroyed 30 percent of the state's apple crop.

Southerners largely accepted blemished fruit at the beginning of the century, when they dried most apples for storage or fermented them for cider and vinegar. As consumer taste for "snack" apples developed in markets far from Southern orchards, so did the demand for "perfect" fruit. Wormholes, scabs, asymmetry, scald, and bruises made most Southern fruit unmarketable. Enforcement of the Pure Food and Drug Act of 1906, requiring proper labeling and quality standards of all fruit shipped out of the state, further cut profits.

In the latter half of the 1920s and early 1930s, severe climate and economic events assaulted the entire state of Arkansas. The Great Mississippi Flood of 1927 began in the late spring and affected the Mississippi River valley from Cairo, Illinois, to the Gulf of Mexico. Broken levees along the Mississippi, Arkansas, White, and St. Francis Rivers flooded five million acres in the state. Although crop damage was primarily confined to the cotton-growing regions of the Delta, the economic damage to the state was catastrophic, affecting all Arkansans. Unusually harsh spring rains and late freezes after the blossoms set often resulted in near-total crop failure for the year.

Like other Mississippi River states, Arkansas had not yet recovered from the agricultural depression after the Great Flood when the stock market crashed in 1929, spinning the Arkansas banking industry out of control and plunging the nation into the Great Depression. Land foreclosure and bank failure were commonplace throughout the agricultural regions in the South. Northwest Arkansas was no exception.

As if flooding and credit loss were not enough of an assault, in 1930 and 1931, a severe drought spread across the Mississippi and Ohio River valleys and over to the mid-Atlantic states. Rainfall in June and July 1930 was the lowest in Arkansas's history. Crop failure was catastrophic, especially in Arkansas and Oklahoma. By November, food shortages were commonplace; pellagra and typhoid fever became epidemic. The Dust Bowl and the Great Depression had just begun.

What was once an Arkansas yield of five million apple bushels a year dwindled to less than two million by 1935 and less than 250,000 by the 1960s. The industry never recovered from the Great Depression. Some blame environmental factors such as frost, rain, and drought. Others point out that Arkansas orchardists failed to adapt to a changing market that demanded high-quality fruit shipped around the country. Arkansans had a reputation for mislabeling and mixing fruit from different varieties in the same barrel and supplying poor-eating apple types, such as the Ben Davis, long after their demand dwindled. Most importantly, Arkansas farmers could not absorb the increased pest and disease control costs and remain competitive in the national market.

The collapse of the Arkansas apple industry in the late 1920s coincided with an uptick in "apple fever" in Washington State's Columbia River Basin. With the help of the refrigerated railcar, favorable shipping rates, abundant sunshine, and federally assisted irrigation, Western farmers outcompeted apple growers in the South and Northeast. Washington State consistently supplied large, colorful, flawless apples such as the Red Delicious to grocers worldwide. Today, Washington grows 123 million bushels of apples a year, 42 percent of the US market, including all popular varieties such as Gala, Golden Delicious, Fuji, Granny Smith, and Honeycrisp.

Many authoritative texts attribute the origin of the Arkansas Black apple to the orchard of John Braithwaite (Brattwait) in about 1870. The Braithwaite red-brick farmhouse, built in 1862, still stands in the northern part of Bentonville. "Uncle John," as he was known to his friends and kin, was born in England in 1811. By 1840, he lived in Benton County and later became accomplished in fruit tree grafting. Other sources credit DeKalb Holt, the son of the early Washington County settler Jack Holt, for developing the Arkansas Black in the 1870s. Yet another story suggests that John Crawford of Lincoln, Arkansas, in the 1840s, first identified the variety. Crawford propagated a cross between the Limber-twig and the Black Twig apple, which he called the Arkansas (also known as the Mammoth Black Twig), which undoubtedly caused confusion.

Farmers often misused heredity lines and labels in the nineteenth-century, leading to unique local nicknames of emerging fruit lineages. One can see how these monikers obscure the exact origin of the Arkansas Black. What is not in dispute: the apple is a true Arkansas native.

Southern heirloom apples still grow in small orchards in Northwest Arkansas, and fruit stands occasionally sell Arkansas Black apples from late November to early February. No commercial market exists for what was once the pride of Arkansas. Saplings, available from online nurseries for purchase, are advertised as the "baker's favorite" with "sharp flavor . . . sweet aftertaste with notes of sugar and cinnamon." The tree is hardy in zones 4-9 and is best pollinated by a Gala or Granny Smith variety.

Born of chance on a Bentonville farm in the 1870s, the Arkansas Black apple, whose skin turns deep red—almost black—with storage, caught the attention of the nation and the world when it won first place at the 1900 Paris (World) Exposition. Subsequently, it showed well at the 1904 St. Louis World's Fair and the 1915 San Francisco Panama-Pacific International Exposition. In the 1890s, the artist Paul Cézanne claimed he would astonish Paris with a still-life painting of an apple; the Arkansas Black did just that and more.

Extra

Seed

"It is remarkable how closely the history of the apple tree is connected with that of man."

—Henry David Thoreau

Born on the Silk Road, the domestic apple, *Malus domestica,* has implanted itself into human civilization like no other fruit. Forbidden, mystical, golden, magic, fair, and evil, the apple graces the writings of Homer to Thoreau, the paintings of Caravaggio to Magritte, and the religious traditions of Germanic pagans to Christians.

Wild apple trees bearing big, sweet fruit evolved several million years ago in temperate Eurasia. Glacial fingers of the Ice Ages then isolated their genetic material into distinct regions, producing unique wild apple species. The fossil record from Western Europe to China shows that humans collected wild apples for food as early as 10,000 BC. However, it was not until the establishment of trans-Eurasia trade routes in the first millennium BC, known as the

Silk Road, that these wild apples were brought together through hybridization to develop the domestic apple.

The modern apple contains the genetic material of at least four wild apple species with origins in Europe and Asia. Much of the genome originates from *Malus sieversii,* a wild apple still found in the Tien Shan Mountains of Kazakhstan. It is generally thought that this large, sweet apple was carried east and west along the Silk Road, where it came in contact with hardy European wild crab apples and hybrids from Siberia and Iran. Because of the hundreds of thousands of years of genetic isolation, these wild apple hybrids may have shown robust growth and sizable, sweet fruit, attracting the attention of orchardists throughout Europe and Asia.

But apples are victims of their own genetic creativity; they are incredibly heterogeneous, like humans, and produce offspring that may have little resemblance to the parent trees. Domestic apples cannot self-pollinate or even pollinate from the same variety. Therefore, an apple grown from seed will not "come true," looking and tasting nothing like the fruit from which it came. Most of these seedling trees will produce undesirable wildling apples. Only one in ten thousand seedlings will have new apples worthy of further regard. Genetic variation is favorable for creating new cultivars with new tastes and textures and flourishing in new environments but frustrating for apple growers who want to preserve a favored variety. The answer to this problem came thousands of years ago from China with the art of grafting, whereby a scion (twig) from a chosen tree is inserted into the rootstock of another. The resulting tree will produce the desired fruit. All modern apples known today are exact clones of others born by chance.

Blight

> *"Even if I knew that tomorrow the world would go to pieces, I would still plant my apple tree."*
> —Martin Luther

William Denning noticed sweet sap oozing from a canker on the cracked bark of a quince tree in his prized New York orchard overlooking the Hudson River valley. He noted this in his journal; the year was 1780. The Northeast was recovering from the most severe winter in the eighteenth-century, and the Continental Army had just suffered a significant defeat by the British at the Siege of Charleston. Two weeks later, the leaves and fruit on an entire branch wilted and eventually turned brown and died as if they had been scorched with fire. Over the next fourteen years, as his young country struggled with its formation, Denning watched the destruction of his entire pear and quince orchard, one branch, one tree at a time. He could see no external cause of the "malady" but surmised it must be from an insect, a "stem borer." However, his similarly affected farming neighbors concluded their trees had been "blasted by lightning." By 1817, fire blight, as the condition was then referred to, was felt to arise from "the rays of the sun operating on the vapor, or clouds, floating in the atmosphere, either by concentration or reflection."

It would take almost seventy more years before scientific inquiry conclusively determined bacteria caused fire blight, the first known contagious plant disease. Four years later, M. B. Waite showed insects spread the disease, the first such example of any plant pathogen, either microbe or virus. By then, germ theory had been well-established and proven in the animal kingdom, but many botanists still resisted extending this concept to plants.

The bacteria *Erwinia amylovora*, responsible for fire blight, is indigenous to the American Northeast and can infect all members of the rose family, such as hawthorn, wild crab apple, serviceberry, and mountain ash. With the introduction of European apple, pear, and quince trees to the American colonies in the 1600s, fire blight had a new host. The disease spread rapidly with fruit cultivation through the Ohio River Valley and the Southeast. California and the West initially escaped the disease because the Spaniards brought Western fruit directly from Europe to California via Mexico, bypassing the Northeast endemic. The Western settlers grew fruit trees throughout the Pacific Coast for over one hundred years before fire blight eventually spread across the continent in 1887 and destroyed a third of the Californian pear and apple crop between 1900 and 1910.

Fungicides and insecticides had no effect on the bacteria. Treatment remained reactive—prune and destroy infected branches as they became visible. Fire blight favored recent growth and water shoots, so farmers starved heavily diseased orchards of fertilizer and forced dormancy until they could prune out the infection. Fire blight could destroy a tree in one season and an entire orchard in a few. Because insects, birds, and even tools spread the bacteria, neighbors cut and burned fallow and abandoned orchards to protect their own. In the end, perhaps the British orchardists of the English

Isles, while hearing of the plight of their American counterparts after their revolution, had the last laugh.

Scale

> *"Time ripens the substance of a life as the seasons mellow and perfect its fruits. The best apples fall latest and keep longest."*
>
> —Amos Bronson Alcott

When James Lick died of a stroke in his San Francisco hotel on October 1, 1876, he was the wealthiest man in California, possessing vast real estate throughout the West Coast, including the entire island of Santa Catalina. After arriving in the then-sleepy town of San Francisco in 1848 from South America, he capitalized on the emerging gold rush by selling 600 pounds of Peruvian chocolate to would-be-miners with pockets flush with cash. This led to the first of his three notable lifetime achievements: convincing his one-time neighbor in Lima, confectioner Domingo Ghirardelli, to come to the Golden State.

Lick was an avid astronomer and philanthropist, establishing the world's first permanently occupied mountaintop observatory—The University of California Lick Observatory—on Mt. Hamilton, southeast of San Francisco. A thirty-six-inch refracting telescope mounted at the site made the first new moon discovery on Jupiter since Galileo's time—his second notable achievement.

An amateur botanist and lover of plants, Lick imported ornamental and fruit trees worldwide for his manor house in San Jose. In the early 1870s, workers found a tiny scale-like insect on one such tree. This pest scattered throughout his orchard and neighboring groves of apple, pear, apricot, plum, and other deciduous stone fruits. Within twelve years, the scale had spread to all significant fruit-growing regions of the Pacific coast, causing extensive crop loss and economic damage. The Department of Agriculture determined James Lick unintentionally imported the San Jose scale, as they labeled it, on a peach tree from a remote area between Peking and the Great Wall of China—Mr. Lick's third and most significant notable achievement, albeit destructive.

For several years, the scale was confined to the West and unknown to have infected the important pear and apple orchards in the Middle and Eastern states. However, in 1893, the scale was identified in a Virginia nursery, brought over on a California plum tree, and spread throughout the region. Soon, the scale emerged over the American Northeast and South, Europe, Japan, Hawaii, and Australia. The scale first appeared in Northwest Arkansas in 1903 on mail-order peach trees.

The San Jose scale weakened the leaves on recent growth and caused purple-red blemishes on the fruit. A lime-sulfur-salt wash and oil emersion spray, applied in the winter, could control but not eliminate the pest. To offset the increased cost of spraying, California farmers began short-pruning and shaping their trees to facilitate insecticide application, a practice not adopted in Arkansas for decades. In the early 1890s, the San Jose scale was the first insect observed worldwide to develop resistance to an insecticide. Hyped-up national and global attention to this tiny bug led to the first of many interstate and international regulations controlling the distribution of orchard fruit and nuts.

In Japan and China, traveling research entomologists discovered an Asiatic ladybird beetle dined on the scale, controlling damage and allowing local farmers to cultivate their crops. In 1902, scientists shipped hundreds of these beetles back to the East Coast in an unsuccessful attempt to introduce them to American orchards.

The female San Jose scale is a soft, yellow, immobile insect without legs or wings and lives under a hard cap. It sucks sap from branches, leaves, and fruit, robbing vigor and stunting growth. In the late spring, short-lived males emerge with legs, wings, and antennae and fly from tree to tree to mate with females. After mating, the female produces about 400 crawlers that travel short distances to attach themselves to the tree and create their own hard cap. Two to three adult generations can occur each season in Arkansas and destroy an apple tree in just a few years if left uncontrolled.

At the turn of the century, renowned entomologist C. L. Marlatt appropriately petitioned his colleagues to refer to this pest as the Chinese scale. But alas, the moniker San Jose scale had already villainously attached to the South Bay orchard of James Lick, the man who also introduced America to the sweetness of Ghirardelli chocolate.

Moths

"For when man migrates, he carries with him not only his birds, quadrupeds, insects, vegetables, and his very sward, but his orchard also."
—Henry David Thoreau

John Chapman (a.k.a. Johnny Appleseed) began his legendary spread of apple trees to the frontier wilds of Ohio, Pennsylvania, Illinois, Indiana, and Ontario in the early 1800s. He carried seeds, seedlings, and shoots from one farm to the next, planting orchards and nurseries along the way. Undoubtedly, he spread the destructive codling moth as well.

The codling moth has followed apple cultivation from Asia Minor to Europe and worldwide for thousands of years. Its name derives from the frequent infestation of codlin apples, small, firm, green apples first grown in pre-Victorian England. These apples required parboiling (coddling) before they were edible. By the early 1700s, the moth was well-established in American apple orchards, having arrived on European fruit stock.

Moments after hatching from tiny white eggs on the surface of apple leaves and twigs, the codling moth caterpillar, one-eighth of an inch long, makes its way to the calyx (bottom of the fruit where the flower once was) and bores its way into the pulp. Once inside, it seals its entry with scraps of apple skin, pulp, and excrement. The worm works its way to the seminal chamber of the fruit, where it consumes the seeds, thus halting the growth of the fruit and causing premature ripening and dropping.

After three to four weeks of feeding, the worm exits the apple and finds a protected location in the tree bark or under fallen leaves to spin a cocoon. The adult moth, one-half inch long, soon emerges, mates near the tops of the trees at twilight, lays eggs near the developing fruit, and dies. Arkansas orchards could see three generations of codling moths in one season, each more extensive and damaging than the preceding.

Control of the codling moth in the 1920s was difficult and often ineffective. Farmers collected and destroyed dropped apples. They wrapped trunks with burlap to discourage larvae from using the rough bark to shelter a cocoon. Last, they sprayed lead arsenate on the developing fruit, giving partial protection from caterpillar infestation. Spraying was costly, especially on the tall trees of Arkansas, where the damage was worse at the top. Fruit sprayed with lead arsenate required acid-washing to remove the pesticide residue before market. After washing, packers waxed and polished the apples to show they had been cleaned. Consumers came to associate waxing with purity, and the practice persisted long after growers stopped using lead arsenate.

Indeed, John Chapman helped spread the codling moth westward by planting seed nurseries for local farmers to tend. Because he shunned grafting, his seedling apples, contrary to popular folklore, were not especially edible and primarily used for hard cider. By supplying means for "drink,"—a Bacchus of the wilderness—he was welcomed by pioneers on every farm in the expanding frontier.

Rust

*"It was from out the rind of one apple tasted, that
the knowledge of good and evil, as two twins cleaving
together, leaped forth into the world."*

—John Milton

In the late nineteenth century, French winemakers pressed
renowned botany professor Pierre-Marie-Alexis Millardet of the
University of Bordeaux to solve an urgent problem affecting local vineyards. A downy mildew fungus, accidentally introduced
from America into the premiere Bordeaux wine-growing region,
was causing extensive economic damage and tainting its stellar reputation.

Millardet visited the expansive Château Dauzac, growing ex-
clusive wines, once classified by Napoleon as one of the eighteen
Cinquièmes Crus of Bordeaux. He noticed that though the fungus
affected vast swaths of Cabernet Sauvignon and Merlot, it spared
thin strips of the vinery along public roads. Speaking directly to the
caretakers, he learned workers routinely sprayed a solution of copper
sulfate on the fruit closest to the road to temporarily impart a bitter
taste and discourage theft by passersby. This led Millardet to begin
a series of experiments at Château Dauzac. He learned copper ions
inhibited the germination of fungal spores and halted the spread of

the infection. In 1885, he developed a blend of copper sulfate and quicklime, nicknamed the "Bordeaux mixture," that proved highly effective in controlling fungal diseases, including the cedar-apple rust native to North America.

On the first warm, wet spring days from Maine to Louisiana, round galls (*Gymnosporangium juniperi-virginianae*) on the branches of the eastern red cedar swell and extrude dozens of bright orange gelatinous horns like a postmodern medusa. The tendrils release millions of microscopic fungal spores (basidiospores) into the wind, drifting for several miles.

Spores landing on the moist leaves or fruit of native crab apples or cultivated apples will attach, germinate, and embed. Infection takes only a matter of hours. Yellow-orange rust spots with a bright red border enlarge to a quarter inch over the next few weeks. The center becomes stippled with black pimple-like bodies, exuding a sticky substance to attract insects. Aphids, flies, and ants unwittingly carry spermatia from one rust spot to another, fertilizing the fungus. The lesion soon grows to extend through the leaf, emerging on the underside with reproductive bodies called aecia. Apple leaves react to this invader by thickening and cupping the aecia, but to no avail. The leaf becomes deformed and weakened, no longer capturing the sun's energy to perform photosynthesis—the magic of making sugar from carbon dioxide and the foundation of all life on earth.

By mid-summer, the aecia free millions of aeciospores into the air. These new spores are harmless to apples but must land on an eastern red cedar to continue the life cycle. In the fall of the first year, small green-brown galls form on infected cedar needles. Eighteen months later, after a few warm spring days, the tiny galls mushroom in size to two inches in diameter and explode into flowering tendrils of two-celled teliospores, releasing the airborne cedar-apple rust spores once again. This is one of nature's most complex life cycles, requiring two different host plants, four different spore types, and two years to complete.

For the red cedar, the fungal damage is slight. For the apple, it can be devastating. Heavily infected leaves will turn yellow and drop in mid-summer. Fruit will blemish, under-develop, and deform—becoming unmarketable. Once the rust spot is visible on the leaf, the damage is irreversible for the season.

In 1922, the United Fruit Company introduced Millardet's Bordeaux mixture to South America, where locals nicknamed it "Perico" or "Parakeet" for it could turn exposed farmworkers blue. Overuse of the mixture polluted water and soil, killing fish and livestock. Despite this, farmers throughout North America adopted copper sulfate and lime because it was highly effective against many agricultural fungal diseases. They sprayed the mix in the early spring on apple trees throughout the twentieth century to prevent cedar-apple rust damage. The bitter-tasting mix would remain on the leaves and fruit for several weeks before eventually being washed off by rain.

ACKNOWLEDGMENTS

First, I would like to express my sincere gratitude to my wife, Marcia, for her unselfish patience while listening to me ramble on about this novel from its inception to publication. She lived through each character flaw, plot hole, historical misrepresentation, and publishing woe with me. Without her encouragement and unwavering support, I would not have been able to write this book. Thank you.

I extend my heartfelt thanks to my daughters, Carly and Meghan, and my sister, Kathryn, for their commitment to reviewing early drafts and providing constructive feedback, which significantly contributed to shaping the plot and bringing the historical era to life.

I am fortunate to have found a group of local writers, known as the People of Writing (POWs), who provided a platform for exchanging ideas and fostering creativity. Scott Lenoir, Drew Estabrook, Ashley Karcher, Tom McGraw, and Valerie Winn, I will forever cherish our friendship and late-night meetings at St. Pierre's. Thank you for your inspiration.

I also wish to acknowledge those who read and critiqued various iterations of the novel: Cecil George Smith, Linda Peters, Linda Healy, Bruce Leonard, Charles Wilson, Dee Meadows, Faith Wilson, Loretta Scott, Susan LeGrand, and John Anthony Miller. Your feedback was essential in refining the manuscript.

Special thanks to Dr. Pete Mitchell, retired obstetrician, for his insights into complications during childbirth, and Dr. Brooks Blevins, the Noel Boyd Professor of Ozarks Studies at Missouri State University, whose works and personal correspondence enriched the portrayal of the "Hill Folk" of Northwest Arkansas.

I am deeply appreciative of my editors, John Ledwith, Kimberly Coghlan, NancyKay Wessman, and Johnnie Bernhard, for their meticulous efforts in connecting the dots, addressing gaps, polishing, and revising the content, thereby enhancing the final product.

Gratitude is also due to Tracy Crow, my former literary agent, for her belief in Arkansas Black and her willingness to take a risk on its publication, which instilled confidence for pursuing this endeavor further.

Rob Samborn, your encouragement and support during challenging times have been instrumental, and I thank you sincerely for your assistance.

I would like to commend Srjdan Vulovic for his exceptional cover art that captures the essence of the story and extend my appreciation to the staff at the Rogers Historical Museum, Shiloh Museum of Ozark History, and Bella Vista Historical Museum for their guidance through collections that provided valuable insights into life in Northwest Arkansas a century ago.

Thank you all.

RECOMMENDED READING

Old Southern Apples by Creighton Lee Calhoun, Jr. This is the "Bible" of Southern apple varieties that once graced commercial and kitchen orchards throughout the South.

Apples of Uncommon Character by Rowan Jacobsen. An heirloom and modern apple lover's compendium of unique and notable varieties.

The Botany of Desire by Michael Pollan. A delightful mix of botany, philosophy, and evolution, which dips into the complex relationship humans have had with plants for eons.

Fruit from the Sands by Robert N. Spengler, III. A surprisingly informative book of how many of the foods we eat today trace their genetic origins to the Silk Road, including apples.

Hill Folks by Brooks Blevins. A comprehensive profile of the people and land that shaped Arkansas Ozark culture, history, and stereotypes.

John Barleycorn Must Die by Ben F. Johnson, III. A brief account of "The war against drink in Arkansas" during the prohibition era.

Arkansas: A Concise History by Jeannie M. Whayne, Thomas A. DeBlack, George Sabo III, and Morris S. Arnold. Modern comprehensive history of Arkansas, including the progressive reform era of the early twentieth-century.

ABOUT THE AUTHOR

Alexander Blevens is an Air Force veteran and retired orthopaedic surgeon who lives and writes on the Mississippi Gulf Coast. While growing up in Northern California, the gritty writings of John Steinbeck and Jack London influenced his literary taste. He relishes stories of adventure, human frailty, family bonds, sacrifice, and endurance.

In Alexander's debut novel, *Bycatch*, Southern and Vietnamese cultures clash on the shrimp-rich waters off the coast of Biloxi when two Vietnam War veterans meet unexpectedly in America. Their families must heal old war wounds through reconciliation and forgiveness to find peace in the present and past.

The idea for his second novel, *Arkansas Black*, grew from a faded early twentieth-century family photo taken in Bentonville, Arkansas, showing twin brothers with their sister wives in front of a fruit tree nursery. This sparked the author's desire to know more about this era and the people who lived it. *There was a story here.* Alexander combed through historical records, periodicals, historical accounts, land deeds, local museums, and period maps to bring this unique time in American history to life. The collapse of the Southern apple industry in Northwest Arkansas is only briefly noted in history books, and rarely appears in historical fiction, despite its rich stories of prohibition, corrupt politicians, and natural disasters. This period is frequently overshadowed by the subsequent calamities of the Great Depression and the Dust Bowl.

Actual events frame the story of *Arkansas Black*; however, all the characters are fictional. Alexander Blevens included four short essays on apples and diseases at the end of the book to add depth and create connections to the broader world of which Arkansas farmers in the 1920s were most likely unaware.